W9-BNR-846

Killer Praise for Sara Rosett and the Ellie Avery series!

GETTING AWAY IS DEADLY

"A fast-paced romp through Washington, D.C., with super-sleuthing Air Force wife and professional organizer Ellie Avery. No mystery is a match for the likable, efficient Ellie, who unravels this multilayered plot with skill and class."
—*Romantic Times Book Reviews* (four stars)

"Rosett skillfully interweaves a subplot about a Korean War veteran recovering his memory and provides practical travel tips from Ellie's organizational Web site, Everything in Its Place."
—*Publishers Weekly*

"Hyperorganized Ellie is an engaging heroine, always ready with tips for ordering your life."
—*Kirkus Reviews*

"*Getting Away Is Deadly* keeps readers moving down some surprising paths—and on the edge of their chairs—until the very end."
—*Cozy Library*

STAYING HOME IS A KILLER

"If you like cozy mysteries that have plenty of action and lots of suspects and clues, *Staying Home Is a Killer* will be a fun romp through murder and mayhem. This is a mystery with a 'mommy lit' flavor. . . . A fun read."
—*Armchair Interviews*

SEP 2005

"Thoroughly entertaining. The author's smooth, succinct writing style enables the plot to flow effortlessly until its captivating conclusion."

—*Romantic Times Book Reviews* (four stars)

"A satisfying, well-executed cozy . . . The author includes practical tips for organizing closets, but the novel's most valuable insight is its window into women's lives on a military base."

—*Publishers Weekly*

"Sara Rosett is a great storyteller as she creates a magnificent protagonist who is a bloodhound once she gets the scene. The author infuses her delightful cozy with humor . . . readers will eagerly await the next installment in this special cozy."

—Harriet Klausner, *midwestbookreviews.com*

MOVING IS MURDER

"A fun debut for an appealing young heroine."

—Carolyn Hart

"Armed with her baby and her wits, new mom and military spouse Ellie Avery battles to unmask a wily killer in this exciting debut mystery. A squadron of suspects, a unique setting, and a twisted plot will keep you turning pages!"

—Nancy J. Cohen, author of the Bad Hair Day mystery series

"Everyone should snap to attention and salute this fresh new voice. Interesting characters, a tight plot, and an insider peek at the life of a military wife make this a terrific read."

—Denise Swanson, author of the Scumble River mystery series

"An absorbing read that combines sharp writing and tight plotting with a fascinating peek into the world of military wives. Jump in!"
>—Cynthia Baxter, author of the Reigning Cats & Dogs mystery series

"Reading Sara Rosett's *Moving Is Murder* is like making a new friend—I can't wait to brew a pot of tea and read all about sleuth Ellie Avery's next adventure!"
>—Leslie Meier, author of the Lucy Stone mystery series

"Mayhem, murder, and the military! Sara Rosett's debut crackles with intrigue. Set in a very realistic community of military spouses, *Moving Is Murder* keeps you turning pages through intricate plot twists and turns. Rosett is an author to watch."
>—Alesia Holliday, author of the December Vaughn mystery series

"A cozy debut that'll help you get organized and provide entertainment in your newfound spare time."
>—*Kirkus Reviews*

"Packed with helpful moving tips, Rosett's cute cozy debut introduces perky Ellie Avery . . . an appealing heroine, an intriguing insider peek into Air Force life."
>—*Publishers Weekly*

"Ellie's intelligent investigation highlights this mystery. There are plenty of red herrings along her path to solving the murderous puzzle—along with expert tips on organizing a move. The stunning conclusion should delight readers."
>—*Romantic Times*

Harlan Community Library
718 Court Street
Harlan, Iowa 51537

Getting Away
Is Deadly

Sara Rosett

KENSINGTON BOOKS
http://www.kensingtonbooks.com

KENSINGTON BOOKS are published by

Kensington Publishing Corp.
850 Third Avenue
New York, NY 10022

Copyright © 2008 by Sara Rosett

All rights reserved. No part of this book may be repro-
duced in any form or by any means without the prior
written consent of the Publisher, excepting brief quotes
used in reviews.

All Kensington titles, imprints, and distributed lines are
available at special quantity discounts for bulk purchases
for sales promotion, premiums, fund-raising, educational,
or institutional use.

Special book excerpts or customized printings can also be
created to fit specific needs. For details, write or phone
the office of the Kensington Special Sales Manager: Attn.
Special Sales Department. Kensington Publishing Corp.,
850 Third Avenue, New York, NY 10022. Phone: 1-800-
221-2647.

Kensington and the K logo Reg. U.S. Pat. & TM Off.

ISBN-13: 978-0-7582-1341-9
ISBN-10: 0-7582-1341-7

First Hardcover Printing: April 2008
First Mass Market Paperback Printing: March 2009

10 9 8 7 6 5 4 3 2 1

Printed in the United States of America

To Mom and Dad,
who always believed I could do anything.

Chapter
One

"Now, if you'll follow me, we'll go down to the crypt," the tour guide said.

I let our small group flow past me as I waited for my best friend, Abby Dovonowski, to catch up with me. "You know, if everything had gone according to my plan, right now Mitch and I would be lounging on a private beach on St. John, working on our tans. But instead, I'm about to tour a crypt. Kind of ironic, isn't it?"

Abby pawed through her huge purse and didn't look up as she said, "Why did you think things would go according to your plan?"

"You're right. I forgot about Murphy's Law as it applies to military spouses: 'If you plan it, they will ruin it.' "

"Well, at lease we've got FROT," Abby said as she unzipped a compartment inside her purse and dug around it.

"Yeah, where would we be without FROT?" I asked.

"At home in Vernon, Washington, where it's raining. Again. For the record-breaking thirty-fifth day in a row. I checked the weather this morning."

"I guess you're right. I'll take Washington, D.C.'s, humidity and sun along with FROT over rain and being at home."

We shared a smile over the acronym of the class our husbands were taking. The military has to have an acronym for everything, so Foreign Reciprocity Officer Training was shortened to FROT. Originally, Mitch and I had planned to go on a Caribbean vacation after he returned from his Middle East deployment. I had the airline tickets, a room reserved at a secluded beachfront cottage, the grandparents lined up to watch our daughter, Livvy, and a reservation at a kennel for our dog, Rex, where he'd be so fawned over and catered to that he probably wouldn't even miss us.

Then Mitch returned from his deployment and learned in his absence he'd been "volunteered" to attend a weeklong training school. Mitch could have begged and pleaded and tried to get out of it, but since his squadron commander had handpicked Mitch to attend the school, he felt like he had to go. The fact that he'd forgotten to turn in his leave paperwork had an impact on the decision, too.

So what was I going to do? Cancel each carefully planned detail? Nope. I exchanged my airline tickets and mentally kissed my days at the beach good-bye. The only redeeming thing about the whole vacation switch—besides the fact the military was picking up the tab for the hotel room—was that Abby's husband, Jeff, had been picked to be the alternate to the FROT program and he had to attend as well. Since the trip fell during Abby's spring break from teaching third grade, she'd promptly made airline reservations, too.

Abby repositioned her purse on her shoulder. "Do you have anything to eat? You've always got chocolate. I'm starving."

"Of course I've got chocolate, but we can't eat in the Capitol!" I whispered back as we navigated around another clump of people with their heads tilted back to gaze at the dome mural. I always had Hershey's Kisses. I was addicted to them.

"Why not?"

"Abby, this is the *Rotunda*. We can't eat in here." The chamber echoed with the voices of the guides and the shuffle of feet as tourists made their way around the circular room, studying the oil paintings.

"I'm starving," Abby repeated. "I have to eat. I'm pregnant. It's my right."

After struggling for months, Abby was finally pregnant and she was playing it for all it was worth. It was a bit different for me, even though I was pregnant, too. Life with a preschooler tended to make everything else fade into the background. Sometimes I'd gotten so wrapped up in parenting Livvy, our almost two-year-old, that I'd actually forgotten I was pregnant again. Well, except for the nausea. That's hard to ignore, but, thankfully, that stage seemed to be over. I rubbed my slightly protruding belly. I hoped this mini-vacation would help me tune into my pregnancy. I felt a tad guilty that I didn't think about our little Nathan more. Abby looked at my purse with a longing expression. "Come on. Why can't we eat in here?"

"The sense of history. The artwork." I nodded at the center of the Rotunda as we walked. "Presidents lie in state here. It would be disrespectful."

"Yeah, you're right," Abby conceded.

As we reached the lower level of the Capitol, Abby and I merged back with our sightseeing group made up of several Air Force wives from different bases whose husbands were also in Washington, D.C., for FROT training.

Our guide said, "Forty Doric columns of brown sandstone support the Rotunda directly above this room. Does anyone know what the star at the center of the floor represents?"

The gaze of our Capitol tour guide, a young woman in her early twenties, roved over our group, as she tried to avoid making eye contact with the petite, dark-headed woman planted directly in front of her. The rest of us were clueless, so our guide said, "Nadia, I bet you know. You've known everything else."

"Oh, I do." Nadia bounced with excitement and her dark hair bobbed against her cheekbones. "It's the exact center of Washington, D.C." Her Capitol brochure crumpled as she squeezed it. "The very heart of Pierre L'Enfant's grand plan. The diagonals that divide the city into quadrants originate from *right here.*"

Our guide gave a perfunctory smile. "That's correct. As you can see, there aren't any tombs in this crypt and it has never been used as a burial chamber. It was intended to be the final resting place for George Washington, but his family buried him at Mount Vernon instead. Today, the space is used for exhibits. Feel free to take your time looking around. This concludes the tour. I'll leave you to explore." She gave us directions on how to exit the Capitol and we dispersed around the room.

Nadia headed to the gift shop, which was really just a few glass display cabinets stocked with postcards and touristy items set up on one side of the room. Abby and I set off on a slow circuit of the room. I loved reading the small print inside the exhibit cases. Abby indulged me until another member of our group,

Irene, joined us. She pushed her subtly highlighted blond bangs off her forehead and checked her watch. "Shouldn't we be going? Where is everyone?" Irene had taken on the roll of den mother. Abby and I knew Irene because she and her husband, Grant, had been stationed at the same base as Abby and I, Greenly in Washington State, until a few months ago when Grant got a new assignment to Alaska.

Irene shoved a plastic bag of postcards and souvenir books into her massive tote bag, which was emblazoned with a flag and the words *Military spouse: the toughest job you'll ever love.* She pulled the lapels of her black wash-and-wear travel blazer together over her busty figure and looked around the room. "Nadia's in line to check out and there's Gina, leaning on a pillar." Irene checked her watch again. "I'll go round everyone up. Don't you think Wellesley will be waiting for us outside by the reflecting pool by now?"

Wellesley Warner was our tour guide for the D.C. area. She'd handed us off at the Capitol to their expert guides and told us where to meet her when the tour was over. Some companies had tour programs for spouses who accompanied their significant others to conferences and training programs. Not the military. An expense like that would be an easy target for complaints about waste, fraud, and abuse. Can't have our tax dollars going to entertain the wives, so our group had pooled our money and hired Wellesley, the owner of Inside Look Tours, a "boutique" tour company specializing in small tour groups for people who didn't want to spend their time on a bus, lumbering from one site to another.

Irene bustled everyone together and we emerged from the Capitol on the west side. We paused at the balustrade to take in the view down the Mall, the grassy open space lined on each side with the Smithsonian museums. Straight ahead, the Washington Monument rose vibrantly white against the blue sky. I knew from studying the map earlier in the day that the Lincoln Memorial was directly beyond the Washington Monument. "I love the symmetry of this place," I said.

Abby snorted. "You would. You like everything lined up in a row. Neat and squared away."

Gina Trovato was on the other side of me. Abby noticed her puzzled look and leaned over to explain. "Ellie's a professional organizer. She helps people get things in order. Her business is called Everything In Its Place."

Gina smiled. "Too bad we aren't at the same base. You could experiment on me since I'm chronically unorganized. If you could help me, you could help anyone." She turned back to the view and said, "It is awesome, though. Even someone as messy as I am can appreciate good lines when I see them."

"What do you do? You're in Oregon, right?" I asked.

"I'm a social worker at a hospital in Portland." Gina leaned her bony arms on the balustrade. She looked a bit like she'd been run through a wringer and had all the color and contour squeezed out of her body. She was tall and flat-chested with gray eyes, pale skin, and long straight hair that was somewhere between a washed-out blond and a dingy brown. The only exception to the linear lines of her body was her slightly upturned nose.

"We're not that far away from you. We're at Vernon in eastern Washington State. At least for now," I said.

Gina turned toward me. "Due for a move?"

"Yes. Well, not for the next six months or so, but we should be hearing pretty soon. We've turned in the dream sheet and now we're waiting."

"Dream sheet. That's an accurate name, if there ever was one," Gina said with a laugh. A dream sheet was a form on which Mitch listed the bases where he'd like to be stationed. It was called a dream sheet because that was what it was: basically, a dream. The Air Force pretty much sent you where they wanted you. If it happened to coincide with your dream sheet, you were lucky.

Gina continued, "Not that you're going to get it, but what did you put down as your first choice?"

"Hawaii. We know it's a long shot, but after the winters in Washington State we're ready for sunshine. Of course, we'll probably get one of the other bases down the list, like the one in Kansas or Georgia. Abby and her husband are up, too. We're hoping we'll get the same base again."

"Okay, everyone," a loud, perky voice rang out. "Time for a snappy."

"Not another picture," Gina muttered. "She's got to have taken at least fifty already."

Nadia must have sensed a mutiny brewing because she said, "Come on, just one more. Last group picture of the day, I promise. I just have to have this for my scrapbook."

"All right, then let's get it over with," Gina said. We all swung around with our backs to the view and Nadia recruited another tourist to take our picture. We squished together and grimaced.

"Now, that wasn't so bad, was it?" Nadia asked as we went down the steps to the Mall.

I heard Gina mutter, "Not if it shuts you up."

We made our way down to the Capitol Reflecting Pool through the beautifully landscaped grounds. I wondered how much money was spent on maintaining the grounds. Did it rival the defense budget?

"Where is Wellesley?" Irene asked, scanning the

clumps of people gathered around the pool. Abby plopped down on a low wall and I joined her. I pulled some energy bars and several Hershey's Kisses out of my Coach backpack purse and handed them to Abby.

"Ah. Nourishment." She ripped open the bar and downed it in three bites. I offered a bar to Gina, but she shook her head. Abby crumpled the wrapper and said, "You have to teach me all this mom stuff, like carrying food in your purse. I'm going to be so toast as a mom."

"You're going to do fine," I said and pulled out my cell phone. I'd turned it off during the tour.

Two messages. The first one was from my parents' phone number. They were taking care of Livvy during my week away with Mitch. I punched the numbers for voice mail and I tensed, waiting to hear Livvy crying. To put it mildly, she'd had some issues with separation anxiety. I'd even debated canceling my trip several times. My mom's voice came on the line. "Hi, honey."

No sounds of screaming in the background. I relaxed a little.

My mom said, "Sorry we missed your call. We were in the backyard. Livvy loves the sandbox. She's doing great. We're having a wonderful time. Don't try to call us back for a while. We're going to the mall and the toy store. Bye." Okay. No crying. That was good. Wasn't it? I had a hard time believing Livvy wasn't in the throes of separation anxiety, but my mom wouldn't lie to me. *Would she? No. Of course not.* I just hoped all Livvy's new toys and clothes would fit in our suitcases for our flight back to Vernon.

I checked our little group. Irene paced to the edge of the Reflecting Pool and scanned the Mall for Wellesley. Abby and Gina were talking and Nadia was busy snapping pictures of the Capitol dome. A noisy group of teenagers swarmed around the pool. Their matching green T-shirts proclaimed they were from Crocket Middle School. We were engulfed in a chattering, giggling, hormone-energized crowd.

My next voice mail message came on the line and I heard my sister-in-law's breezy voice. "Hi, Ellie! Great to hear you guys are in town. Give me a call back and we'll get together. I know you said you had a free afternoon today, but I can't get away. I'm babysitting the Little Terror. She's sleeping now, thank goodness, but call me later."

Abby saw me close my phone. "So, did you hear from your sister-in-law? Are you getting together with her this afternoon?"

"Yes. That was Summer, but she's babysitting for her landlady."

Abby's eyebrows crinkled down into a frown. "Isn't she a little old to be babysitting?"

I smiled. "Not if you're babysitting for your landlord, who happens to be a high-powered Washington lobbyist. Summer figures it can't hurt her chances of getting a job once she graduates in May." Of course, that was assuming that Summer actually graduated.

Mitch's youngest sister was as flighty as a hummingbird and changed majors as fast as some teens changed their shoes. I was amazed that her hodgepodge of college credits was going to add up to a degree in political science. Even with her short-lived detour to beauty school a few months ago, she'd pulled everything together this spring and was about to get her degree.

The green mass of teenagers departed and I recognized Wellesley striding across the Mall, her black skirt rippling around her legs. The name Wellesley conjured images of headbands and preppy plaid. Wellesley had a headband, but it was a long white scarf that held back an explosion of dark corkscrew curls. Definitely no plaid for her. She went for the minimalist look. Today she wore a white sleeveless shirt and black flared skirt with tiny white embroidered dots. The ends of the scarf fluttered behind her.

"And what about Debbie? Has she checked in again?" Abby asked.

"No. And she only called to make sure I made it to town."

Abby leveled a look at me. "And to make sure you had his phone number. And again to make sure you didn't lose it. And a third time to make sure you didn't forget to call him."

I sighed and pulled out another Hershey's Kiss for me. "I know she's being kind of annoying, but this is really important to her. She's always wanted to know what happened to her dad in Korea. It's a taboo subject. Her mom won't talk about it. No one else in the family will either, so this guy, MacInally, might be her only chance to find out about her dad. The whole situation is kind of sad. Since she couldn't get any details out of anyone in the family, she used to make up stories about what happened to him, like that he died rescuing a family from a fire, stuff like that. Once, she told me that she used to pretend that he wasn't really dead, that he'd somehow escaped death and was a spy and it was too dangerous for him to return home."

"That *is* sad, but I still don't see why this guy who knew her dad doesn't just e-mail her or call her," Abby said.

"I know. I don't understand it either, but I'm doing it as a favor for Debbie. She used to babysit me when I was a kid. I idolized her. She was my cool older cousin. She was nice to me at family get-togethers. She didn't make a big deal about me following her around and asking her a thousand questions. She even sat at the little kids' table with me and my brother when she could have sat with the grown-ups." I popped the Hershey's Kiss in my mouth.

"Okay, okay. But don't you think you're taking on too much? This is supposed to be a vacation, remember? Well, a vacation for us, even if Jeff and Mitch are working during the day," Abby said.

I swallowed the chocolate and said, "No. I have to see Summer. It would be rude not to stop in and see her while we're so close. And the thing with Debbie—that won't take long—a couple of hours. Just a quick meeting. Besides, it means a lot to her. It's the least I can do for someone who endured the rickety card table with me at Thanksgiving when she didn't have to."

My phone rang in my hand. It was the same Texas area code as my parents' house, but not their number.

"Ellie! It's Debbie. Did you meet him yet?" A mixture of expectation and fear mingled in my cousin's voice.

"No. It's tomorrow," I said as I watched Wellesley's approach. I raised my hand to wave at her. She'd almost reached the Reflecting Pool when a man joined her. He was shorter than her and had black hair and heavy dark eyebrows. I lowered my arm and said to Debbie, "I'm going to meet MacInally in the hotel lobby tomorrow for breakfast. I promise I'll call you as soon as I talk to him."

"Okay." Debbie's voice was strained. "I've waited thirty-plus years to find out what happened. I guess I can wait one more day."

"How's Morgan?" I asked as I watched the man and Wellesley. He pulled at the neck of his thin white T-shirt, which distorted the logo of a tree and the outline of the Capitol above the words *Capitol Landscaping*. His dark green pants were paint-splattered and had muddy patches on the knees. He shifted his weight from one heavy work boot to the other as he talked rapidly to Wellesley. She shook her head and stepped away. He caught her arm and spun her back toward him.

Debbie said, "Itchy and mortified. Thirteen is a difficult age without the chicken pox. I still can't believe she got it even after she'd had the shot. I'm so—ugh—so disappointed I can't be there, but I can't leave Morgan right now and I can't wait any longer. I *have* to know what MacInally has to say."

I divided my attention between Debbie's voice and Wellesley's encounter with the man. The rough way he'd jerked her arm worried me a bit, but she didn't seem to be bothered by it. She tugged her arm away, said a few terse words, and strode away from him.

I tuned into the silence on the phone line and said cautiously, "Debbie, MacInally may not know anything." Debbie had such high hopes for this meeting, but I was afraid I might not bring much more back than photos of her dad's war buddy.

The dark-headed man on the other side of the Reflecting Pool watched Wellesley walk away, his face under his heavy eyebrows expressionless. After a long moment, he turned and walked in the other direction. I expected him to join a landscape crew that was trimming bushes, but he passed them and continued on toward the Washington Monument. "Debbie, I've got to go. Our tour guide is here. I'll call you as soon as I talk to him, I promise."

Wellesley spotted Irene and they walked over together. Wellesley didn't seem shaken by the encounter with the man. She asked, "How's my band of mothers doing?" When she'd found out that morning that both Abby and I were pregnant and that everyone else in the group either had kids or stepkids, she'd dubbed our group the band of mothers. It was a cute designation, but I thought she might not think we were so endearing after a few more days of constant pit stops for bathroom breaks, since one of the less exciting parts of being pregnant was the need to keep within sight of a restroom at all times.

She asked about our tour of the Capitol and then said, "Your afternoon is on your own. There's a nice exhibit at the Natural History Museum." She handed out brochures. "But we're going there tomorrow, so you might want to wait. If you want to see more of our founding documents, visit the National Archives, across the Mall."

"I'm ready for a nap and room service," Abby said.

"Okay, I'll head back, too," I said. Maybe Abby was right and I was trying to squeeze too much into my vacation itinerary. Lounging around the pool or even lounging around my hotel room for a few hours completely alone sounded pretty good. It might not be the Caribbean, but at least it was a four-star hotel.

"I think I'll go to the Library of Congress," Irene said as she studied the map.

Gina and Nadia agreed they were ready for a break, so Wellesley gave Irene directions to the Library of Congress and then walked with the rest of us back to the Metro stop.

The day had started out a little on the cool side, but now Washington's famous humidity was creeping in. By the time we reached the escalators and descended into the cavelike darkness of the Metro stop, I was glad to get out of the sun. We inserted our Metro cards into the machines connected to the turnstiles and pushed through them. Then we took the second escalator down to the platform. It was quiet, almost peaceful, under the barrel-vaulted ceiling, except for the occasional shrieks coming from two kids running in tight circles at the far end of the platform. They were so close to the edge it made me a little nervous. Nadia had her camera poised in front of her as she took more "snappies," but she didn't ask us to pose for her, which was a good thing since I thought Gina might yell at her if Nadia told her she wanted another snappy.

Wellesley stood beside me as we waited for the train, so I asked, "Do you have another tour this afternoon?"

"No. I'm heading back to my office to work on my other business."

"You run two businesses?" I asked.

"With the cost of living in this place, you've got to have two incomes to live here. Unfortunately, I'm not married so I have to bring in both of them," she said with a smile.

"What's your other business?"

"Household Helper. It's more of a resource for people looking for a gardener or a housecleaner. We've got some handymen, too, for small remodeling jobs. If someone wants to update their bathroom—and believe me, there's a lot of that going on around here with people buying older homes for the inside-the-Beltway location and fixing them up—but they don't want to pay a contractor, I've got tile guys, plumbers, and someone who can hang cabinets. All with references and a record of actually showing up for work."

"Wow. Your clients must love that," I said.

A new group of people arrived on the platform, led by two women, both in suits and heels, a marked contrast to the usual tourist uniform of T-shirts and shorts. The shorter woman in a navy suit lugged a load of equipment, including a video camera with the name of a local news station on the side. She extended the legs of a tripod and said nervously, "This look okay? I'll set up as close to the tracks as I can, all right?" The other taller woman wore a cream suit that complemented her blond hair twisted up in a chignon. She stalked over to the edge of the platform and positioned herself in front of the camera while dialing her cell phone. She pressed the phone to her ear, then barked, "Speak up. The connection's bad." After a few seconds she said, "You're cutting in and out. Call me back in fifteen minutes. We should be done here by then." Frowning, she ended the call, pulled off a lanyard with an ID tag dangling from it, and tossed the lanyard and the phone at a man standing off to the side.

It's funny how group dynamics play out, even in impromptu groups, like random people waiting for a train. I realized the news camera had the attention of everyone on the platform, including the kids at the far end. Since I'd just had some less than pleasant encounters with the media, I was glad the camera wasn't focused on me.

The reporter threaded a small microphone under the blond woman's collar and stepped back. "Okay, we're ready." A bright light attached to the camera clicked on and, just as quickly, a smile lit the woman's face, replacing her frown. The reporter said, "Ms. Archer, tell us why the Women's Safety Initiative is so crucial."

"We're all concerned about safety. Our nation's security has been our top priority recently, but we can't overlook individual safety, especially for women. Women must be safe in their homes, at work, and on public transportation, like the Metro. That's why the Women's Advancement Center has worked closely with Senators McKay and—"

There was a burst of noise from the top of the escalator and we all turned to look. Another group of teenagers, this time wearing dark blue shirts, flooded down the escalator in a gush of chatter and the flutter of miniskirts.

I noticed the lights in the floor of the platform near the edge of the track flicker on and off, a signal the train was arriving.

Ms. Archer snapped at the man holding her phone, "Tell them to keep it down. We're recording," but her voice was overpowered by a high-pitched shout from a girl in a blue T-shirt. "Here comes one. We can make it, if we hurry!"

The train sped into the station and a whoosh of air swept across the platform, stirring my hair as a scream rang out. I thought it was one of the teenagers horsing around, but then little waves of panic rippled across the platform.

People started shouting. Someone yelled, "Call 911." Suddenly, we were pushed forward. "What happened? What's wrong?" A few people pushed back, fighting against the surging tide. The noise level on the platform swelled. "An accident."

I heard someone crying.

". . . horrible . . ."

"Can you believe—"

The reporter disconnected the camera from the tripod, yanked the microphone off the other woman, and pushed into the fray.

A woman behind me said, "Oh God. I hope it's not terrorism. Is there a bomb?"

The whole platform descended into chaos as the word "terrorism" was repeated. We all turned and ran for the escalators. Hands pushed at my back. I looked around for Abby, but didn't see her. I was caught in the horde of people in the bottleneck at the foot of the escalator. The tide of people shoved forward and smashed me against the wall of the escalator. *Trampled. I'm going to be trampled.* The crowd surged again. The sense of fear permeated the air like the heavy stench of sweat. *I'm going to be crushed.*

"Wait! Calm down!" A man had jumped up on one of the benches. "Someone fell off the platform." The crowd swirling around him slowed. The pressure against my back eased. "It's okay," he repeated. "Slow down. No terrorism. Someone fell. It was just an accident."

An Everything In Its Place Tip for an Organized Trip

Travel planning
   The Internet is a great place to start your research for a trip. Major cities usually have Web sites with extensive information. Some sites like TripAdvisor.com and IgoUgo.com have firsthand traveler reviews of hotels, restaurants, and tourist sights.

Chapter
Two

"Ellie, have you seen my belt?" Mitch tossed the suitcase down and stomped to the closet.

I clicked off the morning news and snuggled farther into the luxurious layers of the bed. "You're sure it's not in the suitcase?"

"Yes," Mitch said shortly and picked up our carry-on bag. "I know I packed it, but I can't find it." I cocked my head to the side and watched him as he patted the closet's top shelf. It was so unlike him to be frantic. That was usually me.

"Well, there's military bases everywhere around here. We're not that far from the Pentagon. Couldn't you buy one there?"

He slid the closet door closed with a thump. "You can't just walk into the Pentagon. And I don't even know if they have a uniform shop."

"I thought I was the one who was supposed to be crabby. Pregnancy hormones and all that."

That made him smile. "I've learned to never mention those words—or any variation of them. Sorry, I'm stressed."

He looked different in his "blues," a uniform with a light blue shirt and dark blue pants. He didn't wear it too often because he was usually in a flight suit. "You look good," I said. That distracted him from his search for a moment as he glanced at me and smiled slowly. That slow smile gets me every time.

A quick knock on the hotel door interrupted anything interesting that might have happened. "Mitch, are you coming down or not?"

I recognized Jeff's voice and I said, "Why don't you see if he's got an extra belt?"

He did. Wardrobe crisis averted. Mitch returned with the belt, slipped it on, then shrugged into the dark blue jacket. He brushed at his shoulders and smoothed his hands down over the silver wings and lines of ribbons. Then he turned to me and leaned on the bed, squashing down the pillow with his elbow as he kissed me good-bye. "Love you. Be careful today. Don't overdo."

"I won't. We're just doing the American Indian museum and the natural history museum."

He smiled. "Hey, don't try and fool me. I know how you are with sightseeing. You think it's an endurance sport. Kind of like you shop for purses. So take it easy."

"You know I get my purses online."

He tilted his head down and raised his eyebrows.

"Usually," I amended.

"Right," he said. "Like I said, just take it easy. You brought, what, four purses?"

"You know I only brought two." I didn't want to lug more suitcases around than we absolutely had to, so I'd pared my clothes down to a week's worth of casual capri pants, shirts, and skorts. Actually, Abby had

helped me pack. She's the best at coordinating out-
fits. I'd limited myself to two purses, my trusty ma-
hogany Coach backpack purse, and my roomy Louis
Vuitton Luco Tote.

"I know. I'm afraid you're going to go into with-
drawal," Mitch said.

"Watch it," I joked. "If you keep teasing me I might
skip the sightseeing altogether and go shopping for
a new bag instead."

His tone turned serious when he said, "And watch
out in the Metro."

"I will. That was scary yesterday. Besides, today is
my meeting day. MacInally at nine and Summer at
four. She's going to meet me at the natural history
museum. We'll come back here and get you, then
head out to dinner. Sound good?"

"Yes, as long as she actually shows. You know Summer. She's not good at follow-through." He kissed me
again and picked up his paperwork.

I sighed. "You always say that. Sure, she's a little
flighty, but I think she's growing up. She'll be there."

Mitch laughed. "She's never stood you up before,
has she? We'll see how you feel after that happens."

I let it go. Sometimes your closest family members
are the last to notice changes.

"Didn't you want to call the squadron today? See if
there's any news on the move?"

Mitch checked his watch. "Too early. I'll call them
during the lunch break," he said as he headed to the
door.

I called out, "Don't have too much fun in your class."

"Yeah. My goal is not to snore."

I stretched and grabbed the phone. My mom answered and put Livvy on right away. "Hi, Mommy."
Her voice came over the line squeaky, but upbeat.

"How are you?"

Long silence. "Okay." Was she talking to me or my parents?

"Do you know that I miss you?" I asked. I didn't want to start a crying bout, but I did want her to know that I missed her.

Her undistinguishable muffled answer could have been *yes*. Then she laughed, said bye-bye, and I heard a thump.

My mom's voice came on the line. "She had to go. *Barney's* on."

"Have you ever watched *Barney*, Mom?"

"No."

"You're so lucky. Don't start now. Get out of there before the music starts," I said. I was only half joking.

My mom's voice sounded slightly gleeful. "Livvy's in charge of the TV and that means no sports."

"Must be killing Dad. So, how are things going?"

"Fantastic. She's fine. We're fine. You have fun and don't worry about us. We're having a great time."

I felt slightly depressed when I hung up. Livvy didn't need me. She obviously got along great without me. When she was crying and clinging to me with a death grip, I'd often wished she'd get over her separation anxiety, but now that she had, it was kind of sad. For me, anyway.

I put my hands on my stomach and closed my eyes. It was too early to feel the baby move, but it didn't hurt to be quiet for a few minutes and *see* if I felt anything.

I waited as several minutes ticked off the clock. Nothing, except a few growls from my stomach. Maybe by the end of the week. I tossed back the fluffy duvet and went to the closet. No use wallowing in self-pity because Livvy was too busy to talk to me. I had to get up and have some fun. Everyone else was having fun, I might as well try and have some.

I rolled the closet door back and contemplated my clothes. Picking out clothes to wear when you're pregnant is always an adventure. So far I was still able to wear most of my clothes, but sometimes it seemed that the baby grew overnight and what I could fit into one day was an absolute impossibility the next day.

An hour later, I sipped my orange juice and glanced toward the entry of the hotel restaurant again for a big guy with dark hair going gray and a blue-and-white-striped tie. I shifted on the bench and sighed, dreading the phone call I'd have to make if Mac-Inally didn't show. I'd give him thirty more minutes. Debbie would be crushed if he didn't show up. I checked my phone again. No messages.

I grabbed a discarded newspaper from the next table. There was a small article on the local news page about the death in the Metro. The man had been an illegal immigrant who worked temporary jobs. His name was being withheld until family could be notified. I stared the grainy picture of a man with thick brows and dark hair.

He looked like the man who'd talked to Wellesley yesterday. Maybe he was one of her landscapers? I wondered if she'd known he was illegal.

I spotted Irene making her way down the breakfast buffet line and waved her over when she finished. I said, "I'm waiting on someone, but I don't think he's going to show."

"Oh, okay. How about I sit over here?" Irene sat down at the table beside me.

"How are you doing after yesterday? You know, I didn't see you afterward, but you were okay, right?" I asked.

Her silverware clinked to the floor. She quickly bent to pick it up and set it aside before reaching for another set wrapped in a napkin. She slowly unfolded

the napkin and said, "Um, yeah . . . sure. I'm fine."
She lined her silverware up neatly and spread her
napkin in her lap.

"You didn't get hurt or anything?" I asked, puzzled by the way she smiled tentatively. I realized she
didn't know what I was talking about.

"No, I'm fine," she said quickly as her hand fluttered around her face, pushing her blond bangs off
her forehead. Then she smoothed the lapels of her
lightweight travel blazer. Today's blazer was green.

I signaled the waitress for another glass of juice
and said, "Well, that's good."

After a few seconds, she inched her chair toward
mine. "Ellie, I'm not sure . . ." Her voice trailed off.

I said, "You don't know what I'm talking about?"

She smiled quickly and shook her head.

I handed her the newspaper. "A man died yesterday in the Metro. He fell off the platform as the Blue
Line train came in."

"Oh, goodness. That's terrible," she said, but I
could have sworn I heard relief in her voice.

"So what happened to you?" I asked.

"Me? Oh, I remembered I had an . . . appointment."
She nodded her head and her voice became more
sure. "I had an appointment and didn't want to bother
anyone, so I left the group right before everyone went
into the Metro."

"That's right." *Good grief. I'd completely forgotten.* Had
being pregnant addled my brains or was it everything
else that had happened? "I can't believe I forgot. You
were on your way to the Library of Congress. You
didn't get to see it?"

"No." Now she looked completely at a loss. Apparently that was all she was going to say, because she
put down the paper and cut her omelet with intense
concentration. I paid my bill and calculated the tip.

Irene had never puzzled me before. I'd always thought she was as transparent as a plate-glass window, but there was something about her today, a furtiveness, that I'd never seen before.

"Well, I'll see you in the lobby. I've got a call to make," I said and Irene nodded, distractedly.

I found a sofa in the lobby and dialed Debbie's phone number. She picked up immediately, her voice eager. "How did it go? What did he say? What was he like?"

"Debbie . . ." I paused and it seemed like I could feel the hope being sucked out of her. "I'm sorry. He didn't show."

"It's okay." Her words were a monotone now. "You know, I don't know why I do this to myself. It's always the same. No one will talk about it."

"Have you tried talking to your mom again?" I asked as gently as I could.

There was a bitter laugh. "Are you kidding? No. Wouldn't do any good. Subject is closed. She doesn't even know I contacted MacInally. Or how hard it was for me to track him down. I didn't want to get into the whole why-can't-you-move-on thing. I can't move on. I just can't."

"I'm really sorry," I said. I hated hearing the anguish in her voice. "I'll try to get in touch with him again. I'll be here all week. Maybe he'll meet with me later."

"You know what really gets me?" I didn't think she'd even noticed what I'd said. Now anger laced through her voice. "No one will talk about it, but if they do happen to accidentally mention it, then it's with shame. Shame! He served his country. What's shameful about that?" Her voice rose and wavered on the last line.

"Nothing," I said quietly.

She took a deep breath. "Yeah. Sorry. You should know. You're living it."

"Look, I'll call him again," I repeated. "Do something nice for yourself today. Tell Derrick you need a break for a couple of hours. Take yourself out to lunch or buy that pair of boots you were telling me about, okay?"

"Okay. Call me if you hear from him."

I hung up, called MacInally, and left a terse message. Did he really understand the hopes he'd raised?

That afternoon, I leaned over a display mounted in the wall. "I don't see anything," Abby said as she peered over my shoulder.

"You have to look closely. The tarantula is right there under the branch," I said.

"I'm glad I can't see it." Abby moved on to a display that showed the interior of a beehive. Live bees thronged over the comb. A few departed through a cleverly constructed transparent tunnel connected to the museum's windows. We watched the bees fly away; then, a few returned through the tunnel to the hive.

"Okay, I think we've done it all," Abby said. "American Indian Museum—check. Dinosaurs—check. Sea fossils—check. Mammals—check. Reptiles—check. Now we can check off the Insect Zoo. I think when you've made it to the Insect Zoo you've seen it all."

Nadia didn't even have to consult her map. "We haven't seen the Hope Diamond yet."

"Jewelry." Abby brightened. "Lead on."

Nadia's glossy dark hair bounced as she strode through the museum. "It's up here on the second floor, too. Did you know the Hope Diamond weighs over forty-five carats? It was donated in 1958." I glanced back at Wellesley. She was at the back of our group, talking on her cell phone. She didn't seem to mind that Nadia had taken over as tour guide.

"Where's Irene?" I asked Gina. She crossed her skinny arms and shrugged. Her pale lemon shirt made her look even more faded and washed-out than she had yesterday. "She said she was tired and headed back to the hotel a few minutes ago." Gina hadn't said much during today's tour. Granted, it was hard to get out more than a sentence or two with Nadia nattering away all day, reporting little-known facts and trivia about the exhibits.

As we walked past the open gallery that overlooked the rotunda on the main floor, I looked around for Summer, in case she was early. She said she'd meet me by the African elephant display. The massive hall dwarfed the elephant. I didn't see Summer, so I still had a few minutes to check out the diamond. I lingered a few seconds, enjoying the dramatic architecture of the museum with its three floors of pillared galleries that rose to the dome. Wellesley had informed us it was a classic Beaux-Arts style. I thought it was a wonderful contrast to the modern museum buildings that I'd been in, which always seemed a bit cold and sterile.

Wellesley ended her phone conversation and I fell into step with her as I searched in my bag for chocolate. I opened my hand, offering her one of the silver-wrapped Hershey's Kisses as I asked, "Irene went back to the hotel? Was she okay?"

"Oh, no chocolate for me," Wellesley said. "I eat an ounce and, I swear, I gain two pounds in my hips. Irene seemed fine. She said she was tired and was going to the hotel to take a nap."

Irene didn't set a marathon pace in anything I'd done with her, but I'd never known her to skip out of activities. I hoped she really was feeling okay. Wellesley interrupted my thoughts as she asked, "So, what's this class that all your husbands are taking? I know you told me, but I can't remember the details."

"Foreign Reciprocity Officer Training. Did you know that our military helps train military officers from foreign countries?"

Wellesley shook her head. "No, I had no idea."

"We do. They're usually from ally countries. Mitch told me that sometimes foreign countries don't have the technology for training that we do here. It's kind of like a foreign exchange program for foreign military officers. Anyway, when these people arrive here for training, each base has to have a point of contact to help them get situated with everything they need. The FROT class trains them in how to handle the paperwork and coordinate everything the foreign officers need."

"How big is this training program?" Wellesley asked.

"It's not that large. The FROT training is an additional duty," I translated for her. "That means the guys will still do their primary job, being a pilot, and they'll do the FROT thing if they have a foreign officer arrive on base. I don't think it will be that often where we are. Now, if we were at a training base where they teach people to fly, then I bet it would be another story."

We walked a few more paces and I said, "I saw the article about the man who died in the Metro. I didn't realize yesterday in all the chaos that he was someone you knew."

She stopped walking and looked at me. "What?"

"The man who died. You talked to him on the Mall right before we went to the Metro."

"I have no idea what you're talking about."

"But his picture was in the paper. You spoke to him by the Reflecting Pool. In fact, it looked like he was angry with you. He grabbed your arm."

Her eyebrows descended and she quirked her mouth to one side. "I don't know what you saw, but it certainly wasn't me. We're holding up the tour." She elbowed her way into a crowd around the display case where the Hope Diamond rotated slowly.

That was weird. Maybe I'd been mistaken? The picture in the paper had been in black-and-white and kind of grainy.

Nadia said, "It's so beautiful. Can you tell us about the curse?" I stood on tiptoe and looked over the crowd to catch a glimpse of the diamond. The color surprised me. I'd expected a deeper blue, but it had a more translucent quality. Wellesley eyed Nadia warily as if Nadia was trying to trip her up before she said, "The gem has a colorful history, but like most curses, the curse associated with the Hope Diamond—bad luck and death—turns out to be mostly myth. Contrary to the legend, the jeweler who brought the diamond back from India, Jean-Baptiste Tavernier, didn't die from being torn apart by wild dogs in India. Instead, he lived to be eighty-four and died in Russia. Even though the diamond was part of the French crown jewels, Marie Antoinette did not wear the diamond . . ."

My cell phone rang. The caller ID read SUMMER AVERY. I checked my watch as I opened the phone. It was four o'clock and I was late. I waved to Abby, who knew I was meeting Summer, and dashed out of the room to the balustrade overlooking the museum's gallery.

"Hey, Summer. I'm on my way," I said, searching the crowds milling around the elephant. "But I don't see you. Are you by the elephant?"

"No. I've been . . . delayed."

Shoot. I hoped she wasn't about to cancel. I didn't want to have to tell Mitch that Summer was a no-show. He wouldn't hold back with the "told you so" comments.

"That's okay. You're on your way, right?"

"Umm . . . I don't know how long this thing will last." Now that I wasn't focused on being late, I noticed she didn't sound like her usual breezy self.

I slowed down. "What thing?"

"Being questioned by the police."

An Everything In Its Place Tip for an Organized Trip

Routines that will take the pain out of packing

- Keep a set of small, travel-size bottles of lotions, shampoos, and other toiletries separate from the items you use day-to-day. You'll have all the items you need in one spot and can pack quickly. Restock used items at the end of your trip or save hotel samples for your next trip.
- If you travel frequently, invest in travel clothing that doesn't wrinkle and that you can wash and hang to dry.
- Containerize your travel items into smaller bags for quick packing and unpacking. For example, separate jewelry, toiletries, and makeup into different bags. You can even use zip-top bags for this.
- To avoid the last-minute search for your airline and hotel confirmation numbers, have a copy of your reservations sent to your e-mail account. Print information and store all travel reservations (airline, rental car, hotel) in a designated place. To make it easy to find your travel documents in your purse or carry-on, place them in a business-size envelope or plastic folder, which will keep them separate from your other items.

Chapter
Three

"Can I get you anything else?" A dark-headed man with an olive complexion set a glass of water on the end table beside me.

"What? Oh no. Thank you. I'll be fine." As he moved across the office's reception area, I noticed he had the compact, solid body of a wrestler. What had he said his name was? Tom? Terry? And what did it matter? Was I focusing on that minor detail so I didn't have to think about Summer being questioned by the police? He did look a little familiar, but after my encounter with Wellesley, I wasn't sure if I'd seen this guy either.

A short, lean man with a shriveled face entered the office and shouted, "Tony!" as he scurried by the reception desk. Tony met him in the hall. They talked about a contract as they walked down the hall and disappeared around a corner.

I pushed my sweaty bangs off my forehead and tried to get my breathing under control. It had been quite a hike from the Mall to K Street, where Summer worked. I probably could have taken the Metro to the offices of the Women's Advancement Center, but I hadn't thought about it, and the truth was that if I *had* thought of it, I'd probably have avoided the underground trains anyway. I still felt a little skittish about the Metro.

I was glad the reception area was deserted. It was frigidly air-conditioned and everything was either clear glass, transparent plastic, or white fabric. Even the receptionist's desk was a plastic and glass concoction that looked like an ice sculpture. I'd gone for the touristy look today with a skort, sleeveless shirt, sunglasses, and tennis shoes. I definitely looked out of place with my vacation duds and flushed face.

I took a sip of my water and noticed Tony had reappeared in the doorway. "Tony, how long has Summer been in with . . ."

He forced a smile. "Only fifteen minutes or so. It won't be much longer, I'm sure. Routine questions. They didn't take long with the rest of us."

"Oh, they questioned you, too?"

"Yes, of course. We were all on the platform in the Metro."

I finally placed him. He'd been the man that the tall, blond woman had tossed her lanyard and cell phone at shortly before the television interview began in the Metro. So the woman had been Summer's employer and landlord. I hadn't made the connection until just now.

I was about to ask what the police wanted to know, but I heard voices from somewhere behind Tony. Summer stopped abruptly in the doorway, her long red curls swirling around her shoulders. "Tony! There you are. I'm out of here. Remember, I told you I had to leave early today—" She caught sight of me and hurried across the reception room to hug me. "Ellie!"

Her long hair tickled my nose as I returned her hug. I pulled away and held her back by her shoulders. "Are you okay?"

She shrugged and broke away. "Sure." She dashed over to the reception desk, jerked open a drawer, and tossed her hobo bag on her shoulder. "I'll see you in the morning, Tony," she said as she leaned over and tapped a few keys on the computer keyboard. "I'll have that spreadsheet finished after lunch tomorrow, I promise."

Summer picked up a denim jacket from the back of the chair, then linked her arm through mine and pulled me out of the office. "I'm so sorry about that! No big deal. Where do you want to go to dinner? Is Mitch still waiting for us?"

"I called him on the way over and told him you'd been delayed. He's tied up anyway. One of his meetings was rescheduled, so we're going to meet at six."

"Perfect. Where do you want to go? Do you feel like Thai?" She kept chattering as she pulled a black beret out of her purse and situated it on her curls at a jaunty angle. "Oh, I'm so glad I got out of there before I saw Mr. Archer. Did you meet him? I heard him talking to Tony right before I left. I *know* Mr. Archer's going to ask me to babysit Emma again and I don't want to see him go ballistic when I tell him I can't. He's unpredictable. Ms. Archer says he has sleep issues and that's why he's so irritable." Summer rolled her eyes. "He's just plain old mean."

I stopped dead in the quiet hallway. "Summer, you were questioned by the police. That is a big deal. Are you sure everything's okay? Why did they need to talk to you anyway? You weren't on the platform at all."

Her green eyes narrowed as she studied me for a few seconds. Her busy, almost frantic manner fell away. "So what they say about pregnancy hormones is true. I've never heard you use that tone."

Why is it that when a woman is pregnant and she displays any emotion from frustration to irritation or just plain crabbiness, everyone in the vicinity has to tell her it's the pregnancy hormones? It's as if a pregnant woman can't have legitimate emotions. Every state is attributed to hormones. "This has nothing to do with me being pregnant or my hormones. It's about the police questioning you. I'm worried about you and you don't seem to have a care in the world."

"Let's go downstairs. There's a restaurant where we can talk."

We sat down at a tiny table in the back corner and ordered. "So what happened?" I asked.

Summer pulled her long hair over one shoulder and raked her fingers down the curving strands. "They wanted to talk to me because they thought I was on the platform yesterday."

"But you weren't. You were babysitting what's her name—the Little Terror."

Summer actually glanced around the restaurant guiltily. "I shouldn't call her that. Her name is Emma. Anyway, they wanted to talk to me because there was someone on the platform who looked like me from the back. Long hair, beret, denim jacket. But it wasn't me. I told them that." She smiled and sipped her latte.

"Summer, why are they still investigating?"

"They're not sure it was an accident."

"What?"

She flipped her hair over her shoulder and leaned across the table. In a quiet tone she said, "They think he was pushed. They've got photos from the security cameras and they're talking to everyone who was on the platform."

"Well, it's a good thing you can prove you were at the Archers' house. Believe me, I've dealt with the police before and you don't want to get . . ." I trailed off as I realized Summer's face had a slightly pinched look. "What? You can't prove it?"

"No. I called you early in the day yesterday and I didn't make any phone calls from the Archers' house. And no one saw me yesterday afternoon either. Well, Emma saw me, but I doubt they're going to take the word of a four-year-old. And she slept most of the afternoon anyway."

"Still. That's no reason to worry. Surely, the video will show what happened—show who pushed him."

"Apparently not." Summer shifted and kept her eyes on the table. "They weren't telling me much, but Tony, that's Ms. Archer's assistant, he found out from Ms. Archer that the video 'isn't conclusive.' There's a crowd of people around Jorge and they can't tell who pushed him."

"But then how are they sure it wasn't an accident?" I pressed.

"They isolated one shot from the camera seconds before he went over the edge. There's a hand on the man's back, shoving him. They're just not sure who the hand belongs to. It's too far away to get any details about the hand—no rings or nail polish. Of course, they were able to eliminate Ms. Archer and Tony."

"Wait. You said a name—Jorge?" It wasn't just the fact that she'd said the name that caught my attention. It was the way she'd said it, casually, like she'd said it before.

Summer studied the table more intently. "Jorge, the man who died."

"But how do you know who he was? His name wasn't in the paper. Did the police tell you?"

"No," Summer said.

"You *knew* him?"

Summer shrugged and said, "It's nothing. He was the Archers' yardman. He was around their house."

"So the police know that you knew him."

"I didn't tell them."

There was something about the way she was determinedly *not* looking at me that worried me. Having a kid taught you all sorts of suspicious body language. "How well did you know him?"

"Not that well."

"Summer."

"Okay." She looked up at me and said, "I knew him. He asked me out. He was good-looking, but there was something . . . I don't know . . . cold about him. You know me, I don't care what people do. It didn't matter to me that he was a landscaper or that some people would think he was a little too old for me. Anyway, I turned him down politely. Then he got—persistent. It was kind of scary, so I went to the police to see if I could get a restraining order."

"So the police know all this?" I put down my glass.

"No," she said disdainfully. "I talked to the police on campus. They don't have any connection with the people who questioned me today."

"They'll find out, though, if you filed a report or a complaint. They'll make the connection eventually. You should call them and tell them. It's not going to look good if they find out later. They'll think you're hiding something."

Summer leaned in again, bracing her forearms on the table. "But I didn't file a report. I only asked some questions." She must have been able to see that I wasn't convinced. "Ellie, do you have any idea how many people die in this city every year? Hundreds. It isn't called the 'Murder Capital' for nothing. Then there's the other crimes—rape, robbery, carjackings. Pretty soon Jorge's death will be buried under the avalanche of other crimes."

An Everything In Its Place Tip for an Organized Trip

Travel guides

A good travel guide can be your most valuable resource on the road. Find the one that best suits your type of trip. Some travel guides focus on bringing the place alive visually with lots of color photos and maps. Others are heavy on text. Some guides specialize in off-the-beaten-track locales, while others spotlight traditional stops that are usually on the most popular tourist itineraries. There are even guides for traveling with kids and pets. Your local library will probably have a wide variety of guides that you can browse before purchasing some for your trip.

Chapter
Four

Later that night, Summer swung her RAV4 into the hotel's drop-off lane and hopped out. I'd suggested Italian instead of Thai, since I was avoiding spicy food. We'd gorged ourselves on breadsticks and pasta. When Mitch asked what delayed her, she'd dismissed the police questioning as a routine interview. "They talked to everyone in the office because they were all in the Metro that day." She'd jumped to another topic and kept the conversation away from Jorge's death. After dinner, she'd driven us around on a night tour of the capital. The monuments were majestic and imposing as they glowed against the black sky.

As she hugged me, she whispered, "Please don't tell Mitch about Jorge. He'll overreact." She released me and looked at me with raised eyebrows. I didn't want to keep anything from Mitch, but this was her brother and I'd let her tell him about the investigation in her own time. Maybe she was right and the investigation would peter out on its own and that would be the end of it. "All right," I said.

She grinned. "It was so good to see you all. Have a

great time on the rest of your trip. Call me if you have more free time, Ellie."

She hugged Mitch and he said, "Good to see you, too." We turned to walk into the hotel, but Mitch swiveled around and rapped on the passenger window. Summer rolled it down and he leaned an arm on the top of the car. "Hey, stay in school. You're not going to drop out before the semester is over, right? You're not thinking of, I don't know, going to cooking school or heading off to walk the Great Wall of China, are you?"

Summer scowled at him. "No. Bye." She rolled the window up before he could tease her anymore and roared into the traffic.

Mitch cringed as a truck slammed on its brakes to avoid the RAV4's bumper.

I said, "You know she's only driving like that to get back at you for teasing her. She was a great driver the rest of the night."

"I couldn't help it. She's always been so erratic that I have a hard time believing she's not going to do something crazy like drop out."

"Hey, did you get a chance to call the squadron today?" I asked.

"No news."

"Oh." I tried to be philosophical. We'd find out soon and it wasn't like there was anything we could do about getting ready for a move while we were on vacation, but I just wanted to *know*.

We were almost to the elevators when a man stepped in front of me and said, "Ellie Avery?"

He didn't look like anyone from Mitch's training class. Everything about him was long and thin, from his sheer blond hair that drooped over his forehead to his skinny nose that parted his elongated face. Even his extended hand had long slender fingers.

"Yes, I'm Ellie," I said as I shook his hand.

"Detective Mansfield from the Metropolitan Police." He showed us his badge and shook hands with Mitch after he introduced himself.

"If you'll just step over here, I need to ask you a few questions." He led the way to a set of four square ottomans. I picked the orange one and plopped down. My jean-clad knees popped up above my waist. There's really no elegant way to sit on an orange ottoman when you're pregnant and tired. I shifted around a bit, but I still felt like I was sitting on a beanbag. Mitch sat down beside me and Detective Mansfield took the yellow ottoman across from us. "Did you talk to Jay MacInally today?"

I'd braced myself for questions about Summer and the man in the Metro, so it took me a few seconds to place the name. "Jay? Oh. MacInally. I think of him as Mr. MacInally. Um . . . no, I didn't talk to him today. In fact, he was supposed to meet me here this morning, but he didn't show up."

"I'm afraid Mr. MacInally was involved in an accident. He's in the hospital."

"Is he okay?"

"You know how doctors are. They don't like to give any info anymore." He hadn't really answered my question. Instead, he asked one of his own. "How do you know Mr. MacInally?"

I scooted around on the ottoman, trying to find a place that didn't make me sink down several inches. "I don't really. My cousin tracked him down and wanted to talk to him because he knew her dad, my uncle. They were stationed together in Korea. Her dad died over there and she wanted to talk to MacInally about it."

"So you've never met him?"

"No. Debbie, that's my cousin . . ." I noticed he

was jotting her name down in a notebook, so I slowed down and said, "Debbie Corder. She lives in Texas, I can give you her phone number. She talked to him several times. At first, I think she contacted him by e-mail, but I know that they talked on the phone when she had to cancel her trip. That's why I was going to meet with him. Debbie couldn't come and she asked me to talk to him."

"And he knew you were coming in her place?"

"Yes. I called and set up a time to meet." I looked at Mitch. "It was Sunday, right?"

He nodded and switched his attention back to the police detective. I tried to read Mitch's expression, but he kept it neutral. I bet he wasn't thrilled, though. I can't say he'd ever been happy when I'd had to talk to the police before.

"So you talked to him Sunday and didn't hear from him again?"

"Right. Can you tell me what happened?"

Mansfield put the notepad and pencil away in his jacket and rubbed his slender hands down his long legs. I wondered if he played basketball. He had the build for it. "Apparently, MacInally was slugging this morning." He paused, realizing we didn't know what he was talking about. "Slugging is like carpooling, except people don't usually know the people they ride with. Commuters park their car in a commuter lot and catch a ride with any car that's going into town. Drivers pick up passengers so they can drive in the carpool lane.

"MacInally's car is still parked in the commuter lot, so we think he parked and caught a ride with another driver. Whoever picked up MacInally pulled off the interstate about twenty-five miles away from the commuter lot, beat him up, took his wallet and briefcase, and left him. A woman walking her dog behind her condos found him this afternoon. He'd managed to crawl to a gravel access road that wrapped around the back of the condos.

"We found a paper with your name and this hotel phone number in his pocket. That's how we found you."

I sat there, stunned. "That's terrible." Violence, even at a distance, was shocking. Finally, I asked which hospital he was in.

"St. Simon's Memorial. He can't have any visitors now. Here's my card. Let me know if you remember anything else that might be helpful."

I thrashed about for a few seconds and finally managed to stand up from the ottoman. Mitch and I went to the elevators in silence. Once the doors closed I said, "Can you believe that?"

Mitch shook his head. "No. I thought the crime rate was down in D.C."

"Well, if it is, I'd hate to be here when it's up. And that slugging thing. I wouldn't get in a car with a stranger."

The doors opened and we walked down the hall to our room. "The guy that taught our class today mentioned it. He does it every day—must be pretty common around here."

I felt disoriented like I'd spun around a few times and then tried to walk while the room revolved around me. Mitch put his arm around my shoulders. "You okay?"

I registered that he wasn't mad about the police visit. His easy smile and manner were back. "That whole conversation has thrown me off. What was it that we were supposed to do when we got to the hotel? Livvy. What time is it?" I asked as I pulled out my phone.

"Nine-thirty."

"That makes it seven-thirty in Texas." Livvy would

probably still be up. I dialed my parents' number as
Mitch slid the key card into our door. My mom answered and I asked, "How's everything going?"

"We're fine. Well . . . a little tired, but we just got
Livvy to bed and she's already asleep. We took her to
the park this afternoon and it really tired her out."

"Oh. Well." I forced some cheerfulness into my
tone. "That's great. I'm glad it's going so well."

I heard my mom stifle a yawn. Keeping up with a
preschooler could really wear you out. "Look, I know
you're tired. I'll call back in the morning."

We said good-bye and I tossed the phone back in
my purse and flopped onto the bed. "What kind of
mother am I? I forgot to call and tell Livvy good
night."

Mitch came over and sat down. He pulled off one
of my shoes and rubbed my foot. "You're a good
mom. You've been enjoying yourself and Livvy is
fine."

"I know she's fine, but doesn't she miss us?"

Mitch said, "I'm sure she misses us. Besides, you
wouldn't want her to be miserable, would you?"

"No. I'm glad she's happy, but I wish she missed
us—well, okay, *me*—a little bit. I mean, I've taken care
of her since birth and she doesn't miss me *at all?* And
I do feel bad that we forgot to call."

"Well, having a police detective show up unexpectedly will throw you off your stride," Mitch said as
he moved to my other foot.

"I know."

"Why are you frowning?" Mitch asked.

"Summer seemed awfully nonchalant about talking to the police today. I'd have thought she'd been
more, I don't know, worried or bothered by it."

"Yeah. That's Summer. Nothing fazes her. I just
hope she stays in school. I can see her dropping out

next month to do something insane like become a mime or something."

"You're awful. You know she's not going to do that. I think she's grown up a lot more than you give her credit for."

"We'll see."

"Do me a favor. Set the alarm on your watch so I won't forget to call Livvy in the morning."

"She'll probably talk your ear off," Mitch said as he set the alarm, then went back to rubbing my feet. "Now where were we?"

Wednesday

The next morning, Livvy still wasn't interested in talking. I was in a huff when I went down to the lobby. I knew it was silly to feel disgruntled because Livvy wouldn't say more than two or three words to me, but I couldn't help it. I was so distracted that I almost collided with a young guy in a gray hooded sweatshirt, who was listening to music on his iPod. I maneuvered around him and went through the breakfast buffet, then joined the tour group at the tables.

Abby put down a plate heaped with waffles, fresh fruit, and eggs beside me before she sat down. "What's wrong? You look upset."

"I'm a little disappointed. And I know it's ridiculous, but Livvy is having such a good time at my parents' house that she barely has time to speak to me. This morning she said exactly two sentences. She likes Lucky Charms and she wants to know why we can't have them at *our* house every day. Then she dropped the phone because my dad was going to the store and she wanted to ride along. She probably didn't even brush her teeth."

Across the table from us, Gina dumped a pile of pills of all sizes and colors into her palm. "Vitamins," she explained and downed them with several gulps of juice, then said, "Just be glad she's eating breakfast. When they get to be teenagers they barely get up in time to get dressed and run out the door. And forget about them brushing their teeth."

"How old are your kids?" I asked as I cut my French toast.

"Stepkids. Seventeen and fifteen. Two boys."

Nadia set her camera on the table beside her plate. She looked scandalized. "But breakfast is the most important meal of the day. I can really tell a difference between my students who've eaten breakfast and the ones who haven't. The ones who haven't always get cranky before snack time."

Gina peeled her banana and said, "Teenagers are always cranky. What grade do you teach, again?"

"First. I love it. The kids are cute and they're so excited to be in school."

"Teenagers aren't excited about anything," Gina said.

Nadia sat up straighter. "I'm sure it's an act with them. They're just trying to be cool."

"Of course it's an act," Gina said.

In an obvious effort to keep them from coming to blows, Abby pulled out her itinerary. "So let's see. What's on the agenda today? It's 'Memorial Day.' Jefferson, Lincoln, and Washington plus a few war memorials."

Wellesley arrived, her corkscrew curls bobbing against the barrettes that held them back. "Good morning, ladies," she said. In her sleeveless white sundress she looked like she was ready for a garden party. "This is our group today. Irene isn't feeling well, so she won't be joining us. As soon as you're ready, we'll go to the Lincoln and Jefferson Memorial. Then after lunch, we'll see the Washington Memorial."

"Are we taking the Metro today?" Abby asked.

"Not this morning. It would be quite a hike from the nearest Metro station, especially for our moms-to-be. I was planning on driving us to the Jefferson Memorial first and then up to the Lincoln Memorial. From there, we can walk to the war memorials and the Washington Monument."

"That would be great. I don't know about you, but I'm not ready to go back to the Metro." Nadia shivered. "It was awful."

Gina shrugged. "I don't think it will bother me. It was just a onetime thing. And we'll have to ride the Metro again sometime. It's the easiest way to get around this city."

Wellesley nodded. "That's true, but we can skip it for today."

Should I tell them the death wasn't an accident? I wondered what their reactions would be, especially Wellesley's. My cell phone rang before I could decide. I was surprised to see Summer's name on the caller ID. I hadn't expected to hear from her again while we were in town. "Hi, Ellie," she said brightly. "You're probably surprised to hear from me, but I have a favor to ask. You're not in the middle of a tour or something, are you?"

"No, we're just getting started."

"Good. Well, you see, the thing is, Ms. Archer's got this big interview coming up with *Mom Magazine*. They want to do a feature on her and Emma."

I didn't see where this was going. I mouthed to Abby that it was Summer on the line and shrugged. I signed my bill, stood up, and moved with the group to follow Wellesley. "Anyway"—Summer's tone became upbeat—"the feature is going to be fabulous. A big photo spread of Emma's room. Pictures of Ms. Archer reading to Emma. It'll be a huge publicity coup for the Center. Tons of promotion."

"Fascinating, Summer. That's great. I have to get on the elevator to go down to the parking garage with the tour group. I might lose you." I hoped she wrapped it up.

"Well, the thing is, I told Ms. Archer about you yesterday. About your organizing business and, well . . ."

"Do you really call her Ms. Archer? All the time?"

"She hasn't asked me to call her anything else, so that's what I call her. Anyway, there's a small problem. Emma's room is a mess."

"So I guess you'll be cleaning it up."

"That's the thing. It's really terrible. She has every toy ever made, no shelves, no storage. Her closet is a big tangle of clothes. You can't really *walk* in her room because there's so much stuff and her closet kind of scares me. So"—her voice rose on the word—"when Ms. Archer heard about your organizing business, she said wouldn't it be great if you'd come organize her daughter's room?"

For a few seconds, I was actually speechless. I found my voice and said, "Summer, I'm on vacation."

"I know and I'm sorry, but Ms. Archer has already pitched the idea for the article to the magazine and they love it. Before and after photos of Emma's room. They can show how a busy mom with a full-time job can organize her kids' rooms. And Ms. Archer is sold on it." I had to strain to hear Summer's voice as she practically whispered, "I think Ms. Archer is about to transition to something new. Maybe a run for Congress. I don't know, but there's been a lot of talk about softening her image and everyone loves the idea of this article. Please, Ellie, if you help me pull this off, I might get a job out of it, maybe even as a congressional staffer. That'd be huge. And it would be good for you, too. *Mom Magazine* will interview you. You'd be the organizational expert." She spoke more quickly, her words almost bumping into each other. "It's a national magazine. Think of the publicity. And I'll help you. You wouldn't even have to do the actual work. You'd be like a consultant. You tell us what to do and we'll do it. I'll get as many people we need." She finally ran out of steam and I realized everyone was in the elevator waiting for me to step inside.

"I'll call you back from the van," I said.

The elevator doors closed, shutting out the guy in the hooded sweatshirt, who was sprinting toward the elevator. I said to Abby, "That was Summer and she wants me to organize a room for her boss while I'm in town."

"You've got to be kidding." Abby stepped back a pace, nearly knocking over Gina, who was so slight it wouldn't take much more than a heavy breeze to topple her.

"I know. I told her I'm on vacation."

"You didn't tell her 'no,' though, did you?" Abby asked.

"I had to get in the elevator. I'll call her from the van."

Abby exchanged glances with the other women in the elevator. "Her sister-in-law," she explained to everyone. "Ellie can't say no to save her life."

Nadia patted my arm as we emerged from the elevator. "I know, honey. I hate to disappoint people, too."

Abby sighed. "How much work is she talking here? A whole house?"

"No. One room. It sounds bad, but I could probably pull it off in a day or two. She said she'll get as many workers as I need. In fact, she says I don't have to do the work at all, just tell them what to do and they'll do it. I'd consult. I have to admit, I do like the sound of that."

"Who does your sister-in-law work for?" Nadia asked.

"Ms. Archer. Apparently, she doesn't have a first name."

Gina glanced quickly in my direction. "Vicki Archer, from the Women's Advancement Center?" I nodded and she whistled. "That was her doing the TV interview in the Metro before . . . Anyway, she's supposed to be one of the fastest burners in D.C."

"Really? You recognized her? I haven't heard of her. I mean, I don't watch the news as much as Irene does, but I'm not totally out of it."

Gina climbed into the van and sat in the backseat. "I was reading an article about her a few days ago. She's listed as one of the 'Women to Watch in Washington' this year. They think she'll run for Congress. Her name is already popping up as a potential vice presidential candidate."

I slid into the seat beside Gina. Was it too early for chocolate? I definitely needed some. Chocolate was my go-to stress-relief mechanism. I pulled out a few Hershey's Kisses and offered some to everyone. Wellesley shook her head, but everyone else grabbed one. I said, "How am I going to be able to say no now? Summer's hoping to get a full-time job with Vicki Archer after graduation, and if Archer has such great prospects, it would be an amazing job for Summer." I popped the chocolate in my mouth and sat back to try and think of a kind way to let Summer down easy.

Nadia belted herself in and leaned forward to talk to Wellesley. "This afternoon, is it free again?"

"Technically," Wellesley said as she reversed and pulled out of the parking garage, barely missing two pedestrians before she merged into the traffic of

Crystal City. "I don't have anything scheduled, but I was leaving it open for you to choose what you'd like to do. I thought possibly Union Station."

"Perfect." Nadia turned back to me. "I'd like to see where a potential vice presidential candidate lives."

An Everything In Its Place Tip for an Organized Trip

Pick the right bag
- Choose a bag made with a durable material, preferably one that is water-resistant. Check zippers and handles for sturdy construction and look for reinforced side panels.
- Pick a color besides black to avoid confusion at baggage claim.
- You can also use colorful luggage tags to help distinguish your bag from similar ones.
- Luggage wheels that rotate 360 degrees make maneuvering easier.

Chapter
Five

After our tour of the monuments, Wellesley parked the van on the street in front of a white 1950s Cape Cod–style house with a red front door. The neighborhood, a mix of bungalows and Cape Cods with tiny square footage and surrounding mature land-scaping, reminded me of our neighborhood in an established section of Vernon in Washington state. Except this neighborhood had an air of aggressive maintenance. No peeling paint or scruffy lawns marred these streets.

"It's so tiny," Nadia said with dismay.

Wellesley said, "It may not look like much, but this is prime real estate, an inside-the-Beltway location. These houses go for over half a million dollars."

Nadia stared at her. "You've got to be kidding. For that little thing?"

"I'm serious. Fairchurch is a primo location."

I climbed over Gina to get out of the van. "Thanks for dropping me off. Summer can give me a ride back to the hotel."

As I stepped out of the van, a blue four-door car pulled into the driveway. A man in a suit and a woman in a pantsuit got out and paced toward me. They didn't look threatening, but suddenly I felt nervous.

"Detective Jason Brown, Metropolitan Police," said the heavyset man as he ambled across the grass to me. He didn't remove his aviator sunglasses from his face, which was narrow near his forehead and salt-and-pepper crew cut, but widened around his chin and lower checks because of his jowls.

The approach was so similar to Mansfield's last night that I thought of MacInally. Were they here to ask more questions about him? Had he gotten worse?

"I'm looking for Summer Avery," Detective Brown said as the young woman followed him.

"I'm Ellie Avery, Summer's sister-in-law. She lives in the converted apartment in the back," I said and pointed to the small building at the back of the lot. It was obvious that the apartment had once been a detached garage, because the driveway still ran right up to the edge of the small building. "Is there something wrong?" It dawned on me that a detective wouldn't bring me news about MacInally's health.

"Thanks. Just usual inquiries," he said and walked up the slight incline of the driveway with the woman.

I turned back to the van. "I'd better go."

Abby leaned forward. "Do you want me to stay? Do you think everything is okay?"

I shrugged. "I don't know if it's okay, but I think it'll be better if I go by myself."

"All right. Call me if you need me. I can get a cab or something and come get you."

By the time I got to Summer's door, the police were already seated on her futon couch. Summer had pulled a bar stool over to the "living area" and perched there with one high-heeled foot dangling. She hopped up when she saw me walking up the driveway and let me inside. "Just be a sec," she said to me as I headed to the other bar stool in the kitchen area. "Help yourself to something to drink."

I really couldn't believe her sometimes. A second session with the police and she was acting like all she needed to do was put on her lip gloss and she'd be ready to go. I know I wouldn't be so blasé.

Summer went back to the living area and I found a bottle of water in the fridge. One of the first mantras of pregnancy is to stay hydrated. Not that I'm very good at following mantras, but I like to at least give the hydration one a shot every once in a while. I climbed onto the other bar stool, wishing I could kick off my shoes. I hadn't thought I was tired from the day, but suddenly my feet and calves ached and I wanted to stretch out and take a nap. The monuments had been amazing and I'd been caught up in their massive scale.

I couldn't see Detective Brown's face, but the set of his shoulders seemed to telegraph his disapproval. He asked, "So you met Jorge Dominguez six months ago?"

Summer shrugged. "I guess so. I don't remember the date. He came to work for the Archers' last fall. Probably around October. I'm sure they'll have the date."

"Did he have any family?"

"I don't know."

"How often did you talk to him?"

"I don't really know. Whenever he was here doing the yard I'd say hello to him if I was leaving to go to class or coming back home. And I saw him in the Metro a few times."

"When did you start dating?"

It was a good thing I hadn't taken a big swig of water because, if I had, I would've spit it across the room. I managed to choke down my drink with only a muffled cough. Summer didn't seem to notice my reaction. She laughed, a short, you've-got-to-be-kidding laugh. "We didn't date."

"Your neighbors say you rode in the landscaping truck with him."

"He gave me a ride to class once when the battery in my car was dead. It was on his way to his next job. It was nothing."

"When did he start bothering you?" Summer's foot swung into a higher gear, but that was the only sign his question bothered her. I bet Brown picked up on it, though.

"He asked me out for a date. It was probably a month ago. I said no, thanks. End of story."

The woman stood up and strolled around the room. Since I'd missed the introductions, I wasn't sure exactly what her role was, but I assumed she was another detective.

"Then why did you talk to your campus police about how to file a restraining order? And why didn't you tell us this when we first talked to you?"

Summer gathered her long red hair, pulled it over one shoulder, and leaned forward. "Look, the guy was getting to be a nuisance. He asked me out. I said no, but then he kept on asking. I found out what my options were. I didn't tell you earlier because I didn't know who had died. You only wanted to know where I was on Monday afternoon. You didn't mention his name."

I felt myself go very still as I thought back over my conversation with Summer. She *had* known the name of the man who died. At least, she had when we talked. Why was she lying now? Why had she held back before? Was she afraid of the police?

"And why didn't you file a restraining order?" Brown

didn't seem to be aware of the other detective moving around the room, but it bugged me. Her light brown hair was pulled off her puffy face into a ponytail. Her slightly uneven bangs were plastered to her forehead. I watched her as she strolled around the studio apartment like she was browsing in a store, but the gaze from her small, closely spaced eyes roved over everything.

Everything Summer owned was out there in the open. Was the detective seeing anything she shouldn't? I gave myself a mental shake. Of course the detectives could look around all they wanted. Summer had nothing to hide.

"After I found out how involved the whole process was I decided I'd just talk to him. It worked. He left me alone after that," Summer said.

"So you threatened him."

Summer sat up straight and assumed a rather haughty air. "No. I did not threaten him. I told him to stop asking me out, to stop watching my house, to leave me alone or I'd have to go to court."

Brown jumped on her slip. "So he was watching your house, too? How often? Did you record the dates he was here?"

"No. At that point, I didn't realize how persistent he was going to be. I didn't know I needed to write stuff like that down. Are we through here?"

"Not quite." Brown turned to me as he flipped though his notebook. When he looked up, his gray eyes were cold as they focused on me. "Mrs. Avery. You were in the Metro station that afternoon as well."

Surprised, I choked on another swallow of water. "Yes, I talked to the police Monday. They took everyone's contact information."

"And were you aware of your sister-in-law's conflict with Mr. Dominguez?" His jowls vibrated a bit as he tossed his head in Summer's direction.

I didn't like the turn his questions had taken. "No, I didn't even know she knew him. I didn't know who he was."

"I see." His tone clearly said he didn't believe me.

"You'd been in touch with your sister-in-law before you arrived here?"

"Of course. We talked about getting together while we were in town."

The female detective made another loop of the room. For some reason, her slow, silent circuits made me think of a shark. I felt a prickle of sweat break out at my armpits. I tried to push my nervousness down.

Summer said, "You can't be serious. There's no way we'd do what you're insinuating."

Brown ignored her indignant voice and kept his monotone as he turned back to her. "We're not insinuating anything, just confirming information. Where were you Monday afternoon between three and five?"

I could tell Summer relaxed just a bit, because her foot stopped swinging so frantically. "Back to that again? I was right here, babysitting the Archer's daughter at their house. And before you ask *again*, I didn't make any phone calls or talk to any of the neighbors."

"Then why was your Metro card used at four-oh-five in the afternoon at the Metro station where Mr. Dominguez died?"

"What?" All the hauteur went out of her. She looked truly disconcerted for the first time in the interview. "My Metro card?"

"Yes. The one you purchased with your Visa credit card two weeks ago Thursday at seven-thirty in the morning. It was used twice before Monday. No activity since Monday."

Summer jumped off the bar stool and grabbed her hobo bag from the kitchen counter. Pens, notebooks, a pack of tissue, sunglasses, a long scarf, and her beret scattered onto the counter as she pawed through the pockets. She looked up from the disarray, her eyes wide, a completely shocked expression on her face. "It's gone."

Chapter
Six

"How could I have been so careless?" It was probably the sixth time she'd said that since the detectives left. I pushed away my own worry about the questions Brown had asked me and focused on Summer. She looked dazed and listless, a state I'd never seen her in. I'd made her sit down on the futon couch and look through her backpack, her jacket, and her purse again while I retrieved a Red Bull from the fridge for her. I figured she could use the caffeine and sugar. I grabbed a couple of Hershey's Kisses from my purse for me. There must be something to that hydration thing, because I'd finished the water and I didn't feel sleepy anymore. After I downed a couple of dollops of chocolate, I could probably stay up until bedtime, well, dinner, at least.

Summer collapsed back against the cushions. "How could I lose it? I always put it right back in this little pocket. It fits perfect. I know I'm kind of scattered, but I've never lost my Metro card. Those things are expensive."

She held the narrow can, but didn't drink from it.

"I know this is going to sound crazy, but do you think someone could have . . . taken it?"

"What are you saying?" I asked.

Summer twisted a strand of hair around her finger. She'd put on a good front for the detectives, but their visit had unnerved her. "I heard Ms. Archer talking about it today. She wants to use the death in the Metro to play up the need for the Women's Safety Initiative. She's going to keep it in the news and that'll keep the pressure on the police. It's not going to go away like I thought." She blew out a deep breath and unfurled the hair from around her finger. "So what if—" She got up and paced into the kitchen area and back. "What if someone intentionally took my Metro card and used it that day so that it would look like I was there? Am I crazy to think like this?"

"No. Believe me, I'm no stranger to crazy speculation." I smiled, but Summer didn't notice my attempt at a joke. "You may be right. Or it may just be the police checking everything out. Being thorough."

"Maybe." Summer didn't look convinced. "I don't know. I mean, they've interviewed my neighbors. Tracked down my Metro card and checked when I ride the Metro."

"So this guy had asked you out and you turned him down?" I was surprised Summer hadn't mentioned this before. It wasn't a small detail.

Summer dropped back onto the futon, her shoulders slumped. "He was stalking me. I didn't want to put it like that to the police, but that's what he was doing. Following me around and sitting out there at the curb in his beat-up pickup with binoculars. It was the binoculars that did it. Seeing those made me realize he was a little beyond normal. So that's when I checked out the restraining order."

"Did you tell anyone else then?"

"No. It only got weird about two weeks ago. He asked me out about a month ago and it was a few weeks later that I noticed he seemed to be doing a lot more yard work here. Then I saw him sitting in his pickup, watching me, and I knew I had to do something."

"Do your parents know?"

"Are you kidding? That's not something you want to call home about and tell Mom and Dad. Or Mitch. Don't tell him anything about this, okay? He'd react just like Dad." She shook her head. "Back when it happened, there was no way I was telling Dad. He might have shown up with his rifle one morning, just to scare Jorge. *That* wouldn't go over well inside the Beltway."

I had to smile at that image. Mitch's dad was a true southern gentleman, from his impeccable manners to his love of hunting.

"Besides, they already think I'm a flake. Mom puts it much more politely, of course. She says I'm 'eccentric.' " Summer smiled sadly. "The funny thing is that I'm not going all conventional—doing the college and job thing—for them. I really like it. The political stuff fascinates me. I think I've finally found what I want to do. And if Ms. Archer even *thinks* I might be involved in Jorge's death, well, I can kiss my inside track to a job in politics good-bye."

"Summer, if she believes for a second that you had anything to do with his death, you don't want to work for her anyway."

"You're right." She nodded and replaced the contents of her purse. "If I could just see those pictures they have, I'd feel better."

"Can Ms. Archer get them?"

"No. Tony already checked on it. If Tony Zobart can't get them, it can't be done."

I thought of the endless pictures Nadia took. I could have sworn she took some in the Metro, too, although why she'd want to photograph the Metro, I had no idea. I'd ask to see them, but I wouldn't mention it to Summer in case I was wrong and Nadia hadn't taken "snappies" in the Metro. I mentally shuddered at the word because I'd heard it so often. And I *like* pictures.

I glanced over at Summer. She was sitting motionless, her purse in one hand and her sunglasses in another.

"Are you feeling all right?" I asked and went over to her.

She shook her head and shrugged. "Yeah, um, no. I was thinking about Jorge. I saw him a couple of times in the Metro." She carefully put the sunglasses into her purse, then picked up her scarf and folded it. "Every time I saw him, he was right down there at the edge of the platform. Some people do that, you know, get as close as they can to the edge so they'll be one of the first people on the train." She tucked the scarf down into the purse and looked up at me. "Either someone knew Jorge always waited right by the tracks or someone happened to see him there . . ." Her voice trailed off and she looked back down at her hands.

"And saw an opportunity," I finished her sentence grimly. I watched her. It wasn't like Summer to be so quiet and still. She looked pale, too, which was understandable after the encounter she'd just had with the police.

I changed my mind about mentioning the pictures Nadia might have. "Summer, I think a woman on our tour took some pictures in the Metro. I'll check with her and see if she has any, but until then there's not a lot we can do." It seemed like a good idea to try to distract Summer so I said, "Where's this room that's in such bad shape?"

Summer checked her watch, said the Archers wouldn't be home for another hour, and headed across the driveway. "Emma is back in preschool today. She was sick yesterday. That's why Ms. Archer asked me to watch her." Summer unlocked the back door of the Cape Cod house. We stepped into a blindingly white galley kitchen with older appliances.

"This room looks great," I said. Usually the kitchen was the messiest room in the house, so it was hard for me to imagine a trashed room in the same house with this kitchen.

"Takeout. I think they've eaten maybe a banana here once." They don't even have cereal, if you can believe that. They both stop at Starbucks on the way to work in the morning. Emma has breakfast and lunch provided at the day care. I mean, school. Got to be politically correct, even with preschool."

Summer led the way through the small living room with hardwood floors. The angular, modern furniture seemed at odds with the cozy architecture of the house. "The master, a tiny guest room, and a bath are on this floor," Summer said as I followed her up a narrow flight of stairs to the second floor. "This used to be an attic, but it was converted into a—"

"A mess," I said. I wouldn't have been so blunt if the Archers were around, but there was stuff everywhere. A tsunami of toys had overflowed a toy box in one corner and dolls, stuffed animals, blocks, and books drenched the rest of the room. I couldn't tell if the floor was carpet or hardwood because I couldn't see it through the tangle of stuff. A crib sat opposite the toy box, and an open closet door beside the crib exposed a mishmash of clothes of all sizes. The only concession to decorating was room-darkening shades over the two dormer windows. Pink and green stripes were painted on one wall, but the pattern gave way to the plain white wall after about three stripes. Summer crossed the room. She nudged a blanket, shoes, and a few toys out of the way to close the closet door, then opened the shades.

I realized Summer was looking at me tentatively. I said, "Despite how terrible it looks, it's really not all that bad. It could be quite nice, actually. Those two dormers could have window seats under them for storage. And how would Emma feel about a big girl bed? A twin would fit perfectly between the windows."

She sagged with relief and picked her way back to me, stepping on a miniature piano and a bathtub duck, before she squeezed me in a quick hug. "Oh, thank you. Thank you so much. If you'll tell me what to do, I'll get everything and we'll make it happen."

"So what's the timeline?"

"Didn't I mention that? Three days. They want to shoot the photos on Saturday morning, so that gives us three full days. That'll be plenty, right?"

An Everything In Its Place Tip for an Organized Trip

Theme park vacation tips
- Bring a backpack with bottled water, snacks, sunscreen, and bug spray.
- Arrive early! Some parks actually open their doors before the scheduled opening time. Take advantage of the thinner crowds early in the day and hit the most popular rides before the lines form.

- A quick overview of the park map or Web site will help you save time and energy and avoid backtracking from one end of the park to another.
- If you've got younger kids in your family, check age and height limits on rides before you arrive to make sure there are enough activities for smaller children so that they won't feel left out.
- Since water rides have a tendency to soak you, consider bringing a change of clothes in a sealed plastic bag in your backpack.
- Bring a small spray bottle. A mist of water is an easy way to keep kids cool.

Chapter
Seven

I tapped on door number 521, Nadia's room at the hotel, and waited. Did I hear giggling?

Nadia opened the door. "Oh, Ellie. Come on in."

I stepped inside and paused, surprised to see everyone from our tour group. Gina perched on the windowsill, Abby sprawled against the bed's headboard, and Irene sat in one of the chairs near the small table. Wellesley had been sitting at the end of the bed. "Here, you can have my place. I have to go, but thanks for the fudge, Nadia." Wellesley didn't seem nearly as irritated with Nadia as she usually did. Nadia wrapped up a few pieces of fudge from the table and tried to press them into Wellesley's hands before she opened the door.

"No, no more, but thanks. I've got a little willpower left. I think I've eaten all of tomorrow's calories. See you tomorrow at nine. The Archives first and then Union Station."

"Would you like some fudge?" Nadia asked me. She was in full hostess-mode. "I always try and bring some snacks with me when I travel. Those vending machines are so expensive. I have oranges, too. Is your sister-in-law okay?"

The first question was easier to answer than the second. "Sure, I'll take some fudge." How could I turn it down? Besides, I was on vacation. "Summer's . . . worried."

Nadia brought me a piece of fudge from the cardboard tray on the table, then took the other seat at the table across from Irene, who said, "So, the police were at your sister-in-law's house?"

Obviously the tour group had filled Irene in on what she'd missed and she was feeling better if she was interested in the news. I finished chewing a bite of the rich fudge, considering how to answer. I decided I'd better tell them about Jorge. "The police think the man who died in the Metro was pushed."

There was a brief silence and then Nadia said, "Well, that is the most awful thing. I thought seeing a man die was the worst thing, but if he was pushed—that's even worse."

"Did you see it?" I asked.

"Well, no. I didn't actually *see* anything. But the whole experience, being swept up in the crowd was frightening. That's what I meant."

I noticed Abby looking at me with a disapproving frown and I realized my question probably sounded insensitive and a bit ghoulish. "Sorry. It's just that the police have a video of the platform and they're trying to narrow down who was near the man who died. His name was Jorge Dominguez," I said with a glance at Irene, who popped the last bite of her fudge in her mouth. "That's why the police came to talk to Summer. Since she works for Ms. Archer they thought Summer was on the platform. There was someone who looked like her in the video, but it couldn't be her because she was babysitting Ms. Archer's daughter that afternoon."

Irene stood up and said, "I just remembered I have to check in at home, you know? Thanks for the fudge, Nadia. No, don't get up." Irene sketched a wave in our general direction and slipped out the door.

"Anyway, that's why I came by. Since the video they have shows someone who looks like Summer on the platform, they think it was her and she can't prove she was at the Archers' house with a preschooler. Did you take any pictures on the platform before the man was pushed?"

Nadia hurried over to her pile of Vera Bradley quilted luggage. She pulled out a small case covered in a country Provencal print and removed a laptop. "Of course I've got photos. I wonder why the police didn't ask for them when they interviewed us that afternoon."

Abby rearranged a pillow at her back and said, "Well, at that point, everyone thought he'd fallen."

"Except for the idiot who yelled it was a terrorist," Gina said with derision.

"Right," Abby said. "So, after the panic died down, we all thought he'd fallen. The police had a lot of people to talk to. I bet if you'd offered them the photos they would have taken them, but they probably didn't even think about it."

"I wouldn't give my photos to the police," she said as she plugged in the laptop and powered it up. "I might e-mail them copies, maybe, but never my originals. Let's see. I've already downloaded that day."

She pointed and clicked a bit and then swiveled the laptop toward me. She'd put it on a slide show view and the full-screen photos flicked across the display.

The first photos were of the Capitol, the requisite shots of the dome and exterior. And there we were grouped in front of the Mall. Then a close-up of a pink flower filled the screen, reminding me of Georgia O'Keeffe's paintings. The next was a black-and-white photo of a gardener as he worked in one of the many flower beds around the Capitol. He was wiping his forehead with the back of his hand. His curved back and drooping hand conveyed the arduousness of his work.

I was stunned. "Wow, Nadia. These are amazing."

"Thanks," she said as she cleared away the crumbs of fudge and fiddled with a stack of napkins.

There were more black-and-white photos in the Metro, the children swirling in their game, a shot of a man, a commuter, shoulders sagging as he waited.

"Nadia. These are incredible," Gina said and I realized she was peering over one shoulder and Abby was looking over my other shoulder. Gina continued. "I had no idea. I'm sorry I made fun of you for taking so many pictures."

"You like them? I get so nervous when people look at my pictures. It's like looking at a bit of me, I guess. But you don't have to apologize. I know I'm sort of a fanatic about it. I go overboard."

"Wait," I said. "That one there. How do you stop this thing?"

Abby leaned over my shoulder and hit a few keys. "There you go. You hit this key and you can look through them. You're going to have to get over your high-tech phobia."

"I don't have a phobia. It's just that I've never really needed to know how to do a slide show. I mean, what am I going to do, create a slide show of the ABC's for Livvy?"

"That's an excellent idea!" Nadia said. "You could add graphics to go with each letter. Oh, the kindergarten and pre-K teachers would love that idea."

I studied each photo of the crowd. "Look, there's Ms. Archer and her assistant," Gina pointed out.

"That's Tony," I said, glad to have photo proof that Summer wasn't in Ms. Archer's entourage.

"There we are again," Gina said, but she didn't sound so snide about Nadia's extreme photo habits.

"Look, there's the end of the platform," Abby said and zoomed in on the image. I studied Jorge's face and felt uneasy. This photo was probably one of his last moments alive. I tried not to think about what he looked like a few seconds later or what his death must have been like, but I got a funny feeling in my stomach and I knew it wasn't morning sickness. The tenuous hold we had on life was enough to freak me out if I really thought about it. And better not think about it, especially while I was pregnant.

In the photo, Jorge turned slightly toward the camera. With his heavy eyebrows drawn down, he still looked a bit angry. Even with the slight fuzziness of the extreme close-up, I could see the back of a woman wearing a denim jacket. A beret topped her long red curls.

I shook my head. "Oh God. That *does* look kind of like Summer. I can see why the police wanted to talk to her." I slumped down and rubbed my forehead. How could she prove it wasn't her in the Metro?

"But it's only her back. Do you think they have a photo from the front?" Gina asked.

"I don't know, but look how low that beret is on her forehead," I said. "I doubt if anyone will be able to see her face. Those cameras are mounted pretty high on the walls. I noticed one while we were waiting during our first ride on the Metro."

"Wait," Abby said, shifting the zoom to another section of the group around the man. "Who's that?"

"That's Irene," Gina said. "What's she doing on

the platform? Didn't she say she was going somewhere else that afternoon?"

"She did. She said she was going to the Library of Congress, which is the opposite direction from the Metro stop we were at," I said as my cell phone rang. I didn't recognize the number. I answered and a soft voice murmured, "Ellie Avery?"

"Yes, this is she."

"Hi. I'm Lena, Jay's sister. I know you've left several messages, but I haven't been able to call you back until now."

I pulled my thoughts away from Summer and focused on Jay MacInally. "Yes. The police interviewed me and told me what happened. I'm so sorry. How is he?"

"He's doing much better. They're going to move him out of the ICU later." She hesitated for a moment, then said, "I know he was supposed to meet you on Monday." There was a hint of a question in her tone. I guess MacInally hadn't told his sister what our meeting was about.

"Yes. He was actually going to meet with my cousin, but she couldn't be here and since I'm in D.C. this week she asked me to meet with him instead. He knew my cousin's dad in Korea."

"Oh." I thought I could detect relief in her tone and it puzzled me. Why would his sister care if he met me? Now, if she were his wife and she didn't know about the meeting—I'd understand her being upset. I wouldn't like it if Mitch met someone, a woman in particular, and hadn't told me about it. She seemed even more guarded as she continued. "Well. I don't think Jay will be able to talk to you any time soon. He won't be up to having visitors for quite a while."

"Of course." This was going to devastate Debbie. "I hope he recovers quickly."

Abby watched me close my phone and said, "Not good news? You look like you could use another piece of fudge."

"We ate it all," Nadia said apologetically.

"That's okay. I've got some Hershey's Kisses." I pulled them out of my purse and tossed a couple to her and Nadia.

Gina shook her head. "I've already had enough sugar to last me the rest of the day."

"So what's wrong? Nothing with Livvy?" Abby asked.

"No, nothing to do with Livvy. I'm not going to be able to meet the man who knew Debbie's dad. Debbie's going to be so disappointed. She really had her hopes set on this guy."

My phone rang again. I expected it to be Mitch, but it was the same number as before.

"Is this Ellie Avery?" a man asked, his voice rough.

"Yes."

"This is Jay MacInally. Sorry I didn't make it on Monday. You heard what happened?"

"Yes, I did. In fact, I just talked with your sister and she said you wouldn't be able to see me. I completely understand—"

His scratchy voice interrupted me. "Yeah. Well, she's a little overprotective. She doesn't know what she's talking about. I'm fine. Come on down to the hospital, if you want to talk to me. I'm not going anywhere."

"Are you sure? I mean, if you're in intensive care, I don't know if they'll even let me in to see you."

"Shouldn't be a problem. I moved to a regular room this morning."

Why would his sister lie to me? "All right. I'd love to talk to you, if you feel up to it. Do you want me to come tomorrow? In the afternoon?"

"That would work. Or now's fine, I've got nothing else to do. Television stinks and they're not letting me out for another couple days. Damn tests and more tests."

I checked my watch. I had plenty of time before Mitch finished with his class this afternoon. "Okay. Let me get something to write on."

He gave me his room number and rough instructions on how to get to the hospital. Before he hung up, he said, "You're not squeamish, are you?"

"Not really."

"Good. Apparently, my face is quite a sight. Thought I'd better warn you."

I wasn't sure what to say to that, so I just told him I'd see him soon.

An Everything In Its Place Tip for an Organized Trip

More theme park vacation tips
- Consider buying a line pass, if available, which will let you skip to the front of the line. Some parks also have timed entry options at popular rides.
- Save on multiple day and multipark passes if you'll be in the area for several days.
- Avoid scheduling your trip on school holidays, if possible. Visit theme parks midweek and off-season for the best experience. Rainy days are also less crowded.
- Staying at hotels associated with the theme parks may get you special privileges like early or late entry to the park.
- Themed dining requires reservations. Book early!

- Take advantage of the package relay service that some parks offer. You can purchase souvenirs and have them sent ahead to exits, or, in some cases, they can even be delivered to your hotel.

Chapter
Eight

I paced down the hospital corridor, profoundly grateful that I wasn't a patient. There wasn't anything disconcerting about the hospital. Everything was shiny and the pathway to the patient rooms was well marked, but that hygienic smell lingered in the air and there were those oversized doors leading to departments with scary names like oncology. Debbie was going to owe me big time for this. I hadn't bargained on having to visit a hospital. There were about a thousand other places I'd rather be. Even the Metro. Actually, riding the Metro over had been easier than I thought. No screaming, no pushing or shoving. It was a little crowded, but I could deal with that. Hospitals were a different matter. I decided it was the stringently clean chemical smell that bothered me the most. I pulled the bouquet of fresh flowers closer to my nose.

At MacInally's room, I tapped on the door and recognized the raspy voice that called out, "Come in."

I paused for a second, steeling myself. I didn't want to react to MacInally's appearance at all. I pushed open the door and walked in. I swallowed hard, but managed to keep my smile on my face. "Hi, Mr. MacInally, I'm Ellie, Debbie's cousin," I said and extended the flowers. He hadn't exaggerated about his face. He was pretty beat up. Almost every exposed area of skin was either covered with gauze and tape or had protruding tubes taped to it. Bandages swathed his forehead, right eye, and right ear. His left eye was uncovered and the swollen skin around it bloomed with multicolored bruises. He had some sort of bandage on his nose, too.

"Jay. Call me Jay," he said as he took the flowers gingerly. Even the palms of his hands had bandages. I remembered what Mansfield had said about how MacInally had dragged himself along a gravel walking path.

"Thanks." He gave a little laugh. "Who would'a thought I'd be getting flowers? Now, there's a laugh," he said as he pulled the rolling tray over and stuck the flowers in his water pitcher. "Nurses'll love that."

I smiled. It seemed Jay MacInally might be physically beat up, but his humor was excellent.

He gestured with his bandaged and IV-taped hand. "Have a seat." I sat in a chair that was already drawn up to the bedside. A purple sweater draped over the back of it. I bet his sister wasn't far away and might pop in any minute, so I decided I'd better get to the point quickly, but first I had to say something about his injuries.

"I was so sorry to hear about your . . ." What to call it? Attack? Mugging? I settled for "accident."

"Wasn't anything accidental about it." MacInally wasn't nearly as delicate as I was. "I guarantee you that"—he glanced at me and amended what he was about to say—"thug didn't expect me to be sitting up, talking to you. I don't remember much of what happened. The dinner I had the night before, I remember that pretty good. Lena was there. And the commuter lot. I got that, too, but the ride in the car . . ." He shook his head. "Not much. They say that's normal, but I know it wasn't an accident. He didn't realize what a tough old bird I am." MacInally flashed a smile at me, then ran his bandaged hand over the tuft of black hair tinged with gray that stuck out above his forehead bandage. "Reminded me of Korea. I guess you don't forget those survival skills, even if you did learn them forty-odd years ago. Course, you don't expect something like that to happen on your way to work." He stopped, cleared his throat. "Sorry. Had a tube down my throat until this morning."

"What kind of work do you do?" I asked, hoping to get him off the subject of the attack. It seemed to rile him up.

"Consulting. Best job in the world, if you can get it. Charge an arm and a leg and set your own hours. After I retired from the Army, I opened a consulting firm. I help military bases and the surrounding communities stay off base closure lists."

"You're never short of clients, then." Base closure lists came out every couple of years as the military reassessed its needs and adjusted to changes, closing some locations and shifting personnel around. It was like a high-stakes poker game for the communities involved and they fought tooth and nail to stay off the lists. The income and jobs military instillations brought to communities boosted those economies and every community wanted their base to stay open.

"But that's not what you're here to talk about. Your cousin wanted to know about Korea." He paused and his laid-back manner left him. He said quietly, "It's not something I wanted to tell her about on the phone. It wouldn't be right. That's why I wanted to talk to her face to face." He settled into the pillow a bit deeper. "I'm not used to talking about it. They call it the forgotten war, you know."

I nodded and felt a bit guilty. We'd toured the World War II Memorial and the Vietnam Memorial, but had skipped right over the Korean Memorial.

"I was there from October of '67 to November of '68."

I tilted my head to one side. "The war was over by then?"

"Police action, was the term they used. There was never a surrender, just a cease-fire in 1953. And things heated up again in 1966. When we went in the Army, we were all so sure we'd end up in Vietnam, and then there we were freezing our buts off in Korea."

I thought I was fairly well read in history, but, obviously, this was something I'd missed. "Heated up? Do you mean combat?" I'd grown up hearing that Debbie's dad died in Korea, but since it was in the late 1960s, I'd assumed it was an accident.

"Hell, yes, there was combat. Vietnam got all the attention, but we went through the same thing they did. I think the North Koreans were coordinating with the Soviet Union and the North Vietnamese." He leaned forward and his bandage flexed as he gripped the handrail on the bed. "The North Koreans seized one of our Navy ships, the *Pueblo*, and held its crew prisoner for something like a year. The North Koreans raided the South, tried to attack the presidential palace in South Korea and assassinate the South Korean president. Combat patrols were ambushed. There were barracks bombings, firefights, and psy ops. It was the real deal."

"I had no idea," I said, feeling like an ignoramus.

"Ah, it's not your fault that you don't know this stuff." He relaxed back into the pillows and waved his hand, dismissing my ignorance. "It was way before you were born. And we all know they don't teach history in school these days. You want to hear about Noel, not get a history lesson." MacInally cleared his throat again, ran his hand over the top of the tray, and then shifted the water pitcher to the far end of the tray. Finally, he said, "Noel Corder was a short-timer when I got there. That meant he only had a few more weeks to go before he went back home. We called him "Pops" because he was one of the oldest guys around. He had a wife and a baby daughter. He was so proud of her, of Debbie. Every picture he got, he passed it around, showing her off.

"Looking back now, I realize he was probably about twenty. But that seemed old to us. Combat does that to you—ages you—messes with time.

"Most of the time we were up north at our compounds, but once Pops, I mean Noel, and I both had passes and we went down to a USO show. It was a morale thing, you know one of those programs. Bob Hope. Now, there was an entertainer who knew how to support the troops. Noel kidded me the whole time that I wouldn't have any fun on leave since I was with him, an old married man.

"Anyway, Noel. He was a great guy, easy to get along with. And funny, kind of a clown. He could make us laugh when things looked bad, but we looked up to him. He had the most experience on patrol and we respected that."

The words stopped and he brushed his hand down the tray again. "Look, there's no easy way to say this. He died during a firefight while we were on patrol. He shot me and another guy from our patrol."

I couldn't speak for a moment. I finally managed to say, "It was a friendly fire incident?"

MacInally just shook his head and went back to

his story. It seemed he needed to tell this his way, so I tried to turn off the questions that were running through my mind.

His scratchy voice went on in that same measured pace. "There were five of us. We'd moved into our primary ambush location and were in our positions, waiting, getting eaten alive by the mosquitoes. This was during the summer. Korea had the biggest temperature swings you can imagine. Cold like I'd never felt in the winter and then, in the summer, the heat came and it was sticky and muggy. The mosquitoes were terrible. When we were on patrol we couldn't swat them away either. Only wipe them away with our hand. Makes me itch right now, thinking about it. Maybe it was the mosquitoes that did it, I don't know. It was our last day out. We'd been on patrol for two days and I know Noel was close to heading back to the real world. Maybe he just couldn't handle it anymore.

"We had our claymores out. Those were mines we could detonate. I'm not clear on everything that happened that day, but I do remember a couple of rocks landing around us. The North Koreans used to do that, toss rocks, to see if they could get us to fire and give away our location. Anyway, I remember a couple of rocks thudding to the ground. You're so tense. You don't know if they *are* rocks. They could be grenades, but you have to wait.

"After a couple of minutes with nothing, there was a movement to the front left that triggered the claymores. I don't remember anything after that. They told me I was hit during a couple of minutes of rifle fire. It was Noel." MacInally shrugged helplessly. "He just lost it. We had marked out our lines of fire and everything, but he lost it and was shooting at anything. I was hit and I don't remember what hap-

pened. They told me later, another guy in our patrol,
Stretch, had to shoot him to keep him from hurting
anyone else. They radioed for support. Another patrol came in, put down cover, and got us out of there."

I closed my eyes. I felt sick to my stomach. How
was I going to tell Debbie this? She'd be devastated.

I opened my eyes and realized MacInally was rubbing the bandage across his forehead. His voice was
almost gone. "That was the way it happened."

"I'm tiring you out. I shouldn't stay much longer,"
I said.

"No. I'm all right." He dropped his hand back to
the sheet and his face cleared. "Sorry. It's horrific—
to know your own guy shot at you. It's unbelievable.
They said Clark died from a mortar fired by the
North Koreans. Noel shot me and Shipley. He probably died instantly. I was in a coma for a couple of
weeks."

I couldn't say anything now. I simply shook my
head.

MacInally said, "Look, what happened with Noel.
It was shell shock. Now they'd call it post-traumatic
stress. He snapped. There's no blame in it. I don't
blame him. It was war. You can't live like that day
after day, on edge all the time, and not have it change
you."

I sniffed and swallowed because my throat felt
prickly. "I see why you didn't want to tell Debbie this
over the phone. I don't know how I'll be able to tell
her." I realized a tear was trembling on my lashes and
I wiped it away with a finger. "She wants the hero story.
She wants to hear that her dad was great."

MacInally swallowed and nodded his head. He
couldn't talk for a few seconds; then he said, "We all
want the hero story, but it doesn't usually happen in
real life. I'll leave it up to you. I won't call her back or

reply to her e-mails. You know her better than I do. You decide if she can handle this. If you think it would be better, you can just say I never showed up." He cracked a small smile. "And it would be true, too."

"I'll have to think about it." I stood up. "Thanks for talking to me today. I appreciate it."

The door opened and a woman sailed into the room, but she stopped abruptly when she saw me.

"Ah, here's my sister," MacInally said and I could hear a smile in his voice. "Lena, this is Ellie Avery." Her lips pursed in disapproval, but MacInally continued. "Don't get upset. I called her and asked her to come over."

She didn't lose the pinch at her mouth, even when she said hello. There was something about the way she carried herself with smooth movements and an unhurried step that made me wonder if she'd been a dancer or an actress. It was almost as if she willed you to look at her, notice her. She was certainly beautiful enough to be an actress with her high cheekbones, glossy dark brown hair with auburn highlights, and curvy body.

The lines that fanned out from the corners of her eyes and around her pursed mouth hinted that she was probably older than she seemed at first glance and I upped my initial guess from late forties to late fifties.

As I moved to the door, she pushed past me to reclaim the chair with her sweater draped on the back. She sure was possessive for a sister. I guess having someone beat up so badly might make you a little overprotective.

I left the hospital and walked past a conglomeration of business offices. I decided I wouldn't call Debbie right away. She didn't know MacInally had contacted me. She thought he'd been a no-show, so I could take time to decide what to tell her. And I definitely needed time to think about this. *Should I even tell her?* She'd always built her dad up to mythic proportions. How would she handle the truth that was so far from the fantasy she'd created about her dad?

I could sort of understand why Debbie's mom hadn't talked about it. It was very painful, but to hide it from her daughter? Didn't Debbie deserve to know the truth? I thought she was strong enough to handle it, but it would mean dismantling all those fake endings she'd dreamed about. The cold, hard reality of Noel Corder's story was that he'd killed a man and wounded another. Why had he snapped? Other people went through the same thing he did, but didn't snap.

I shook my head in frustration. Why was I the one to make this decision? *Because you can't say no,* whispered a little voice in my head. True. I hated to disappoint anyone, but I had no idea I'd be in this position. I'd hoped for a few incidents I could take back to Debbie. Like that about him being funny. Debbie would like that.

I rotated my shoulders to relax them. I realized I'd passed my Metro stop. I turned and retraced my steps to the area of high-rise offices. I saw Irene's familiar tote bag with the words *Military spouse—toughest job you'll ever love* on the side and stepped toward her, but then stopped. *It was Irene, wasn't it?*

It looked like her. The woman was on the plump side and the clothes were right. I'd seen the no-wrinkle travel blazer and pants paired with several different tops already, but this woman had on a floppy canvas hat and huge sunglasses.

I hesitated, waiting for her to get a little closer, but she was almost even with me and I still wasn't sure if it was her or not. I followed her down into the Metro and waited, positioned slightly behind her. If it *was*

Irene and we both got off at the same Metro stop and walked to the hotel, I was going to feel really silly.

But that's what happened. By then, I couldn't walk up to her. It was obvious she didn't want to be seen. She'd huddled in the back corner of the train, slouched down against the plastic seat, and stared determinedly at the blackness out the window. Well, I couldn't go up to her and pretend to see her now, so I sulked along behind her as we exited the Metro and walked through the underground complex of shops and restaurants to the hotel. Once inside the glass doors of the hotel, she slipped around a corner and took one of the less busy elevators. I punched the button for my floor. What was all that about?

An Everything In Its Place Tip for an Organized Trip

Airline, hotel, rental car reservations

Travel search engines let you compare prices on airfare, hotels, and rental cars. Tuesdays, Wednesdays, and Saturdays are usually the cheapest days of the week to fly, but use the "flexible dates" option, which brings up a calendar with the lowest-priced, recently booked flights.

Chapter
Nine

The next morning, I was waiting in line to go through the metal detectors at the National Archives. I set my Louis Vuitton Luco Tote with its classic brown monogram pattern on the conveyer belt. I stepped through the metal rectangle and realized that was my phone ringing as it went through the scanner. Well, at least it was just the basic ring, annoying, but anonymous. I know way too much about people's taste in music from their cell phone ring tones.

I pulled out my phone before I slung the long straps of my purse over my shoulder. I dropped back from the rest of the group a few steps. Wellesley, dressed in all white again today, seemed to glow in the dim room as she gave us the background on the interior of the building and described the two murals on either side of the building's rotunda. I was relieved to see Summer's name on my caller ID. I was dreading the callback from Debbie. I'd left her a rather vague message on her answering machine last night about MacInally being delayed. I'd said I'd call her later, but I was sure she'd call me today.

By the time I got the phone open it had already gone to voice mail, so I lined up with everyone else to see the documents that established our rights and our nation. Summer's message was brief. "Ellie, *please* call me back. I'm scared."

I inched forward in the line and dialed her number. She answered right away. "Summer, I got your message. What's wrong?"

"They really think I did it. They were back again this morning and asked more questions and it was . . . horrible. I can't believe it." Panic edged her voice higher. "And there's no way to prove I wasn't there."

"Summer. Stop. Take a breath. Now tell me exactly what happened."

She inhaled, exhaled, and said more slowly, "The police detectives came back this morning. Detective Brown and that creepy woman who never says a word. Anyway, they spent about an hour here. Brown asked the same questions over and over again. Then they went next door to talk to the Archers before they left for work. Oh, Ellie. This is awful. I have a test this morning. How am I supposed to concentrate? And I don't even know if I have a job to go to this afternoon."

"Summer—"

"Wait, I'm getting another call," Summer said and switched to it.

The line had moved pretty quickly and I leaned over the Declaration of Independence, amazed at the intricacy of the lettering and the names. Those names. I could hardly believe I was looking at the actual document.

Summer's voice sounded in my ear. "It's me again. Well, I still have a job." She sounded slightly calmer.

"That was Ms. Archer?"

"Yes. She said she totally supports me and knows I wouldn't hurt Jorge." The pace of her words picked up again. "Of course, that means you still have an organizing job and we have to get started on it."

"Okay, your test is this morning?"

"Yes."

"You go take your test. Pick me up at the hotel after lunch, say one o'clock, and we'll go back over to the Archers' house. I made a detailed list of my ideas this morning. Any chance I'll be able to talk to Ms. Archer about what she'd like for the room? Or am I just supposed to make it look great and they'll rip it all out if they don't like it?" We'd moved on to the Constitution, but I stepped back from the group. It was too confusing to talk to Summer and take in history at the same time. Besides, the lady in line behind me was giving me dirty looks.

"Oh, they're not going to rip it out. They're not the weekend home improvement types. And anything would be better than it is now. They'll be home later today so you can talk with them then."

"Great. I'll bring my ideas and a list of materials you'll need to get. Now, about the other thing. Nadia did have some pictures from the Metro. I'll bring them."

"Wonderful." Summer sounded relieved as she confirmed that she'd meet me at the hotel and we hung up. I merged back into our tour group in time to see the Bill of Rights. I took a moment to really look at it, taking in the fragility of the script and the yellowing paper.

Abby said, "Hey, are you coming? We're off to the next place, Union Station."

"Feel like a walk, ladies?" Wellesley asked as we emerged into the sunshine on the Mall after Abby and I made a quick detour to the restrooms. "We're only a couple of blocks away from Union Station."

Gina nodded and set off at a quick pace with Wellesley. Nadia was busy photographing other tourists and the buildings we passed. Irene trailed along at the end of the line, her tote bag stuffed with her purchases from the gift shop at the Archives.

I told Abby what Summer had said about her being a suspect and Abby asked, "Do you think it's true or is she being melodramatic? Maybe they're just following up on all the loose ends, that sort of thing."

"I don't know, but she did sound worried. Hardly anything worries her." I glanced back and saw that Irene had fallen a few more paces behind, so we slowed down. "Do you think Irene is feeling okay?"

Abby said, "I don't know. She hasn't been doing her usual mother hen thing, has she?" And because Abby usually says exactly what she's thinking, she called out, "Hey, Irene, are you feeling okay?"

Irene lifted her head and hurried to catch up with us. "Yes. Of course. Just a little tired, you know? All this walking. I'm not used to it."

"But think of all the calories we're burning," Abby said. "We can have a huge lunch."

Irene smiled and I realized it was the first time I'd seen her smile in days.

I was surprised to find out Union Station was still an actual train station. It buzzed with tourists shopping and travelers rushing for their trains. We found a restaurant on the second floor and ordered hamburgers and pizza. I handed my menu to the waiter and glanced around as everyone else ordered. From where I was sitting, I could see the television in the back corner. A reporter stood in front of the skinny rectangular sign with the "M" on top that marked the Metro. I leaned in to concentrate on the reporter's words.

". . . unnamed source within the police department . . . made progress . . . person of interest . . . believed the dead man was stalking a woman . . . possibly killed her stalker . . ."

Oh no. This was not good. I had to call Summer and let her know I'd seen this. It would be better if she found out from me than from someone at school or at Vicki Archer's office. At least they hadn't used her name in the report. I hopped up, said I had to make a call, and kept walking until I got reception on my phone, which was actually outside Union Station.

I punched in Summer's number. I was going to have to rethink my promise not to tell Mitch anything about the investigation. The phone rang several times. I hung up. She was probably in class by now. I'd have to wait to talk to her until after lunch.

A flash of white topped with dark curls moved quickly through the crowd toward me. Wellesley had left the table with her phone a few minutes before I left. She must have had to go outside to get reception on her phone, too. I waited for her to catch up with me so we could go back inside together.

But she stopped at the base of a large fountain and looked around. A man stopped trimming the hedges in front of the building and walked over to her. He'd pulled off his gloves, and as their exchange continued, he pointed them at her. She swatted them away before any clumps of dirt or grass landed on her white dress. She shook her head defiantly and marched back into the building.

The man hit the side of the fountain with his gloves, and bits of grass and dirt showered to the ground.

He turned back to the hedge and I realized his shirt had the same logo that Jorge's had on it, a tree with an outline of the Capitol over the words *Capitol Landscape.*

I opened my purse and pulled out the photos that Nadia had printed for me in the hotel's business center.·

Maybe the man trimming the hedges knew something about Jorge that the police could pursue besides Summer. I took a step, then hesitated. Should I really do this? Was this crazy? But Summer was a "person of interest." He and the other man began to pack up. That got me moving. I hurried over to him before I could lose my courage and said, "Excuse me, do you know this man?" as I held out the photo of Jorge.

He barely glanced at it, shook his head. "*No inglés,*" he muttered, then turned away to rake the last of the leaves into a garbage bag another man held. He continued to ignore me as he walked around the truck, gathering up their equipment. The man with the garbage bag was younger. He twisted the bag closed and hefted it into the bed of the truck. "Don't mind him. He's pissed."

His English was only slightly accented. He propped one hand on the truck and extended the other for the photo. His casual pose conveyed he had all the time in the world and he felt completely comfortable talking with me, unlike his companion, who tossed the rake into the bed of the truck with a clang and then said a few words to the younger man, before he slid into the driver's seat. My high school Spanish couldn't keep up with the swift words, but I did pick up the words *rápidamente* and *vamos,* which, if I remembered right, meant something along the lines of *quickly* and *let's go*. The sharp slam of the door punctuated his words.

The noise and the gruffness of his companion didn't seem to phase the younger man, but the picture did impact him. His uncomplicated smile was gone when he handed the photo back. "Jorge. Yes. He worked with us."

"So he was part of your crew?"

"No, not every day. He filled in when we needed extra help or when someone didn't show up."

"Did anyone not like him? Were there arguments?"

"No," he said flatly. "We work. There is no trouble."

The engine revved in the truck and he moved toward the passenger door.

"Please, hold on a second. The woman who was here before me. How do you know her?"

"Me? I don't know her. I've heard of her, though. She's the *boda* lady." He nodded his head toward the cab of the truck. "She promised him a *boda*, but now she says no. He will be angry all day." He opened the door and slid into the truck.

"Wait. What's a *boda*?" I asked, but the truck was already pulling away.

He leaned out the window and shouted, "Ask at the Verde Campo on Thursdays."

I climbed the steps, going over the word *boda* in my mind, but I couldn't remember what it meant. Surely, not body. I couldn't come up with anything else that might even be a close translation. And *verde campo*. What was that? He'd said it with the word "the" in front of it, like it was a name. A business?

As I tucked the photo back into my purse, I saw something I hadn't noticed before. I pulled it out again and looked closer. A swath of black fabric with tiny white dots trailed along the left side of the photo.

It was a fabric like Wellesley had worn on the first day of the tour, the day Jorge had died.

So *Wellesley* had been at the other end of the platform, too? She had wandered away from me a few moments before the commotion broke loose, but I had no idea she'd gone to the other end of the platform.

I looked at the other photos, but that was the only one that had captured the edge of the skirt. I put the photos away slowly. I arrived back at the table at the same time the food did. I dug into the burger and chunky fries. "Where's Wellesley?" I asked.

"She had to go," explained Gina. "She gave us an overview of the history of Union Station and then told us about a few stores we might want to hit."

"Oh, okay." Then I noticed Irene's place was also empty. "Irene left, too?"

"Yep. It's just us hard-core shoppers who're left," Nadia said.

Abby studied my face, then said, "You look preoccupied. Anything wrong?"

I debated for a moment. Should I tell them? Abby, I trusted, no question, but Nadia and Gina, I didn't know about. Of course, they were looking at me expectantly now.

"It's not the baby, is it? If you're not feeling good, we can all go back to the hotel right after lunch," Nadia said, and I was touched that she'd give up one minute of her sightseeing to escort me back to the hotel.

"No, nothing like that. I'm fine." I decided I might as well tell them. Maybe one of them could make sense of the things that were happening. I knew none of us had been at the end of the platform and I had a gut feeling I could trust Nadia. She was so open and energetic. Gina held herself more in reserve, but I thought I could trust her, too. I pulled the photo out and handed it to Nadia. "Look at this side of the photo here."

Nadia looked at it, frowned, and said, "What is that? I could enlarge it . . ."

Gina said, "It's the skirt Wellesley wore on Monday."

Yep, she was quick. I was relieved that she'd spotted it and made the same connection I had.

"So that means Wellesley *and* Irene were near Jorge before he was pushed?" Abby asked as she pulled the photo across the table to study it.

"Yes. Along with a redheaded woman who resembles Summer from the back," I said and explained what I'd just seen. "That's the second time I've seen Wellesley talking to a landscaper, and both times the men were mad at her."

Gina leaned back in her chair, her flat face turned up to the ceiling. "But they don't work for her."

"Right," I said. "She told me the name of her company is Household Helper and that wasn't the name of the logo on their shirts."

"Well, I know that *boda* means wedding," Nadia said.

"Really?" I was surprised.

"I minored in Spanish." She shrugged. "And the other phrase would be something like green countryside or green country."

I wouldn't write off Nadia anymore. She might be annoyingly perky, but besides her talent with a camera, she was smart.

Abby shook her head. "I know I've heard those words somewhere, but I can't place them."

"Back to the wedding thing," I said. "It doesn't make any sense. Wellesley's not married."

"Maybe she's getting married." Gina picked up her check.

"But why would she tell two different landscapers about her wedding?" Abby asked.

"To hire them to landscape for the wedding or reception?" I asked. "No, wait. She's got her own referral company. She'd just use them."

I noticed the time and hopped up. "I've got to run, too. I'm supposed to meet Summer."

An Everything In Its Place Tip for an Organized Trip

Once you've found the flight that fits your schedule and budget, be sure to check the price directly on the airline's Web site. You may find an even cheaper price if you book directly through the airline's Web site instead of through the larger travel search Web sites. Airlines run Internet specials that are available only through their Web site. If there's one airline that you always fly, check to see if they have a travel newsletter or e-mail so they can notify you of sales and special travel deals.

Chapter
Ten

"**Y**ou're sure they didn't mention my name?" Summer tossed a worried look at me as she hurried to the Archers' back door.

"No, they didn't." We'd been in such a rush to get to their house that I'd barely had time to tell her about the news report.

"Well, at least that's one good thing, I guess," she said, but her eyebrows were lowered in a frown. "There's no way anyone will know it's me. No one else knows I checked into the restraining order." She rapped on the screen door.

"Don't you think the unnamed source could leak your name?" Then it hit me. "Or mine. Summer—"

She cut me off. "Let's talk about it after we get done with Ms. Archer. She hates it when people are late. There's just one other *little* thing I need to tell you about the organizing job."

It was never good to hear those words "little thing." Somehow that combination of words always translated into something enormous. Before she could let me in on the "little thing," Vicki Archer opened the door.

"Good. You're on time," she said and gestured for

us to come inside the small kitchen. Despite her being tall, thin, and blond, you'd call Vicki Archer striking, but it was more because of the force of her personality than her looks. Her features were a bit out of balance. Her nose was too big for her face and her eyes protruded, reminding me of a bug. Her lips were thin and, since I was closer to her today than I'd been in the Metro, I could see she'd outlined her lips on the outside to make them look bigger. I could also see the stiffness of her hair that had been shellacked into her signature upsweep. Summer performed a quick introduction. "This is my sister-in-law, organizer extraordinaire Ellie Avery."

We shook hands and I said, "So nice to meet you, Vicki." If I was going to work with her, I wanted to start off on an equal footing.

She smiled. Well, to be completely accurate, the corners of her lips rose a millimeter as she said, "Ellie, it's a pleasure," with a slight emphasis on my name, indicating she'd picked up on my informality. "I've heard such good things about you. Summer's been singing your praises. I hope you can live up to them," she finished severely.

Her tone bordered on threatening. Mentally, I put on my dealing-with-a-difficult-customer manner and said, "That depends on what you want, of course. Why don't you tell me about your daughter and what you'd like to achieve in her room?"

"Emma's four. She loves pink and princesses. I just want it to look great in the magazine. Something with clean lines. I'll leave the details up to you and Ivan," she said as she led the way up the stairs.

"Ivan?" I raised my eyebrows and looked over my shoulder at Summer.

She whispered, "Ivan Flint."

The way she said his name indicated that I should

recognize it, but I didn't. "Who?" I whispered back, but before she could answer we followed Vicki into Emma's room, stepping over toys.

Vicki said, "Ivan, here's your helper, Ellen."

"It's Ellie, actually," I said as I reached out to shake hands with the largest man I'd ever seen. His tight black turtleneck and leather pants emphasized his size. He was the size of a professional football linebacker. Except he looked like he could fill out a football uniform without the shoulder pads. He seemed to take up most of the space in the small room. My hand disappeared in his hug paw of a hand.

"Ivan Flint. Flint Designs," he said and I realized he was an interior designer.

Vicki turned in a slow circle and said, "A fairly tale theme. Knights, castles, dragons, everything. Murals?" She switched her gaze back to Ivan. "You can do murals, right?"

He ran his hand with several rings over his shaved head and said, "Of course."

Summer stepped closer and said, "Vicki decided this morning that you and Ivan would make a super team for the redo of this room."

Great. That "tiny" thing had turned into collaborating with an interior designer. I kept my smile on my face, but inside I winced. It was hard enough to get my clients to make decisions about organizing, but now we were adding an interior designer to the mix. I could practically see the speedy job disappearing like fog in the morning sun. Well. Nothing to do about it now. I'd agreed to help Summer and I couldn't back out now.

Vicki seemed to be edging toward the door, so I said, "Let's go over a few things quickly. Storage? Would you like more? We could put in some window seats under the dormers."

Vicki looked at Ivan and he nodded. Vicki said, "Great. Do it."

"What about sorting through the toys? You could probably thin the amount of toys. Some look like they're for infants."

Vicki looked down, seeming to notice the toys for the first time. "Yes. In fact, toss them all. We'll buy new ones to go with the room." She took a few more steps to the door and motioned for Summer to follow her.

"Wait. What about Emma? Doesn't she have some favorite toys she'd like to keep? And it would be really helpful to talk about how you use this room."

Vicki's eyebrows drew together over her buggy eyes. "Emma *sleeps* here," she said as if it was the most obvious thing in the world. "She really doesn't play here because she spends most of her day at school. On the weekends we have activities. Ballet, gymnastics, that sort of thing." She tilted her head from side to side, like a metronome. "She's not attached to any of these toys. She'll love new toys. Now. I have five minutes. I'll leave you here with Summer to work out the details, but I need to go over a report with her before I leave." Vicki headed out the door and Summer hurried after her.

Summer wanted to work for this woman? I shook my head and turned back to Ivan. He smiled and said, "Looks like we have carte blanche. I'm thinking black walls and ceiling."

Maybe I hadn't heard him right. "Black?"

He nodded, gazing up at the ceiling. "I'm thinking nighttime enchanted forest. Paint every thing black, string twinkle lights across the ceiling to simulate a starry sky, rip up the carpet, if there is carpet under all this mess, and paint the floor green for the forest floor. Midnight Enchanted Forest."

I was speechless for a moment. It sounded more like the Brothers Grimm to me. Finally, I managed to say, "Do you have kids?"

"No. I'm single." He took his gaze off the walls long enough to focus on me. He must have been able to tell it was going to be hard to sell me on his idea, because he continued. "It'll be striking. Original. Unprecedented. No one else is going to have a room like it."

"Ivan, kids don't like the dark. I don't think a four-year-old is going to like an all-black room. In fact, I think it sounds a little morbid. Now, if she were a teenager, it would probably be a different story. And what about the murals? You can't have murals on black walls."

"Of course we can do murals. We'll use shades of brown and gray. They won't stand out, but they'll be there, lurking, so that when you look closely you'll see a dragon wrapped around a tree or something."

"Lurking. That's a nightmare waiting to happen. You can't paint that on a little kid's wall. You're going to have to come up with something else. What about pink? Emma likes pink." I was all for using clients' ideas as inspiration for organization. Surely the same principle worked for interior design.

"No pink. Pink is hackneyed. Blasé. Worn out. This space has to stand out. Be unique. One of a kind."

Summer reentered the room and said, "Don't worry about the toys. Emma's got a few favorites and I'll stash them away for her. How's it going?"

"I can't work with her." Ivan threw his thick arm at me. "She has no vision. No inspiration. No insight." He stormed out the door and pounded down the stairs.

"He'll be back. Artistic temperament and all that. Seems he has to storm off every job at least once to keep his reputation."

"So you've worked with him before?"

"Yes. He did Vicki Archer's reception area. An ice cube was his inspiration."

"Well, that explains the subzero temperature in there. Oh, Summer, I don't know if this is going to work."

"I know it looks bad but, please, just give it a try."

"Okay. Let's get everything down on paper."

Two hours later, Summer parked her car in the lot next to the Metro station. "Are you sure you don't want me to drop you at the hotel?" she asked.

"No, this is fine. I'm an old hand at the Metro now." Summer had a night class and I didn't want her to have to go out of her way to drop me off at the hotel. Emma's room had occupied all our time up to this point. We'd made two exhaustive lists, one of things that needed to be done to Emma's room and another of everything that needed to be purchased to get it organized. It seemed like Summer was focusing on Emma's room so she didn't have to think about her new designation as a person of interest.

I pulled Nadia's photos out of my purse. "Here's the pictures my friend took."

Summer didn't snatch them out of my hand like I expected. She took them gingerly and studied each one carefully. The first ones were photos of the crowds in the Metro, commuters and tourists mingled together.

The last one was the clear photo of Jorge with the redheaded woman nearby. "Ellie, that does look like me. I thought I'd be able to see something that proved it wasn't me, but there's nothing—the jacket looks like mine. I have a beret like that. It could be me."

The paper trembled in her hand. "What am I going to do? I'm a 'person of interest.' If my name and face get on the news I won't be able to get a job—probably ever. It won't matter if it was me or not. All people will remember is that I was a suspect. I might as well be guilty. Four years—well, actually five—years of college for nothing. Wasted. No one will hire me."

I didn't have an easy answer for her. She was right. If her name got out and she was portrayed as a murderer, her career would be over before it had begun, never mind that no evidence would have reached a courtroom. This investigation had all the hallmarks that media cable shows gravitated to: young, beautiful woman in danger, a murder, a stalker. There was even alliteration, *murder in the Metro.* I cringed when I thought of what the text and graphics people at the cable news channels could do with that phrase.

But what troubled me even more was that I doubted the police would look too hard for other suspects since they had circumstantial evidence pointing to Summer.

"Look, Summer, we know someone near Jorge pushed him. The woman who looks like you is a coincidence." There was panic in her face and I could tell she wasn't really listening to me, so I used my calmest voice and asked, "Where did you get your denim jacket?"

That got her attention. "The Gap. Why?"

"Okay, there have to be thousands of jackets exactly like yours out there. Someone who had red hair happened to be standing beside Jorge when he was pushed."

"Wearing a beret like mine."

"That's not as common as the jacket, but I'm sure there are lots of black berets in the D.C. area, too." I realized I sounded like a defense attorney, so I quickly moved on. "We just have to find something that will convince the police that one of those other people around Jorge might be a better suspect than you."

I pointed out Wellesley's dress and told Summer about the conversation between Wellesley and Jorge as well as the encounter I'd seen earlier in the day. "We don't have enough to take to the police right now. I don't think they'd be very excited about a scrap of fabric in a photo, but I'll see Wellesley again tomorrow and I'll ask her about it. If nothing else, she might have seen something."

Could Wellesley have pushed Jorge? I didn't know. I did feel a bit guilty about searching the photo for someone else to throw to the police, but I steeled myself. I had to keep my focus on Summer. If Wellesley didn't push Jorge she didn't have anything to hide and she'd be able to dispatch the police quickly. Then there was also Irene's face in the photo and her weird behavior. I shut off any mental speculation about Irene. She couldn't be involved in Jorge's death. Not Irene. She was too sweet, too motherly.

Then a thought jumped into my mind. *Unless it was an accident.* No. That couldn't have happened. Irene would have said something if it had. She wasn't the kind to hide things. She loved the news and would relish being part of the news. I closed off that line of thought and put my attention back on Summer.

Summer looked at the photo again. This time she focused on the faces. "You're right. All we need to do is throw suspicion on someone else."

She looked a bit more in control, so I brought up the other topic that had been bothering me. "I'm going to tell Mitch about the investigation."

"Why? Do you have to?"

"Yes, I really do. I hate to hide things from him, and this is starting to feel a lot like hiding."

"All right." She sighed. "But can you keep it kind of vague? I promise if my name shows up on the news, I'll tell him everything. I know you think this is crazy, me not wanting to tell him, but he's always rescued me and I want him to see that I'm grown up now. If he knows about everything he'll come charging in and take over. I need to work this out without him. Maybe he'll see me differently then."

"You're always going to be his kid sister."

"I know. I don't want that to change, I just want him to see that I'm grown up."

Later as I swayed with the rhythm of the Metro car, I thought about her response to the picture and the different conversations we'd had. Had she ever flat-out said that she wasn't on the platform that day? I didn't think so. And she hadn't told me about Jorge stalking her until the police brought it up. Was there something else she wasn't telling me?

The train slowed down and I braced my hand on the silver pole as I leaned back to counter the motion of the train. I checked the station. One more stop to go. A couple of people squeezed into the already crowded car, erasing a little more of our personal space. A man holding a little girl of about two in the crook of his arm shifted the girl from one arm to the other and changed his stance as the train sped up.

As he moved, I saw a familiar floppy hat and tote bag. I couldn't move around to see better, but it looked like Irene in her incognito getup again. What was she up to?

I didn't want to think about it, but she *had* been in those photos near Jorge, too. As soon as the doors opened, I'd catch up with her and ask her about it. There had to be a simple explanation.

But she was quick. One minute she was digging through her tote bag, and the next, the doors opened and she was gone. I turned in a circle a few times before I left the Metro, but I didn't see her anywhere. I walked through the underground shopping complex, thinking what an odd place it was, keeping an eye out for the hat and tote bag. You never had to actually step outside in this part of Washington. You could do everything in these underground tunnels: shop for clothes, groceries, do your banking, get to and from work. Really, you could live like a mole and never see the sun if you wanted.

I was almost to the hotel entrance when I saw the floppy hat again. I made my way through the small restaurant and sat down at the table across from Irene. Her huge sunglasses were on the table and she was using a paper napkin to wipe her eyes.

An Everything In Its Place Tip for an Organized Trip

Traveling with pets
- Make sure you've got identification tags on your pet as well as any vaccination tags that are expected like rabies tags.
- Book accommodations with pet-friendly hotels, which can be found online or in guidebooks specifically focused on travel with pets.
- Request a ground-floor hotel room with easy access to outdoor areas.
- Don't forget pet food, food and water bowls, collar and leash, and any medications your pet needs.

- If you're traveling by car, a few practice runs around town in your car before your trip will help your pet feel more comfortable in the car.
- If your pet is flying, check for regulations about the type of kennel you can use and for temperature restrictions. Some airlines won't ship pets during times of extreme heat or cold.

Chapter
Eleven

Her miserable face wasn't what I'd expected. Any questions I'd wanted to ask her flew out of mind, except for one. "Irene, what's wrong?"

"Oh, Ellie." She sounded almost relieved. Was she relieved to see me or relieved I wasn't someone else? "It's nothing. I'm fine. Don't worry about me, okay?"

"No. You're not okay. What's wrong?"

She burst into tears and I pulled a few more napkins out of the dispenser for her and patted her shoulder. Could things get any more reversed? Me, mothering Irene?

After a few seconds her sobs tapered off. She wiped her eyes, blew her nose, and set her hands in her lap. "There. Sorry. I'm done. It was too much, you know? I got the results back and then I saw the little girl in the Metro." Her eyes watered but she sniffed determinedly and went on, "I just lost it. I can't go up to the room, looking like this. So I stopped in here and I just couldn't quit crying. I'd been so hopeful . . ."

"About what?"

She tucked her sunglasses away in her purse, then

gathered the wadded napkins. "It's nothing to be upset about, I know that, but . . ." She shrugged and the waterworks threatened to burst again. She fought her surging emotions before she could speak again.

"You don't have to tell me. I just wanted to make sure you were all right."

She dabbed at the corners of her eyes and said, "No. It's okay. It'll be a relief to tell someone, actually. I had some tests done and the results weren't what I wanted." She saw my face and hurried on, "Nothing bad. I . . . well, this is going to sound silly, but I want to have another baby.

"I had some problems last time and the doctor told me I was done. It would be too dangerous to have another baby. But then I heard about this experimental treatment that a research clinic was doing. It was in D.C. and since I was going to be here anyway it just seemed like it was meant to be, you know? I was so sure it was going to work out." Irene paused and looked at the ceiling as she blinked several times.

I wasn't quite sure what to say. I knew Irene had a passel of kids. Five? Or was it six? I knew she'd had twins at least once. Anyway, my first thought, to be perfectly honest, was along the lines of *don't you have enough kids already?* But I managed to restrain myself from saying anything. I took a few seconds and thought about Irene. She did enjoy her family and she was wonderful with kids. She'd even taken care of Livvy for me when Livvy was in the middle of her worst stages of separation anxiety, and Livvy hadn't even missed me. I finally said, "I'm sorry, Irene."

"Thanks. I tried to take it in stride. I thought I was going to be okay, but then I saw the girl in the Metro and I lost it. I know that I have a big, beautiful family and I should be happy with the family I *do* have, but . . ." She shrugged again. "It's hard to describe. I love kids, you know? I don't want this stage of our life to be over, I guess. But it is."

"You don't have to explain it for me. You're a great mom."

At least that made her grin. "Thanks, Ellie. I know I dither about everything, but I do love my kids and this may seem limited to you, but I've always wanted to be a mom and a housewife. You've got your organizing business and you're busy with that, so you might not understand, but being a mom is everything for me. I don't know how to describe it. It's almost like it's a gift or something. I hear other moms complaining about their kids and I know I have bad days where everyone drives me crazy, but I love it and I don't want it to change."

"I think you're right. You do have a gift. Look how you've taken care of us on this trip. You're nurturing and caring and you're so much more patient with your kids than I am with Livvy." I paused, debating if I should go there, but then I said, "Have you ever thought about adoption or foster care?"

"I haven't, not really. Of course, it's kind of crossed my mind, but I've always pushed it to the background, you know? Because I absolutely *love* being pregnant. I feel very special and powerful at the same time, you know?"

"Ah—no. I just feel tired and cranky. And huge."

Irene laughed and shook her head. "You're so funny. Being pregnant is the best. It's something to revel in."

I wasn't making a joke, but I didn't let Irene in on that. If she liked being pregnant, then that was great. I sure knew I wasn't reveling in my pregnancy. I just wanted it to be over so I could finally meet the little fellow.

Irene's face turned serious. "You're right, though, about foster care. I wonder what Grant would think about it. I should think about it, check into it?" She looked at me questioningly.

"Irene, I think any child would be very lucky to have you as a parent or foster parent. I have to ask, why the disguise?"

She plucked the hat off the table and stuffed it in her tote bag. "Guess I'm not very good at disguises since you spotted me, right? I felt self-conscious. I didn't want anyone to know what I was doing. I mean, most people would think we have plenty of kids, you know? And, well, I didn't want to get into the subject of female problems."

I laughed. "You're right. Get a couple of women together and mention pregnancy or birth and you're going to hear everyone's story."

"That's why I slipped off on the first day. It was my first appointment. I thought I had to take a different Metro, but I mixed up the stations and got turned around. I ended up at the same one as you and every-one else. I hoped no one would see me because I didn't want to explain everything, you know?"

"And I've made you do exactly that. I'm sorry."

Irene stood up. "No. I feel much better. It helped to talk about it, but I don't think I'm ready to talk about it with everyone else." She tossed her napkins in the trash and we walked back into the underground tunnel that led to the hotel.

And that's why she'd acted so funny at breakfast the next morning and lied about being on the plat-form. "Don't worry, I won't tell anyone. But I have to ask, did you see anything on the platform?"

"No. I was trying so hard to avoid you guys that I wasn't watching what was happening right beside me." Irene shuddered. "It's awful to think that a man standing so close to me was alive one minute and dead the next. Terrible. But I didn't see anything." Her voice slowed down as she said, "In fact, I was looking *over* my shoulder right before the commotion. I'd just seen Wellesley near me and I was checking to see if she was still there."

"Was she?" I asked as we entered the hotel and hurried to catch an open elevator.

The doors slid closed and Irene said, "I don't know. I looked behind me and didn't see her, but right at that moment someone screamed and I looked back toward the tracks and . . . well . . . You know, the funny thing is that there really wasn't anything to see. The train was streaming in and people were milling around, but you couldn't tell what had happened. I can't say if she was there or not because everything went so crazy after that."

"And did you see anyone who had long red hair?"

Irene shook her head. "No. I don't remember anyone like that." She shrugged. "I wasn't paying attention, trying to notice things. I was more focused on avoiding you guys."

Irene got off at the eighth floor and I continued up to the fourteenth. I pulled out my phone and dialed my parents' number as soon as I stepped out of the elevator. All this talk about babies made me miss Livvy. I'd intentionally not called first thing this morning. Maybe later in the day would be better for a chat. After a couple of rings the answering machine came on and I left a short message. The door across the hall from our room opened and Abby stepped into the hallway. "Guess where we're going to dinner tonight?" she said.

"You sound like you've got it all planned."

"Verde Campo. It's a Mexican restaurant. I saw it on the list the concierge gave us. We're going there tonight for an early dinner since Mitch and Jeff have to meet with their study group later tonight."

"Oh yeah. I'd forgotten about the group project. I think I'm seeing Mitch less often than I do when we're at home."

Abby laughed. "Right. Except, when we're at home, they're usually not home either. They're either deployed or on a trip. We can go shopping after dinner. There's been far too much history on this trip and not enough malls. Shopping malls," she clarified, but she was smiling so I didn't take her too seriously. I knew that her visits to the monuments would show up in her lesson plans when she went back to her classroom.

"I won't be able to. I've got to—" I was about to say I couldn't because I had to get Livvy to bed. "Boy, old habits die hard, don't they? We can stay out shopping until the stores close." Even after I'd been apart from Livvy for several days, her schedule was still imprinted on my brain and impacted the way I operated. Well, except when a police interview totally threw me off.

"How's she doing?" Abby asked.

"Great. Fine. Wonderful. I call at least once a day and it's always the same. She's *way* too busy to talk to me, though. I know that's a good sign, but still . . ."

Abby nodded. "Still wishing she'd miss you?"

"Just a little bit." I tried to shake off the feeling of insignificance and said, "Well, at least we can ask about the *boda* lady at dinner."

"And tonight is Thursday. We might even see her."

An Everything In Its Place Tip for an Organized Trip

Brand loyalty pays when you travel. If possible, book most of your flights with a single airline. You'll rack up points and perks. The same goes for rental car companies and hotel chains. Most hotel chains have a membership program. Sign up and you'll receive better service and discounts because you're a frequent guest.

Chapter
Twelve

The Verde Campo Restaurant was a few blocks from the hotel so we walked, aboveground, that is. It was a busy restaurant with trompe l'oeil murals of the rolling hills and expansive skies. I spent most of the meal trying to figure out who to ask about the *boda* lady and how to go about it.

I heard the word "assignment" and focused on the conversation. "Still no word on our assignment," Mitch repeated for me. A little indentation formed between his eyebrows as he frowned. "Everything okay?"

"Sure. Fine," I said brightly.

"I don't understand why it takes so long," Abby said. "I haven't thought about it nearly as much since we've been here, but it's still there, hovering in the background. I hate not knowing."

Jeff said, "We'll know soon enough. Should be any day."

"We've said that for what? The last three weeks?" Abby said.

Mitch looked like he regretted bringing up the subject of moving. I realized he was trying to change

the subject as he said to me, "You seem really interested in those murals."

"Vicki Archer said she'd like to have a mural in
her daughter's room, so I was checking these out." I
told them about Ivan's idea for a midnight forest
theme. "I was just imagining what he'd say about this
place."

Jeff said, "Oh, I know what he'd say. Abby's made
me watch enough of those design shows that I can do
'design speak.' He'd say something about the 'space'
and how the murals 'bring the outside in.' You only
have to repeat that over and over again, maybe throw
in an 'absolutely' every once in a while."

Mitch said, "Don't forget 'pop.' As in 'that color
really makes the space pop.' "

I couldn't help but smile. The guys had nailed the
jargon. "You're awful, but I'll have to remember those
buzzwords. Maybe they'll help me communicate with
Ivan. And I think I'll try to get the name of the person who did these murals, just in case Ivan's contact
doesn't work out." When our waitress, a young woman
with lush dark hair and beautiful brown eyes named
Gloria, brought our checks I asked her about the
muralist and she said she'd ask the manager.

Mitch gave me a long look.

I shrugged. "I'm just asking."

"Somehow, I don't think that's all you're asking
about."

I hadn't mentioned my conversation with Irene—
I was keeping it to myself—but I had told Mitch that
I thought the police were looking at Summer more
closely than she'd let on and that I'd given her the
photos Nadia had taken. He didn't say much, but I
could tell by the way his face closed down that he was
worried.

I usually liked it when I was the focus of his intense gaze—when he looked at me like there wasn't anyone or anything more important or quite as fascinating as me. It's actually quite heady. This time, though, there was a bit of speculation and assessment in his brown gaze that made me uncomfortable.

Gloria returned to pick up our checks and handed me a slip of paper with a name and phone number. I thanked her and then told Mitch I was going to the restroom, which didn't surprise him. The restroom at every major tourist attraction in the capital might as well be on my sightseeing list. It was just a good thing that the restrooms were free, unlike in Europe where you had to pay to use the facilities. We were saving a fortune by vacationing in the U.S.

I followed our waitress across the dining room and through a doorway to a wide corridor. She turned left to enter the kitchen. Instead of turning to the right to the restrooms, I waited. In a few seconds, she emerged with the folders containing our credit card receipts in one hand and a tray of drinks balanced in her other hand.

"One more question. Do you know the *boda* lady?"

The tray of drinks swayed a bit, but she quickly shook her head. "No." She shifted the tray around my shoulder and stepped away quickly.

I hurried along beside her. "Please. My sister-in-law is in trouble and I need to talk to the *boda* lady. Is she here? I was told to ask for her here." Belatedly, I wished I'd asked the younger landscaper for his name. Knowing his name might have helped.

"I don't know who she is," Gloria said shortly.

"But you've heard of her?"

"Yes." She bit her lower lip for a moment, then said, "Wait here," and hurried off.

I waited in the corridor, where a steady stream of waiters and waitresses hurried by me, but didn't pay much attention to me. I studied the mural of a seascape until my waitress returned, with the empty tray. A worn-down woman trailed behind her, pushing a cart with dirty dishes. I couldn't guess her age. She could be anywhere from forty to sixty. Her sloped shoulders and the hesitant way she raised her head, met my gaze, and then dropped her gaze back to her chapped and wrinkled hands spoke of years of menial jobs.

Gloria said quickly. "This is Estelle. She knows the *boda* lady."

At her name, Estelle's gaze jumped to Gloria. Estelle quickly refocused on her hands, which gripped the dish cart handle. I reached way back to my high school Spanish class and said, "*Hola, Estelle. Me llamo es Ellie.*" I hoped I didn't mangle it too badly.

I must have done okay because Estelle's face creased into wrinkles as she smiled quickly, then ducked her head.

Gloria edged away. I didn't want her to abandon me now. "That's all the Spanish I can remember. Could you ask her about the *boda* lady?"

Gloria sighed and translated my question. Clearly her patience was running out. I'd have to make sure we left a big tip. Estelle mumbled a few words, her head downcast.

"She says the *boda* lady finds you a husband or a wife. She's a—" She circled the empty tray in the air as she searched for the right word.

"Matchmaker?" I asked. Did those exist today?

"Yes. You pay her and she will find you an *esposa.*"

"And where do you find the *boda* lady? Does she come here on certain nights?"

She looked offended. "I don't know. I was born here."

"Could you ask Estelle?"

After a few moments of rapid-fire Spanish, Gloria said, "The *boda* lady is here every Thursday night."

"And how does it work?"

Gloria and Estelle talked and then Gloria said, "You give her six thousand dollars and she arranges the marriage. Tells you when to go to the courthouse for the ceremony."

Six thousand dollars? For a woman like Estelle that had to be a huge sum of money, but a marriage certificate would make it easier to become a U.S. citizen.

For the first time, Estelle spoke directly to me in Spanish. I didn't understand her words, but I completely got her tone—angry. She raged a few seconds, then pushed the cart roughly between us and scurried away.

I looked at Gloria. Her mouth twisted in disgust. "Estelle gave her the money, but now the *boda* lady says everything's off. There's a delay. Estelle says she's not paying any more money."

Wasn't that what the landscaper was angry about earlier today? He'd paid money and then been told the deal was off, too.

Gloria shook her head. "People are so desperate, they do foolish things. Estelle will probably never see any of that money again, much less a groom."

"She'd never say anything to the police, would she?" I asked.

"Of course not."

"Who's the *boda* lady matching them with?"

Gloria hesitated, then spoke quickly. "I know someone else, a girl my age used the *boda* lady. My friend married a sailor. Estelle said she was going to marry an airman."

Wellesley was hooking up illegal aliens with military personnel? Now I really wanted to talk to her. "So the *boda* lady will be here later?"

Gloria nodded. "I know who Estelle's talking about. She's a snob—the bad customers, you always remember. Kinky black hair and she usually comes in on Thursday night, but late, like right before we close at ten."

I found the restroom and then headed back to our table, but I waited to tell Abby what I'd found until we were back at the hotel and the guys were on their way to the study group.

We were in a quiet corner of the lobby. "Should we call that detective and tell him that Wellesley was near Jorge when he was pushed and that she's arranging marriages for illegal immigrants?" Abby asked.

"I don't think we can call yet. What if we're wrong? And is what she's doing—*if* she's doing it—illegal?"

"I think it is," Abby said. "And I know how we can find out." Abby led the way to the hotel's business center.

A few word combinations in an Internet search engine and Abby sat back in the chair. "Marriage fraud. That's what it's called."

"Okay, so it's illegal. A federal offense, too, but so what? We still don't have any proof, only the word of a woman who would never talk to the police."

"Well, we're going back to Verde Campo later tonight, right? We'll just wait and see what happens."

"So you're game?" I asked.

"Of course I'm game. I'm not going to let you go off and have all the fun. And we didn't have dessert. I'm looking forward to those sopapillas," Abby said.

"What are we going to do if she doesn't show up tonight? I don't know if I want to spring this on her in the morning right before we head out for a tour."

After a few taps on the keyboard, Abby printed a page and handed it to me. "Wellesley's home address. If she doesn't show up tonight, we'll go by her house."

"It's scary what comes up when you type a name into a search box. I think I'll call Summer and let her know what we've found out. The *boda* lady is supposed to arrive late, around ten, so it looks like we've got some time to burn."

"Time to shop!" Abby announced.

"What do you think about this?" Abby held up a royal blue tank. The hotel's courtesy shuttle had dropped us off two hours earlier at one of D.C.'s swankiest malls.

I'd called Summer to tell her what we'd found out and she wanted to go back to Verde Campo with us. "Anything to get the police interested in someone else besides me," she'd said and offered to pick us up at the mall entrance after her class ended.

"Too lightweight for eastern Washington. It may be summer here in D.C., but you know I'd only get to wear that a couple of times in Vernon. Besides, I need to look at maternity clothes." Summertime in Vernon was short. July was warm and then August usually announced itself with a heat wave that wilted the town for about three or four weeks; then, fall blazed succinctly, and suddenly, it was winter again.

"We've got plenty of time for that. We can shop for maternity clothes in Vernon. And you could wear this tank every week in August. Here, hang on to it."

"I don't know . . ."

"Trust me," Abby said.

I added the shirt to the pile on my arm. A couple of months ago I'd vowed to take Abby's fashion advice since she always looked stunning and I tended to look . . . Well, probably ho-hum was a more accurate description of my look. I couldn't get fired up about buying clothes that I knew were going to get spit-up stains on them. But Abby insisted you could still look stylish and be a mom at the same time. In theory, I agreed it was possible, but only in short bursts. I could look great for an evening out or at the beginning of the day, but my look usually deteriorated from a combination of dirty paw prints, sticky handprints, and various mishaps involving milk, juice, and assorted small pieces of food.

"I think I'll go look at the purses," I said and drifted in the direction of supple leather. Purses, now, those were different. I could spend hours shopping for the right bag. A bag with style I could manage. The rest of the outfit I had to leave up to Abby.

"I see a clearance sign. Follow me," she commanded. Did I mention Abby was the queen of the clearance bin? She not only looked fantastic, but she did it on a budget.

I took one last look at the leather under glass and followed Abby. I might as well take advantage of having a personal shopper while I had the chance. Abby had already flicked through the sale rack. She gave me two more shirts and checked her watch. "Okay, we've got about thirty minutes before the store closes. Let's go try these on and then we can meet Summer. She said it would take her about thirty minutes to get here after her night class finished, so it'll work out perfectly."

We made it out the mall doors right before they locked them for the night. I was carrying a bag with the turquoise tank, two pairs of capris, strappy sandals, and a light jacket that Abby said would "tie everything together." I probably wouldn't be able to fit into any of it next week, but, hey, I was on vacation. And I could always wear it next summer. I hoped.

I'd also managed to find a khaki weekend bag

edged in brown leather. It would be a perfect carry-on for the trip home. And I'd picked up a little white leather envelope clutch with a splash of turquoise flowers trailing diagonally across it. I could fit it in the suitcase, no problem. It was a clutch.

"Shoot. I forgot to buy anything to take home to Livvy," I said as I spotted Summer's RAV4 and waved.

"That's okay. We'll just have to go again." Abby's haul was bigger than mine. She hadn't bought a new carry-on bag either.

Summer whipped over to the curb, jumped out, and threw open the back. We shoved our bags in and I asked Abby, "How are you going to get all that home?"

She slid into the backseat as I took the front passenger seat. "I brought an extra suitcase," she said as if it were the most logical thing in the world. "I always pack my small suitcase and then put it inside the medium one. That way I have a whole empty one to fill up."

"Sorry," Summer said as she pulled her backpack out of the floorboard at my feet and tossed it in the back. She buckled in and merged into traffic in one smooth motion. "I'm so jealous of your shopping trip. What'd you get?"

Abby itemized our finds, including the regular price and sale price so Summer could fully appreciate what good deals we'd found. Although, from looking at Summer, you wouldn't think she was into fashion. She must have stopped by her house and changed clothes on the way to pick us up. Her long red curls were scrunched into a tight bun under a brown newsboy-style cap. She had on tan cargo pants, a clingy green tank, and leather flip-flops. "Okay, so give me the details on this *boda* lady."

By the time I gave her a summary of Estelle's story

and told her what we'd found on the Internet about marriage fraud, we were stuck in traffic. "We're only a few blocks from the turn." Summer clutched the wheel and pulled herself up a few more inches as she tried to look over the tops of the cars in front of us. "I can't see a thing." The clock on the dashboard counted off five minutes as we sat without moving.

"Good thing I got her address," Abby said. But at that moment, the lane on the right began to creep forward and Summer slid into it, skimming another car's bumper. She crossed another lane of cars as they inched ahead, then hit the off-ramp and accelerated. "I know another way."

I loosened my grip on the door frame. "For a few seconds there I thought I was going to get to see every detail of the grill of that SUV."

Summer flashed me a smile as she changed gears and accelerated through a yellow light. "Don't worry, I'm good at driving in traffic." She zipped into a minuscule opening in another lane and made a hard left turn. "That means I can tailgate without rear-ending and I have nerves of steel. If you go for the opening—even if it isn't there—it'll be there by the time you get there."

I said, "You didn't drive like this with Mitch a few days ago."

"I know. I didn't want him to worry or pester me. Oh, good news, I talked Ivan into pink for Emma's room."

"So he likes pink now?" I asked.

"I wouldn't say that," Summer said as she changed lanes, oblivious of the car horns sounding around us. I glanced in the back. Abby was searching for the seat belt.

"I wouldn't say he's had a change of heart. I'd say he's more resigned than anything else," Summer said.

"I told him it had to have pink because Ms. Archer requested it. We compromised on a pink glaze on the walls with a hand-painted border of black with pink and white."

"That sounds okay," I said slowly.

"It'll be gorgeous, I bet. Sounds like a Mary Engelbreit–inspired style border?" Abby asked.

Summer confirmed, "That's the plan. And if he doesn't stick to it, I'll repaint it."

"It just might work," I said. "Pink for the little girl, but the touch of black will give it sophistication. You could do all sorts of cute things with the black and pink. What about a bedside table lamp? The shade could be pink with black polka dots."

"I'll have to remember to subtly plant that idea in Ivan's head, so he'll think he thought of it. Then he'll love it. I've got all the supplies and workers lined up for tomorrow." Summer made another turn and wheeled into the parking lot of Verde Campo. "Ta-da. And only fifteen minutes late. We would have been early if it hadn't been for the traffic."

We were getting out of the car when I saw a familiar head of springy curls. "There she is." Wellesley walked quickly to a white Land Rover and got in. The brake lights glowed as she backed out of the slot.

"We missed her," Abby said. "She must have come early."

"Come on, we'll follow her," Summer said. Abby and I hurried to scramble back into the car before she left us standing in the parking lot.

Chapter
Thirteen

I gripped the handle on the door as Summer accelerated out of the parking lot and crisscrossed through traffic. She kept about two cars back from the Land Rover. "She's staying inside the Beltway," Summer said as she made a quick right turn and then slowed down so we didn't end up right on the Land Rover's bumper. We zipped through a neighborhood that seemed kind of uneven to me. High-rise condos towered on one block, but on the next, flashing lights on a police car lit up a boarded-up gas station as a police officer handcuffed a man. "Interesting neighborhood." I twisted around to see what was going on at the gas station, but we were already too far away.

Summer hit the accelerator and the engine revved as the SUV climbed a hill. As we crested the hill, the sparkling lights of a shopping complex filled the night. "Yep, this neighborhood's moving on up. It hasn't quite reached into that little corner, but it probably won't take long. In a few months or a few weeks, that gas station will be a chichi drive-through coffee bar or a boutique."

"From the size of the houses around here, I bet you could get two condos on that lot," Abby said.

"You're laughing but that's a real possibility, especially inside the Beltway." Summer hit the gas and made it through another yellow light to keep the Land Rover in sight.

Abby's phone rang and I could hear her in the back saying that we were still running around and we'd be back to the hotel later. She put her phone away and said, "The guy's study group has morphed into a Texas Hold'em tournament. I told Jeff that we're still out. We might want to stop somewhere later for dessert. I never did get those sopapillas."

"Looks like she's almost home," Summer said as she slowed outside a gated apartment complex. Ivy crept up the brick wall enclosing the apartments. Summer paused until Wellesley put in her code and pulled through the gate. When the gate began its slow sweep to close, Summer whizzed through and turned to follow the Land Rover through the complex. Flowers trailed out of window boxes. Patches of landscaped grounds were lit with spotlights that edged the sidewalks. A single-car garage door scrolled open and the Land Rover drove into the square of light. The garage door unwound as we parked on the street behind the passenger van with the words *Inside Look Tours* on the side. The condo with its white-paned windows under the concave copper awnings stayed dark.

I fingered the door handle that I'd gripped so tightly before. I didn't want to barge into someone's house late at night, but I didn't want to have this conversation in the morning with the rest of the tour group as an audience either.

"I don't know if we should do this," I said.

Summer twisted toward me. "All we want to do is

talk to her." She got out and walked up the sidewalk. Abby and I climbed out and hurried to catch up with her.

There was only enough room on the stoop for me and Summer. Summer leaned on the doorbell. I noticed that the window box was full of plastic flowers and ivy. Now, why hadn't I thought of that? Fake flowers were so much easier to keep up than real ones.

Summer pounded on the door and I jumped as the thumps reverberated through the quiet complex.

We waited a few more seconds and Summer pounded again. "Wellesley. We know you're home. Open up."

I put a hand on her arm and leaned toward the seam where the door met the door frame. "Wellesley, we need to talk to you. Please let us in."

Summer shouted behind me, "You don't want us making so much noise that your neighbors call the police, do you?"

I was surprised that Summer was being so aggressive. But Mitch had always said that when she did something she threw herself into it and didn't look back. Wellesley jerked the door open. Her curls vibrated with her abrupt movement. "What is going on? What's all the noise for?"

Summer stepped inside. "Hi. I'm Summer Avery. The police think I murdered a man and Ellie's found out that you knew him. We'd like to talk to you about it." Wellesley blinked and Summer continued into the living room, her shoes tapping on the hardwood floor. Abby and I followed her inside and Wellesley quickly shut the door.

"Hi, Wellesley," I said. "Sorry to barge in on you like this, but we figured you wouldn't want to talk about this in the morning with the whole tour group."

Her place was a mess with a load of white clothes dumped on a leather couch and piles of magazines, flyers, and junk mail sprinkled around every surface of the room. The kitchen trash spilled onto the slate slabs of the floor, and stacks of dirty dishes and take-out wrappers lined the granite countertops in the kitchen.

"All right. Since you're already in you might as well come in here." She stepped into a small living room that connected to a kitchen area. I pushed the pile of clothes over and sat down on a dark leather couch beside Abby. Summer perched on the arm of the couch and Wellesley took the matching leather chair across from the flat-screen TV. Wellesley had taken off her shoes. She tucked her bare feet up under her flowing white sundress and looked at me expectantly. She pulled one curl out and wound it around her finger.

Abby and Summer looked at me, too. I guess I had the lead here. I was the one who'd actually seen her talk with Jorge. I took a deep breath and dived in. "Wellesley, I know you talked to Jorge before he died. Would you tell us what you know about him?"

She frowned and kept circling the curl around her finger. "Jorge? I don't know who you're talking about."

"Jorge Dominguez. You talked to him on the Mall before he was pushed off the platform in the Metro. In fact, you did more than talk. You argued."

"Didn't you mention this before?" Wellesley's voice was weary. "I'm sorry that you're confused, but you have to accept that you're wrong. You must have seen someone else who looked like Jorge."

"I also talked to the man you talked to today out-side Union Station. He was a landscaper, just like Jorge."

Summer leaned forward and said, "We have a photo of you at the end of the platform near Jorge."

Describing what we had as a "photo of Wellesley" was pushing it a bit, but it finally got a reaction out of her. She unwound the curl from her finger and sat up straighter. "What are you saying? That I pushed him? That's absurd. And if you did have a picture of *that* I'm sure you wouldn't be here asking questions. It would be the police."

"Yes, but the police do think he was murdered and they're looking at everyone who was on the platform that day," Summer said. "I wasn't there, but they think I was. Someone used my Metro card and made it look like I was there." Summer stood up and paced back and forth. "So, see, I'm really motivated to find out who else was on that platform and who could have pushed Jorge. It seems like you would be anxious to talk to us instead of the police."

Wellesley's gaze ran over the three of us, then returned to Summer. Her mouth was set in a hard line as she said, "Okay. I'll tell you, but this doesn't go further than this room."

"Fine." Summer stopped pacing.

Wellesley raised her chin and said, "I did know Jorge. He filled in on my landscaping crews."

"Why did you go down to the other end of the platform that day in the Metro?" I asked.

She shrugged. "I like to get on at the front of the train. I'd done my job for your group. I'd gotten you to the right platform."

"Well, did you see anyone with long red hair at that end of the platform?" I pressed. If we could find someone who'd seen that the woman wasn't Summer, we'd at least be making some progress.

Wellesley snorted. "No. You don't look at people in the Metro. You don't make eye contact. You get on your train and get where you're going. You ignore everyone else, so no, I didn't notice anyone at that end of the platform."

I suppressed a sigh, but she was right about people not looking at each other. I'd noticed it, too, when we rode the Metro. Everyone seemed to enclose themselves in their own little box of silence and avoided looking at anyone else. I decided to switch back to Jorge. "So you didn't know anything else about Jorge?"

She paused, frowning. "Not really, except that his last name was Dominguez. Other than that, he was an illegal and he worked whatever jobs he could get. And don't go all self-righteous on me about using illegal aliens. They're here and they work hard."

"What else did he do, besides landscaping?" Summer asked as she began pacing again, moving in and out of my peripheral vision.

"How should I know?" Wellesley shrugged one shoulder. "Probably other manual labor stuff, that's what most illegals do."

I asked, "How did you find him?"

"There's a place, a grocery store parking lot. About six in the morning, they start showing up. I go there when I need more people. You can find any sort of skilled and unskilled worker there—drywallers, painters, framers, roofers, and just general manual labor. He came up and said he could do yard work and drywall."

I tried to keep my face blank, but it was hard. Wellesley was talking about people as if they were items on her shopping list. "So you use these people for your Household Helper referral business?"

"Yes."

So much for her claim of having references on everyone who worked for her.

"You just hire these guys and, let me guess, you

pay them in cash, right?" Abby asked with an accusing tone.

Wellesley stared right back and said, "They prefer cash and it simplifies bookkeeping."

I bet it did. In fact, I bet Wellesley had whole sets of books that the IRS didn't have a clue about, but if Jorge was illegal he wouldn't dare turn Wellesley in. She didn't have a motive to kill him. And during the interaction I'd seen between Jorge and Wellesley, *he* was angry at her, so why would she push him? Unless—

"Was he involved in your other business?" As I asked the question, I realized that Summer wasn't in the room. I didn't turn my head to do the full visual sweep of the room because Wellesley was focused on me and Abby and hadn't realized Summer wasn't there. Somehow I doubted she'd slipped out to go to the restroom. I didn't want to be the one to clue Wellesley in on Summer's disappearing act, so I forced myself to stay focused on Wellesley.

She laughed and relaxed back into the cushions of her chair. "Inside Look Tours? No." She shook her head quickly and her curls quivered. "He could barely speak English. There's no way he'd be able to lead a tour."

"No," I said. "I meant your other, *other* business. Your wedding business." I could see her defenses going back up, as she prepared to deny any other business. "Don't bother to get all huffy. You've already got two businesses operating. What would stop you from having a third? Especially if that business— facilitating marriages between illegal aliens and Americans—could bring in lots of cash that didn't have to be reported to the IRS? You said yourself that it costs a lot of money to live here." I ran my hand over the arm of the couch. "Leather furniture." I looked over Wellesley's shoulder to the kitchen with its pile of dirty dishes and junk mail. "Granite countertops. You drive a Land Rover and have a van for your tour business."

"I don't have to listen to this anymore. I've told you what I know about Jorge. Now leave." Wellesley sprang up from the chair. "You're desperate, you know that, don't you? Your sister-in-law"—Wellesley flung out her arm just as Summer drifted back into the living room—"is in trouble and you're hoping for a new suspect, but it's not going to be me."

Wellesley marched to the door and pulled it open. "Jorge was a good worker, a hard worker, and dependable. He always showed up. He was much more valuable to me alive than dead."

We trooped outside and I'd barely made it across the threshold before she closed the door firmly. She jerked it back open and said, "I'm sure you'll understand that I won't be leading a tour for you tomorrow. You're on your own." The door closed again and I heard the dead bolt slide into place.

"Too bad we paid in advance," Abby said.

"Yeah. Looks like we won't be getting a refund on tomorrow's tour," I said.

We climbed in Summer's car, closed the doors, and sat there for a moment in silence. Finally, I said, "Well, I don't know if that did any good. I need chocolate. How about you guys? Anyone want a Hershey's Kiss?"

"Of course," Abby said as she buckled the seat belt.

Summer clicked her seat belt, flicked on the headlights, and quickly navigated the curving streets to exit the complex. "Sure."

In the backseat Abby rolled the foil around in her hand, her head tilted back on the headrest. "Summer, you sound just like Nadia—all perky. How can you be so upbeat? Wellesley did admit she knew Jorge, but she completely stonewalled on the marriage fraud thing."

I tossed my wrapper back in my purse and pulled out another Hershey's Kiss. "These are so addictive. They're like potato chips. You can't eat just one. But Wellesley did say a few interesting things. Like that Jorge could hardly speak English. You said he carried on conversations with you, right?"

Summer frowned as she worked her way through the thickening traffic. "Yeah, that was weird because Jorge spoke English very well. Not even really an accent and he never had to search for words."

Abby sat up in the back. "And did you notice how she phrased that about when she met him? It sounded more like he sought her out instead of the other way around. I thought that was interesting."

Summer pulled a piece of paper from one of the many pockets on her cargo pants. "I thought this was interesting, too."

I unfolded the paper. It was a list of names, addresses, and phone numbers.

"This is why you look so pleased." Abby leaned over the backseat, reading over my shoulder. "Look, there's Jorge's name. And that must be his address, an apartment on Robinwood Road. Fourth one down."

"And here's Estelle, the woman I talked to at the restaurant," I said as Abby took the paper.

"She's on there, too? That's great. I didn't have time to read the whole thing, I just grabbed it when I saw Jorge's name," Summer said. She glanced over at me quickly with a wide smile. She was fired up. I could tell by the way she gripped the steering wheel and almost bobbed in the seat. Strands of red hair were loose from her bun, and stray curlicues floated around her face.

"There's more than one page," Abby said as she flipped to the second sheet. "Listen to this. Bradley Conner Jenkins, Joseph Harold Tickner, Hunter Jacob Myer, and the list goes on. There's addresses with these names, too, and it sounds like they're all over the D.C. area. A name from the first page is matched up with one from the second page."

"These must be the people Wellesley matched with the immigrants. I wonder where she found them and why they'd do it," I said.

Summer didn't seem to be too concerned with where Wellesley found the American marriage partners for the illegal immigrants because she said, "The important thing is that we've got something that connects Wellesley with Jorge."

"Right, but I can't believe you took this, Summer. I know it's just a piece of paper, but she could accuse us of theft."

Summer made a face. "No way. She'll never even know it's gone. It was in her recycling pile right beside her shredder. That's where I figured all the good stuff would be. You know how it is, you have stuff to shred, but you end up tossing it in a pile on top of the shredder or beside it and then you shred it all at once. By the time she gets around to shredding, she won't even remember what she tossed in that pile."

"Yeah, that's what I do with my junk mail. I don't shred it until the pile's about to fall over." Abby looked at me and said, "Yes, I'm sure you shred your junk mail when you open it, but that's not how most people live."

Sometimes being a professional organizer makes me feel I'm on the outside of things. So I'm a bit compulsive about clutter. So what? I just wish other people didn't look at me like I was some sort of exotic species in a zoo. I wasn't that weird, was I, just because I shredded my junk mail immediately? I filed that away for later and said, "Anyway, what are we going to do with this list?"

"We're going to use it," Summer said. "We're going to visit Robinwood Road."

An Everything In Its Place Tip for an Organized Trip

To-do list (three or more weeks before departure)
- Make hotel, airline, and car rental reservations.
- Reserve space for pets at kennel.
- Schedule an appointment with a vet to update vaccinations for pets, if you're using a kennel. Most kennels require proof of a current rabies vaccination and kennel cough (Bordetella) vaccine within six months to one year.

Chapter
Fourteen

"Not quite in the same league as Wellesley's place, is it?" I asked as Summer parked in front of the small apartment building. The steep slope of the wooden-shingled mansard roof came to within a few feet of the ground and gave the building a heavy, dark look. Dirt fought with stubby grass in the small yards in front of each building. A few spindly shrubs crouched at the corners of the apartment. Like all the other front doors, number 12 had flaking paint. Dried leaves and dead bugs were piled in the corners of the front porch.

The window beside the front door was dark, but blinking Christmas lights outlined the window next door at number 11. The two doors shared the small concrete pad front porch and I assumed the apartments were probably mirror images of each other.

Summer leaned on the doorbell and we heard it ring beyond the thin door. "So, what were you hoping we'd find?" I asked Summer.

She tried the door handle, but it was locked; then, she peered into the dark window. "I don't know. A roommate? Someone we could talk to about Jorge." She pounded on the door a few times.

"We seem to be making a habit of standing on doorsteps demanding entry." Abby took a few steps off the porch and said, "Let's go find some dessert."

Summer knocked on the door a few more times.

"Come on, Summer. There's nothing here," Abby said gently.

"Wait!" She flipped open the lid of the black mailbox mounted on the wood siding near the door. "The mail. Maybe . . ." She pulled out a stack of paper and quickly shuffled through it, beginning with a newsprint advertisement with an unappetizing hot-pink steak on the cover. "Nothing but junk mail."

Still holding the envelopes and brightly colored advertisements, her arms hung limp at her sides. Her high energy had burned away and she looked worn out. "Ellie, I've got to find something . . . anything that will take the police's attention off me. I'd just hoped that there would be something." She banged on the door again.

"I know. There will be something. You have nothing to hide and you're going to be fine." I murmured the soothing words, but while I was speaking them the news reporter's words "person of interest" ran through my mind.

The door to number 11 flew open. "What is wrong with you people?" A short, round woman dressed in an orange sweat suit stood in the doorway with her hands on her hips. She reminded me of a pumpkin, one of the small, squat ones. Two combs held her long gray hair back from her plump face. The frames of her round glasses caught the shine of the Christmas lights as they flicked on and off. "Just what do you people think you're doing? Standing out here yakking and pounding on doors? I got my grandbaby asleep in here."

"We're so sorry," I said.

Summer stepped forward. "I apologize. We're trying to find out about the man who lived here. I'd met him a few times, but didn't know him well. Did you know him?"

The woman used a chubby finger to push her glasses up higher on the bridge of her nose; then, she tilted her chin up and looked at us carefully through her bifocals. She must have decided we were okay to talk to because she folded her hands across her ample tummy and said, "That was real sad about him. We saw it on the news. I didn't know him. I only come a couple of nights a week to watch my grandbaby while my daughter's working. Didn't really know anything about him, 'cept he done yard work and painting, stuff like that. Now, Danielle, she said he was a fine neighbor. Kept to hisself. Never give her no trouble, making noise or anything." She gave us a severe look.

Summer didn't let the look intimidate her. "Did he have any family or friends around here?"

"Don't know. Never had any visitors, except that one time." The woman shook her head and tilted her chin up again. "At first, I thought you was her."

"But I've never been here," Summer said, going into defense-mode.

"She looked kinda like you, same color hair and all, but up close you're much younger and prettier. She came banging on the door late at night, just like you. I came out here to shush her, too, but by then he'd opened the door and she was on her way inside. That was the only time there was any noise from over there. Well, except when she left. She was cryin'. You can hear pretty much everything through these doors."

"So she had red hair?" I asked, just to confirm. The woman nodded. "Was she tall or short?"

"About the same height as her," she said, looking over at Summer again.

"Is there anything else you can remember about her? Did you hear a name?"

"No. She was inside almost as soon as I got out here."

"What about her car?" Summer asked.

"That was one luxurious car. A Mercedes, I think. Black. I noticed it at the curb because, well, this isn't a neighborhood where you see many of those and it kinda stood out, too, because it didn't have any of those fool lights or spinners on it that young people are so crazy about now."

"How long ago was this?" I asked.

"Oh, I'd say it was sometime in February."

There didn't seem to be anything else we could ask her, so Summer said, "Thanks for talking to us. I'm sorry, I didn't catch your name?"

"Rebecca Matthews."

"Thanks for your help, Mrs. Matthews."

She stepped back inside the apartment and we turned to walk down the sidewalk, but then I turned back quickly and caught her before she shut the door. "Mrs. Matthews, have the police talked to you about this?"

"Well, sure. They was here a couple a days ago. Never did see nothing like that. Police tape and everything, just like on TV."

"And you told them about the redheaded woman?"

"Oh yes."

Great. That couldn't be good for Summer. Maybe that's why the police were calling her a person of interest.

"Were they interested in anything else?"

"Not really. Once I told them about that lady they finished up pretty quick."

Friday

The thud of the hotel door closing woke me the next morning. I rubbed my eyes and when my finger-tips came back sooty I realized I hadn't taken my makeup off last night. I scanned the room. Towels heaped on the floor and a razor and shaving cream rested in a puddle of water on the bathroom counter. Then I saw a notepad propped up by the phone on my nightstand. Mitch's bold writing stood out even in the dim light coming in through the fissure in the drapes.

> *Didn't want to wake you since you were sleeping so hard. I'll call you later.*
> *P.S. No news on the move.*

I stretched against the smooth sheet and bur-rowed deeper into the fluffy pillows. That was one great bonus of pregnancy—I slept like the dead. I'd completely missed Mitch's alarm and the never-insignificant noise of him getting ready.

After we talked to Mrs. Matthews last night, a weari-ness had swept over me that I swear went all the way down to the marrow in my bones. Pregnancy seemed to be a state of extremes for me. Either I was feeling great—euphoric—or I was famished or I was so ex-hausted that I could barely crawl into bed. Nothing came on in increments, it seemed. I'd felt so drained last night that we'd bagged our plans for dessert and Summer drove us back to the hotel, but I didn't re-member the drive at all since I dozed the whole way.

Then I'd staggered into the elevator and down the hall to our room and collapsed. I heard Mitch come in later. I have no idea how much later—it could have been ten minutes or two hours—but I snuggled up and reentered REM as fast as I could.

I shifted around, enjoying the warmth of the floaty duvet cocoon and luxuriating in the knowledge that I didn't have to get up. I decided I'd skip sightseeing today. I thought Mount Vernon was on the schedule, but I had no doubt that we'd seen the last of Welles-ley. I figured I should probably call the rest of the group and let them know that we were on our own today. And then what should I do about Wellesley? Did I have a responsibility to tell someone about her marriage scheme? I thought of Estelle's worn face. Could I be the one to ruin her hopes of staying in America? Would she be deported?

The phone interrupted my thoughts. "Hey," Abby's upbeat tone came over the line. "I didn't wake you, did I?"

"No. I was just about to call everyone and tell them Wellesley won't be showing up today."

"Already did it."

"Did they ask why?" No telling what Abby had told them.

"No. I think I phrased it in a way that it sounded like Wellesley had an unavoidable conflict come up."

"Yeah. She hates us now."

"True, but it's not slowing them down. Irene, Gina, and Nadia are going out on their own. Gina got the concierge to hire them a car. I told them to go ahead without us."

"You don't have to hang out with me. You can go, if you want. I'm not going to do anything today."

There was a short pause and then Abby said, "Today would be a good day for that. It's pretty dreary and overcast outside, but don't you remember promising Summer to check everything in Emma's room today? She reminded you of it when she dropped us off last night."

I sighed. Good-bye, blanket cocoon. "I forgot. What time did she want us there?"

"She said she'd pick us up at nine."

I glanced at the clock and threw back the covers. "Gotta go. I'll meet you downstairs."

I showered and dressed in record time and made it downstairs at five after nine, so I was pretty peeved when nine-thirty rolled around and Summer still hadn't shown up. "She's not answering her cell phone," I told Abby, who was munching on a bagel she'd bought at the Starbucks cart in the lobby.

I said, "I've a good mind to go upstairs and go back to sleep." I'd had plenty of time to check my messages. None from Summer. One message from Debbie, saying that her son had now come down with chicken pox and she'd call me later when she had time to breathe. I exhaled a sigh of relief. That would buy me at least one more day to mull over what to tell her about her dad. Honestly, I hadn't even had time to think about it.

The second message was from Livvy, which had totaled two words: good morning. My mom's voice followed Livvy's squeaky one. They were going to the beauty shop and they'd call me later. I imagined Livvy with pink nails and bows in her hair.

Abby grinned. "Don't go all hormonal on me," she teased. She knew how I felt about people tossing that phrase around. "You know you won't be able to sleep now. Why don't we get a taxi over to the Archers' house? Maybe she forgot her phone or the battery's low."

Abby was right. I was awake now. We might as well

go to the Archers' house. I popped the last of my blueberry bagel into my mouth and dug through my purse for Summer's address. "She could have at least borrowed the Archers' phone to call us," I said.

As we paced through the lobby, a young man stepped in my path. "Where is she?" he demanded.

For a second I thought he was asking about Summer, but then he said, "Where's Lee?"

I took a step back. "I don't know anyone named Lee," I said and moved to go around him.

He shifted sideways and blocked me again. Out of the corner of my eye, I saw Abby beckoning to one of the hotel desk clerks, a large guy with black hair.

"She's been here every morning. Your guide. Where is she?"

"Oh, you mean Wellesley? You call her Lee?" He didn't answer me. Instead he untangled the cords attached to an iPod from his hooded sweatshirt. "You were here the other day, weren't you?" I asked, just to keep talking until the desk clerk got closer.

He stuffed the music player and cords into one of the pockets on his baggy jeans and crossed his arms. "Is she here or not?"

He was lanky and tall, over six feet and his light brown hair was cut short. I had to tilt my head back to look at his face, which was sprinkled with a few pimples. With his arms crossed loosely, he had a confident air that broadcast the arrogance of adolescence.

"No, she's not here," I said. The desk clerk crossed the gleaming floor of the lobby toward us. "In fact, she's not our tour leader anymore."

The young guy spun around, cursing, and slammed his fist into the palm of his other hand. I noticed a diamond-shaped tattoo surrounded with circles on the inside of his wrist.

Abby rolled her eyes and said, "Such a limited vocabulary. You'd think he could be a bit more creative than that."

Was this a technique she used to deal with her students? Although I hoped cursing didn't start in third grade.

He turned back to us, hands on his hips. His conceited attitude had slipped away and he looked worried. "You got a phone number, an e-mail, anything, for her?"

The desk clerk arrived, "Everything okay here, ladies?"

I looked back at the young guy as I answered, "Yes, I think so, but we'll call you if anything changes." The clerk nodded and moved a few feet away to a display of maps and brochures at the concierge desk. He began stacking and adjusting papers that were perfectly straight.

The young man leaned in and said in a pleading tone, "Dude, look, I got to get a hold of her. I got to."

I pulled out Wellesley's card from my purse. "This is the phone number from her Web site." Even though she'd been less than honest with us, I couldn't give her home address to this guy.

He grabbed the card, pulled out his phone, and punched a few buttons. "Oh, man. This is the same number I've been calling for a couple of days. She's not answering." He shoved the card back at me, but Abby plucked it from his hand.

"What's your name?" she asked in her authoritative teacher's voice.

"Joe Tickner, ma'am."

Abby didn't look too happy with the designation of ma'am that he'd tacked on to the end of his reply, but I thought it was probably better than dude. She continued. "If we see her we'll tell her you'd like to get in touch. Any message?"

He opened his mouth and shut it again. His gaze dropped and he looked uncomfortable.

"What would you like to speak to her about?" Abby prompted.

He hesitated, then said, "Nothing. It's nothing."

"Joe Tickner," I said and they both turned toward me. I'd been going over his name in my mind. "Joseph Harold Tickner? By any chance, were you supposed to get married soon?"

Now he looked scared. "I've got to go." He turned away.

"We're not going to do anything to hurt you. We won't turn you in or anything," I hurried to reassure him before he sprinted away. "We just want to know more about Wellesley. We know she arranges marriages. Will you tell us the details? She won't talk to us either and we need to know what's going on. My sister-in-law . . . Well, it's a long story. How about this? It's way too early for a drink, but why don't we buy you breakfast and you can tell us about Wellesley?" I said. He didn't actually look old enough to legally consume alcohol anyway, but I figured it couldn't hurt to let him think I'd considered buying him a drink. His gaze ran over the long, decadent breakfast buffet.

"Cooked-to-order pancakes, waffles, or French toast with all the side dishes you can think of," I said.

He wavered, then said, "Okay."

A few moments later he cut into a stack of pancakes swimming in syrup. He had plates of fruit, sausage, eggs, yogurt, and pastries as well as coffee, juice, and a towering glass of milk, too.

We let him eat in peace for a while, and then I said, "So, are congratulations in order? You're engaged?"

He started on the eggs and sausage, shaking his

head. After he swallowed and wiped his mouth, he said, "Nah. Lee, or—what did you call her—Westly?"

"Wellesley," I said.

"Okay, Lee, Wellesley, whatever her name is, called and told me everything was off. I've been trying to find her for days. I need that money, dude."

Since we were back to being dudes, it seemed Joe had relaxed around us. "How did you know to look for her here?" I asked.

He said, "When I met her to talk about the . . . you know, the marriage thing . . . she had a huge stack of paperwork. I saw the itinerary for your group and the name of this hotel. It stuck in my mind, the Grand in Crystal City." He shrugged. "It was easy to remember. And when she stopped answering her phone and e-mails, I figured this was the only place I could find her. I knew she'd be here in the morning. I saw your schedule started at nine. I've been hanging out in the hotel lobby in the mornings."

"You don't go to school or have a job?" Abby asked.

"Shift work. I'm on nights this week."

I wanted to get the conversation back to Wellesley, so I asked, "When did she call it off?"

"Monday night," he said, then chugged the milk.

That would have been right after the incident in the Metro. Maybe she was worried about an investigation and she'd halted all her other less legitimate business deals. I glanced over at Abby. I could see by the look on her face she'd caught the significance of the timing, too. I turned back to Joe and said, "So she was going to pay you to get married? Because you're an American citizen, right?"

He nodded and opened his yogurt cup.

"Who were you going to marry?" I asked.

He shrugged as he stirred the yogurt. "I don't know. Never saw her. We were going to meet at the courthouse and be done. I'd never see her again."

"Why would you do that?" Abby's voice rose with astonishment.

"Money. I need the money," he repeated. "Dude, living off base is off the hook."

"What?" I asked.

Abby looked at me and said, "He means living here is crazy."

He nodded. "Expensive," he translated for me. When did Abby become such an expert in slang? I let that question go and focused on what he'd said. "You said you live off base. A military base?"

"Yeah. I'm in the Air Force. And they don't pay sh—" Abby frowned and he quickly amended his word choice. "Jack. They don't pay nothing."

"So what was she going to pay you? A couple of hundred dollars, maybe a thousand?" I asked. Estelle said Wellesley collected six thousand dollars and I could see Wellesley giving a portion to an American to get them to the courthouse, but their cut couldn't be that big. And what difference could a few hundred dollars make in his life? Even a thousand dollars wouldn't go very far in D.C. Would he splurge on one big item?

"Sure, she was going to pay me eight hundred bucks, but that was nothing. Not compared to what I'd get after I got my increase in pay."

I looked over at Abby as I realized what he meant. I said, "BAQ."

She nodded slowly and looked back at Joe. "And VHA, too, right?"

He looked nervous again. He angled his silverware on his empty plate and put his napkin on the table. "How do you know about that?"

"Basic Allowance for Quarters and Variable Housing Allowance, you mean?" Abby asked. "Simple. We're military spouses. Our husbands are in the Air Force."

Those acronyms could add up to quite a bit of money. The military took into account where you lived and paid more if you were in an expensive area. That number varied according to how many people you had in your family, but even with those increases it would still be hard to make ends meet in Washington, D.C., especially for enlisted folks. A marriage certificate meant another member of the family and a higher pay rate every payday. No wonder Joe was willing to take a small cut from Wellesley; he'd make more money all year long once he changed his marital status.

"How did you find out about this 'marriage thing,' as you called it?" I asked.

"Word gets around. One of my buddies did it and he let me in on it."

"How do you contact Wellesley? Do you call her or meet somewhere?"

"My buddy gave me her e-mail. I e-mailed her and she set up a meeting at a restaurant close to the base." He paused, then said, "It's all legal and everything." He inched his chair backward. "I would really be married. The ceremony and marriage certificate are all legit. It's not like I'm lying or anything."

"You'd just never actually live with your wife," Abby said. "Or see her again, for that matter."

"That system would have its advantages," I said. "No worries about attending the spouse coffees."

Abby rolled her eyes, at me this time, and said, "Look, Joe, you'd be a lot better off finding a roommate or cutting costs some other way. Whether or not you can justify a fake marriage in your mind, I don't think the Air Force would agree with you."

He didn't look convinced so I said, "I don't know if Wellesley's going to start up her marriage thing again anytime soon. I know two other people she canceled on this week. And, besides, what's going to happen when you want to get married for real?"

A bellhop crossed the restaurant and said, "Ma'am, the taxi you called for is here."

Joe snorted. "I'm not going to get married for real."

"I think you're right about that," Abby said as we stood up.

On the way to the Archers' house I said to Abby, "That was crazy, or I should say, off the hook. Can you believe that?"

Abby said slowly, "You know, I think I can. Someone like Joe wants the extra money. It would be easy money for someone who isn't making much to begin with. Just show the marriage certificate and get a raise. Anyway, Joe's so young he probably really can't see himself ever getting married."

I sighed. "I don't know. I still have a hard time wrapping my mind around a scheme like that. But I have to hand it to Wellesley; she created a business that would bring in lots of cash and I don't see the demand for her matchmaking service tapering off anytime soon." I shifted toward Abby and asked, "And how did you know about that 'off the hook' expression, anyway?"

"We had a section on slang in one of my continuing education courses. And being around the kids keeps me up to date."

"Third graders? There's already slang in third grade? I have less time than I thought before I become totally uncool."

By the time we got to the Archers' house, the clouds had sunk down to ground level, swathing everything with a fine mist. The taxi dropped us at the foot of the Archers' driveway, behind a white van with *Flint Designs* emblazoned on the side in a plain black font. So Ivan went for unique and visionary in his clients' homes, but he went conventional for his van. The buzz of a circular saw filled the air. A man with a pencil stuck behind his ear, safety glasses, and a tool belt pushed a piece of wood smoothly through a table saw in the small area between the house and Summer's apartment. "Is the up-and-coming Ms. Archer here today?" Abby asked.

"I don't think so. Summer said Ms. Archer had Emma's ballet lesson and then a birthday party. The interviewer for *Mom Magazine* is tagging along to get a look at a typical Friday."

The back door swung open and a man backed out, carefully balancing a paint tray full of what looked like Pepto-Bismol and a roller with the same paint. I recognized his dark black hair, olive complexion, and compact build. "Hi, Tony," I said as I reached out and held the door open for him. He pivoted carefully, then descended the steps and placed the tray and roller on a plastic sheet on the grass. "You may not remember me—"

"You're Summer's sister-in-law. We met at Ms. Archer's office. Ellie, isn't it?" He looked inquiringly at Abby, and I introduced her.

He wiped his hand on his Washington Redskins T-shirt, adding a few more streaks of paint to the pink splatters before he shook hands with Abby.

"Where's Summer? In the house?" I asked, reaching for the door handle.

"No. She's not here," he said shortly. He didn't look happy. "Something came up last night and she left. An emergency."

Chapter
Fifteen

Clearly, he expected me to know about the emergency. "She left last night?"

"Yeah, she sorted out the toys yesterday afternoon and took the ones she's saving for Emma over to her place to keep them from getting lost or thrown away. She called me late last night and told me where she kept a key to her apartment hidden so I could get in there and get the paint."

"When will she be back?"

"Didn't say. I told her we had everything under control here." He frowned. "And we did until three people canceled on me. We should have been finishing up about now, but, well . . . we're doing the best we can."

"But her car's still here." I pointed to Summer's car parked on the street.

Tony shrugged. "She must have called someone to pick her up." He had other things to worry about besides Summer.

I pulled out my cell phone and saw that I'd missed a call. "Probably her," I said as I dialed my voice mail, but Tony wasn't listening. He'd picked up a lamp and a stack of books from a pile near the door and carried them toward the house. He asked over his shoulder, "Want to see the room?"

We followed him inside. A collection of children's furniture painted a glossy white was squashed into the living room. My voice mail played, but it wasn't Summer's voice. "This is Jay MacInally." His voice wasn't as rough as it had been when I'd met him. "I'll try you again later."

Why had he called? Did he want to know what I'd decided to tell Debbie? Abby looked at me and I shook my head and said, "No, it wasn't Summer." We climbed up the narrow stairs, squeezed past several boxes on the small landing, and entered Emma's room. "Here it is," Tony said and left his bundle of accessories in the middle of the floor; then he hurried back downstairs.

"This is gorgeous," Abby said and I had to agree. Even in its half-finished state the room looked a thousand times better than it had before. Ivan must have used some glazing technique on the walls, because instead of medicine pink, the walls were a soft wash of color. Under the plastic drop cloths, I could see new Berber carpet in a soft gray color covering the floor. The newly painted white trim looked crisp against the blush-colored walls. A woman in cut-off overalls and a baseball cap stood in the center of the largest wall, painting a fairy-tale castle in shades of pink and lavender. Across the room, Ivan looked like a lollipop as he perched on a ladder hand-painting a whimsical border of white, pink, and black swirls around the top of the room.

"Excuse me," a man said behind me.

I stepped aside and the man who'd been working

at the table saw outside carried several pieces of wood into the room and began screwing them into place under the windows.

I thought of those buzzwords that the guys were laughing about at dinner. "Ivan, this space looks wonderful. I think Emma will love it," I said.

Abby winked at me as she said, "The pale blush color with the black accents really makes your border pop."

"Absolutely," I said, grinning.

"Thanks." He came down from the ladder, which squealed and groaned as each step took his weight. His black leather and flashy rings were gone. Today he was in plain red sweats. He did a full 360 turn, taking in the whole room. Then he nodded once and said, "Subtle. Whimsical. Magical. That's what this space is all about." He pointed his paintbrush at the castle mural and said, "We'll place the bed there. The headboard will blend in with the mural. My carpenter is modifying the four posters so they will look like turrets with flags."

"A castle bed, how cool," Abby said, taking in every detail. I bet there would be a fairy-tale-themed nursery in Abby's house before the baby arrived.

"These boxes need to be off the landing, Ivan," Tony said as he entered the room with another load. "Excuse me, Ellie. Got to get these inside in case it starts raining."

Ivan climbed back up the ladder and nodded absently as he studied his border. "Yes. Of course. We'll do . . . something with them," he muttered, but his attention was on the exact placement of his brush.

"Ivan, did you hear me? We've only got a couple of hours left."

"Yes, I heard you, but if we don't get the painting done, the rest doesn't matter."

Tony left without saying anything else, and he crashed down the stairs. I looked at Abby. "I'd better stay and help Tony get everything sorted out. The decorating is coming together, but Tony needs help to finish the organizing. You could call a taxi to take you back to the hotel."

"I'm not going back to the hotel," Abby said. "Nothing there but an outdoor swimming pool. Who wants to swim on a day like this? I'll help you go through the boxes on the landing and then I'll accessorize." She was practically rubbing her hands together at the thought of delving into the pile of pictures, knick-knacks, and books. Home décor was like nirvana to Abby. Her house looked like a spread in a decorating magazine. And the amazing thing was that she decorated with stuff she picked up during her bargain shopping expeditions. Just like with clothes, she knew how to put it together in a way that looked great.

I saw a couple of mismatched china plates at a garage sale and thought, *Those are cute, but what would I do with them?* Abby bought them—after I decided I didn't want them—and hung them on the wall of her dining room in a clever arrangement with a quilt and a sepia photograph of her grandparents.

I knew that if Abby put the finishing touches on Emma's room it would look spectacular. I just hoped she didn't butt heads with Ivan.

I hurried down to talk to Tony in the living room while Abby started on the boxes. "Hey, Tony. Abby and I are going to stay and help—" I broke off as I realized he was on the phone. He snapped the phone off and cursed under his breath as I came down the last two stairs.

He ran his hands across his eyes, then down over his mouth. "Why do I put up with this—" He noticed me and said, "We've got two hours."

"What? Until Ms. Archer gets back? Great, she can pitch in and help."

"Right," he laughed. "No, we've two hours until the photo shoot. The schedule's been changed and the photographer is coming to do the shoot this afternoon instead of tomorrow. The writer for the article will be here, too. She can interview you this afternoon."

"But the light is terrible and the paint isn't even dry. You can't put the furniture and the accessories in with the paint still wet. And where is Summer? She's got all my notes on everything that has to be done."

"I wish I knew. All I know is that we've got to put something together so they can take the photos. The light isn't a problem. They're bringing lights. We may have to tell them to just shoot one side of the room."

"Which side?"

"The side we finish," he said over his shoulder as he went upstairs.

"But neither side of the room is finished yet."

A few seconds later a shout from upstairs seemed to rock the house like a minor explosion. A torrent of words followed. I could make out a few phrases. "Unfeasible . . . can't be rushed . . . impossible." Tony must have given Ivan the new deadline.

Tony trotted back downstairs and flashed a smile at me. "He took it better than I expected. I'm bringing the furniture up as soon as I get everything in from outside."

It seemed he'd gotten over his irritation with the new deadline. Maybe he was one of those people who thrived under pressure. I hurried back up the stairs.

Abby said, "I heard. I'll get rid of these boxes. You see what has to be done in the room." She said something else about reinforcements, but I'd already rushed into the room, the plastic drop cloths crackling under my feet. I twirled around. Suddenly, what

had looked so good a few moments before—a makeover in progress—looked like chaos now. It was anything but organized. And Summer had said that the
article wanted to play up the organizational size of
the makeover—how a well-ordered room makes life
easier for a busy, working mom. I ran my fingers
through my hair. Where *was* Summer?

I grabbed my phone and dialed her number. Why
had I given her all my notes? My precious lists. I needed
those lists. Her voice mail answered and I snapped
the phone off.

Okay. Deep breath. I could do this. I'd just have to
wing it. I *hated* winging it. I loathed working under
pressure. I liked the planned approach with check-
lists and sticky note reminders. I scanned the whole
room again and decided that Tony and Abby could
handle getting the new stuff, the furniture and accessories, into the room. The muralist was packing
up her paints and Ivan did look like he was moving a
little bit faster on the border. Instead of moving at a
snail's pace he'd upped it to a turtle's pace. We might
be okay. If none of the photos in the article were
close-ups.

I decided the closet had to be my priority. Organizing articles loved to feature closets, and Emma's
dark, tiny niche was crying out for an update. I
helped Abby lever one of the boxes down the stairs
on my way to the kitchen. "I'll find somewhere to put
these downstairs," she said. I told her to get the key to
Summer's apartment from Tony and put them in
there.

"Sounds good to me. They can go through it later."

I found the plastic trash bags under the kitchen
sink, ripped several off the roll, and scurried back upstairs. I attacked the closet, clearing the floor and the
top shelf of dusty shoe boxes, unopened plastic baby

bottles, and a few grubby rattles and teething rings. I put everything in one trash bag and moved to the clothes, which were packed as tightly together as pieces of notebook paper in a binder. Most of it seemed to be size 4, which would be right for Emma's size, so I figured they were her current clothes. I wrestled the clothes out of the closet, sorted, and rearranged, pulling out the winter clothes first.

There's lots of different ways to set up a clothes closet. Some people like to group by color. Others like to hang matching clothes together, but Vicki Archer wasn't here so I couldn't ask her what she liked. I sorted the lighter spring and summer clothes together in groups of shirts, pants, shorts, and dresses.

I checked my watch. Fifteen minutes. That was the quickest closet sort I'd ever done. Of course, it was the smallest closet I'd ever done, too, but that was a good thing on a two-hour deadline. Emma must've liked to play dress-up because she had a princess gown and tiara, a mermaid costume with slightly tarnished green scales, and a cherry-colored wig, as well as a butterfly costume, complete with gossamer wings and headband with bobbing antenna. If I'd had time I could have created a special dress-up play area. Maybe even a little theater stage, but there wasn't time for that now and the closet was full.

I folded the costumes to store them in the window seat once it was painted. Scratch that. To save time, we wouldn't paint the inside of the seat, just the exterior. I stashed the costumes and the winter clothes in the newly built window seats.

Abby came back into the room with two large plastic bins. "Hey, do you need these? Looks like organizing stuff. I found it at Summer's when I put the boxes away."

"Yes!" Shoe caddies, matching hangers, and hanging bins spilled out as I checked the items. "I'm so glad you found this."

She handed me a key. "Here. This is to Summer's apartment. She must have really had to leave in a hurry if she didn't have time to even bring this stuff over here."

A clatter of footsteps sounded on the stairs and then the room filled with more people. "This is the most adorable room!" I recognized that enthusiastic voice.

"Nadia! What—" I stopped, speechless as I saw Irene and Gina, too.

"I told you I called for reinforcements," Abby said.

An Everything In Its Place Tip for an Organized Trip

To-do list (one week before departure)
- Put mail on vacation hold—Call 1-800-ASKUSPS.
- Stop daily newspaper delivery.
- Return library books and video rentals.
- Pay bills. One handy way to make sure you don't miss any payments is to use automatic bill pay through your banking institution.
- Enlist a friend or neighbor you trust to keep an eye on your house and give them a key for emergencies.
- Set remote access codes for your home phone. You may have to dig out the manual that came with your phone for instructions. You'll be able to check your messages or forward calls to your cell phone.
- Switch to "no mail" for electric discussion lists

and set an automatic reply on your e-mail to let people know that you'll return messages later.
- Refill prescriptions.
- Withdraw cash from bank or get traveler's checks.

Chapter
Sixteen

"What are you doing here?" I asked Nadia.

"We're here to help. Abby said you were short-handed so we grabbed a taxi and came over," Nadia said.

"What about your tour? You'll miss Mount Vernon."

"Too cold and rainy today." Nadia dismissed one of Washington, D.C.'s, premier tourist attractions with a flick of her hand. "Besides, I love that border." Nadia's head tilted back as she talked to Ivan. "You've got to show me how you do that."

"Watch out," Tony called as he entered the room and set the headboard down in the middle of the room. Gina held it steady so it wouldn't lean against any of the walls. "I'm not any good at that froufrou stuff. I can't even put up a wallpaper border, but I can put this bed together. Irene, hold this and I'll go find a cordless screwdriver."

Irene patted my shoulder. "You look a little dazed."

"I'm just amazed that you're all taking time to help me out."

"Are you kidding? Decorating is fun and it'll be in

Mom Magazine. Besides, I'm a big believer in supporting other military wives. I have no desire to own my own business, but I've known lots of spouses who have. It's hard enough to succeed in business, but throw in a move every few years and it's even more of a challenge.

"Now, after I finish holding this headboard, I'll paint those window seats. They're darling, by the way. White? Like the rest of the trim."

"Sure. Yes, that would be great," I said and realized that they'd all just assigned themselves jobs and gotten busy. I wasn't very good at leading-a-troupe-of-people things. I was more of a one-woman show when it came to organizing jobs, but at least it was getting done.

"Oh, and we saw the news this morning," Irene said with an expectant tone.

Nadia, paintbrush already in her hand, turned to us and said, "We just couldn't believe it. Wellesley, of all people. No wonder she couldn't make it this morning."

I was at a complete loss. "What? Something was on the news?" I just hoped it wasn't me, Summer, and Abby. They'd have mentioned that first thing, wouldn't they?

"It was on the local morning news show. One of those short clips that they play to get you to watch the news at night. You didn't see it?" Irene asked.

"No," I said and moved over as Gina entered the room, carrying the drill. She put it down and began fitting the bed frame together.

"It was one of those hidden camera investigations," Irene said as she obediently followed Gina's instructions on where to stand and how to hold the headboard.

"Hidden camera? Like undercover stuff?" I asked.

Gina didn't look up as she spoke over the whine of the drill. "Undercover news investigation. You know, like when they try to catch sex offenders who want to hook up with kids after chatting with them on the Internet?"

I nodded.

Irene jumped back into the conversation. "The clip they showed had Wellesley in it. We all recognized her right off, even in black-and-white."

"Wellesley was being investigated as a sex offender?" I think my voice sounded kind of shrill.

"No! No, the investigation was about sham marriages. Her tour business is a front. Apparently, she runs a tour every month or so to keep it going, but her real business is arranging marriages for illegal aliens."

"Really? That was on the news?"

"Yes. Full report tonight," Irene confirmed and Gina nodded as she shifted around to the other side of the frame.

Nadia turned to us again. "And she seemed like such a nice girl."

"So the police know about it?"

Gina said, "They do now. They interviewed the reporter this morning and she said they've turned all the information over to the police."

"Well." That was all I could say.

"It does make sense now," Nadia said, "all that about the landscapers and the word *boda*. She was the wedding lady."

Gina said, "*Was* is the operative word there. I don't think she's in that business anymore."

"Well. That's amazing," I said. I'd had a few run-ins with the news media and I couldn't say that I liked the sensationalized state of the media, but, in this case, I was actually glad they'd investigated.

"I know," Nadia said. "But at least we got most of

our tour finished before she showed up on the six o'clock news."

"Yes, I suppose that is a good thing." And it was one thing I could mark off my list.

Two hours later, Ivan was packing up his paints and arguing with Abby about the placement of a window seat pillow. Gina stood on the other window seat, drilling in the screws to hang the last curtain rod. The bedposts didn't get made into turrets, but other than that one item, the room had come together quickly with seven people working on it. Tony and I'd just made up the bed and we tossed the last of the decorative pillows on it. I was sure Ivan cringed at our haphazard placement, but it would have to do.

My phone rang and I whipped it up to my ear. "Summer—"

"Hi, Mommy!" Livvy's voice squeaked in my ear.

"Hi, Livvy. How are you?"

"Okay." Silence filled the line and I did a quick mental check of the organizational items in the room, expecting my mom's voice next since Livvy had only been into one- or two-word conversations with me lately.

"Mommy?"

"You're still there, Livvy? What have you been doing?"

"I got bows. Pink ones."

"I knew you would," I said and surveyed the closet. It looked neat and, well, you wouldn't say spacious, but it was a huge improvement with a shoe caddy and hanging shelves. Clothes were neatly folded in the new chest of drawers, which even had sock dividers. My favorite piece was the bookcase that did double duty with books on the top shelves and bins of toys (with labels, of course) on the bottom shelves.

"Pink's my favorite color."

"I know. What else have you done today?"

"Umm . . . Grammy took me to a store . . . and . . . then," she sighed. "Can't remember."

"That's okay. I'm glad you want to talk to me."

More silence. "Livvy?"

"Hmm?"

"Is Grammy there?"

"Yes, but I want to talk to you."

"Okay." I blew out a breath and tried to focus on the conversation instead of the room. I'd been wanting to talk to Livvy for days and, finally, she wanted to talk to me. There were still several trash bags and bits of paper scattered over the carpet. I closed my eyes. Trash bags could wait. "What do you want to talk about?"

"Don't know."

I blew out another breath. I heard my mom's voice in the background, coaxing Livvy to give up the phone.

Livvy said good-bye and I talked to my mom for a minute, explaining the time crunch we were in, and then hung up with the promise to talk later tonight. I felt terrible. I'd been waiting for Livvy to want to talk to me and now that she finally did, I had to go. Actually, there hadn't been a lot of conversation. She seemed to want to breathe into the phone. But still.

Gina smoothed out the curtain, pink with white swirls trimmed in black ribbon, and stepped down off the window seat. "Is that it?"

"I think so." I grabbed the trash bags. Gina replaced the cordless drill in its case and handed it to Tony. Abby and Ivan had compromised on the placement of the pillow and she came over, took the trash bags from me, and said, "Okay, we're going to get out of your hair so you can have your interview in peace. I called for the hotel shuttle and it's here."

There was a flurry of hugs, compliments, and

thanks. Then it was just me, Tony, and Ivan in the room. Ivan moved the pillow he'd been arguing with Abby about, repositioning it about forty-five degrees to the left, and stepped back to look at it.

Good grief. It was just a pillow. Tony grabbed his jacket off the floor and said, "Thanks so much for your help. They're pulling into the driveway now. I'm going to pick up lunch for everyone at a deli. Can I bring you back a sandwich?" he asked as he folded the jacket and put it in the messenger bag he was carrying.

"No, thanks." I really wanted to get the interview over and try and track down Summer. "And no problem about helping out. I'm glad it all worked out." I still couldn't believe that Summer wanted to work for Vicki Archer. If she had Tony, her right-hand man, painting bedrooms pink and running out to fetch lunch, no telling what assignments she'd give to someone even lower in the office hierarchy.

I called out to Tony, "Hey, before you leave." He paused at the top of the stairs. "Have you heard from Summer?"

"No. I'm going to cover for her with Ms. Archer, but she won't be pleased when she realizes Summer wasn't here today. If you and your friends hadn't helped out, it would have been a disaster."

"Well, maybe she thought she'd be able to help finish up everything tonight. The photos were scheduled for tomorrow."

"Right. The schedule's always fluid. She knows that." I detected a hint of frustration in his tone, but he covered it quickly. "I'm sure she had a good reason."

I could hear voices in the kitchen downstairs, so I said, "What was she like when she called you last night? Was she upset or anything?"

Tony shook his head quickly. "She seemed fine,

excited almost. You know, her usual upbeat self." He trotted down the stairs.

When Summer had dropped us off at the hotel last night, she'd been anything but upbeat. Depressed and worried were more apt descriptions of her mood. What had happened to change that? And where *was* she?

I went back to the room to do a quick visual sweep. Ivan was tweaking a curtain tieback. I felt my shoulder muscles relax as I took in the room. Even though it was still cloudy, the fog had lifted and the clouds were thinning. Watery sunlight glowed in the windows. I noticed a strip of silver on the carpet, just under the edge of the bed's dust ruffle. Expecting a bit of paper or a piece of the metal bed frame, I was surprised to find it was a flash drive, a slim memory chip about two inches long. "Ivan, is this yours?"

He said, "No," and ran his hand over his bare head. I heard someone pounding up the stairs, so I slipped the memory chip into my pocket. I'd figure out who it belonged to later. I noticed Ivan's rings were back on and he'd changed into leather pants and a shirt with a pink and black paisley design. Was he trying to match the room? And when had he had time to change? It must have been while Tony and I were talking on the stairs. Well, I couldn't blame Ivan for wanting to make an impression on the writer. As a small business owner, I knew that any publicity you could get was a bonus. I wished I was wearing something more snazzy than my sleeveless white top and navy skort. Very schoolgirlish next to Ivan's paisley. Oh well. If I'd known what the day was going to hold I would have had Abby pick out my outfit. I just hoped I didn't have any pink paint in my hair.

A little girl in a purple jumper embroidered with kites bounded into the room. Her fine blond hair was pulled back into pigtails secured with pink ribbons, which bobbed as she ran to the bookcase and pawed through the toys; then, she noticed the bed. "A castle!" she squealed as she hurtled across the room and landed with a thud that sent pillows and stuffed animals catapulting through the air. Ivan nearly had a seizure.

"Where's the moat?" she demanded.

As I walked across the Archers' driveway, I pulled the last Hershey's Kiss out of my purse. I'd have to restock. The "interview" had lasted about two minutes and I doubted that my name, or Ivan's for that matter, would end up in the finished piece. He looked as depressed as I felt. In his van, he raised his hand at me, an abbreviated good-bye wave, the weak sun glinting on the gold of his rings, before he reversed out of the driveway.

I'd just spent a good portion of my vacation organizing a bedroom and then I hadn't even heard the words "thank you" from Vicki Archer. She just said, "Oh. It's more cutesy than modern, isn't it?"

What had she expected? Stainless steel and white laminate? And several of my friends had donated their vacation time, too. I felt more irritated about that fact than the lack of appreciation from Vicki. It wasn't like she was a charity case. She could certainly afford to hire help.

Forget about it, I lectured myself. I did it to help Summer. Sure, a mention in *Mom Magazine* wouldn't be anything to pass up, but I was doing it to help Summer get more brownie points with Vicki Archer. The magazine thing was a bonus.

I reached Summer's apartment and peered in her living room window. For someone so energetic and bubbly as Summer, her place felt remarkably orderly. Except for the boxes that Abby had stacked next to several toys in the entry by the front door, the apartment was immaculate.

The dishes were washed and put away, her kitchen counters were clear. Magazines, an eclectic mix of *Elle*, *In Style*, and *Time*, were arranged neatly on the coffee table. Her laptop, which was closed, sat next to the magazines. A tiny green light on the side blinked every few seconds. I smiled when I saw the pile of junk mail on the couch, thinking about how she'd kidded me about shredding my mail right away. Across the room, next to a bookcase, sat two bins, one piled high with newspapers and the other brimming with envelopes and credit card offers. A shredder, its bin empty, sat next to the junk mail.

I studied the far end of the studio, where her closet lined one wall next to the bathroom. Her hats hung from a row of hooks next to the closet. The closet doors were neatly shut and I could see part of the bathroom. No towels on the bath mat or blow-dryer on the counter. It all looked reassuringly normal.

For some reason, it bothered me.

I pulled out my phone and called her number again. This time when the voice mail came on I left a message. "Summer. I'm standing outside your apartment and I'm starting to worry about you. I haven't heard from you since last night. Tony says you had an emergency and had to leave. I'm going to use the key you told him about to go in your apartment and look around. I hope you're not mad, but I'm concerned. Oh, and the deadline for the photo shoot for *Mom Magazine* got moved up to today."

If that last bit didn't get her to call me, nothing would. I stepped inside and paced around the small space. I didn't notice anything up close that I hadn't seen through the window.

I stopped in the kitchen. Her class schedule was posted on the fridge. I checked the list for today's classes. Only a seminar on political jargon and it ended thirty minutes ago.

Her phone rang. Maybe it was Summer returning my call. I hurried across her kitchen area to answer it before the answering machine came on.

"Miss Avery?"

I paused a fraction of a second. "Umm . . . no. Not *Miss* Avery. I'm *Mrs.* Avery. Ellie Avery. Who's speaking, please?"

"Jason Brown, Metropolitan Police. I need to speak to Summer Avery."

Great. Just great. "She's not here. She's—out." I stopped myself from babbling anything else. What I'd told him was true.

"When will she be back? I have a few more questions for her."

"I'm not sure. I can have her call you."

"You do that." The pace of his words, so brisk at the beginning of the call, had slowed down. "She's in class?" His voice was louder. I could picture him pressing the phone closer to his jowly face as his interest sharpened. I had to get off the phone before I said something that would make things worse for Summer.

"No. She only had a seminar today and it's already over," I said and realized the phone was slipping in my sweaty palm.

"So where is she?"

I ramped up the speed of words. "She didn't say. She stepped out a while ago." Again, technically true. I poured confidence into my tone. "I'll tell her you called. I'm sure she'll be back soon."

I certainly hoped so.

I heard someone calling Brown's name and he muttered something under his breath before he said good-bye. I hung up the phone, wiped my hands down on my skort, and crossed the room. My qualms about snooping were rapidly diminishing. Police phone calls can really change your outlook.

I opened her closet door and saw several empty hangers. Maybe she needed to do laundry? I stepped in the petite bathroom and checked the hamper. A mound of clothes filled it to the top. So, yes, she needed to do laundry. Brilliant deduction.

I made the circuit back to the kitchen and checked her answering machine. No messages. I didn't see her purse anywhere, which I took to be a good sign.

I plopped down on the futon couch. Really, I should have been relieved. Everything looked normal, no sign of a hasty exit or—I forced myself to think what had been lurking around the edge of my thoughts—a struggle. So she'd left, by all appearances, of her own choice. In fact, the apartment had the tidied-up atmosphere of a house when someone was gone on vacation.

I hopped up, crossed to the closet, and opened both doors wide. A large suitcase took up one corner, but when I looked at the floor, I noticed several blank spots in her shoe holder as well as another empty space on the closet floor. It was just about the right size for a tote bag or small suitcase.

I went back to the futon couch. Would she really have gone on a trip? With finals approaching and the photo shoot for Emma's room one day away? I didn't think so and, as far as I knew, she didn't have a boyfriend. She'd never mentioned anyone, so that didn't seem to be a possible explanation either.

I opened her laptop and hit a key to bring it out of hibernation. I felt a bit uncomfortable poking around in her things, but my worry about her pushed me to keep looking around.

Her e-mail was open. The most recent messages were from other students about a group project. I opened her sent mail. The recent e-mails were to the office about press releases. No help there.

I leaned back against the couch and let my gaze roam around the orderly apartment. Nothing out of place except for the pile of junk mail beside her laptop. And a mug. I hadn't noticed it earlier. A tea bag string dangled over the edge. Chamomile.

I leaned forward and slowly pulled the mail toward me. I'd seen that grocery store flyer with the pink steak before. *There are probably thousands of these advertisements all over town.* But when I checked the address on the flyer it wasn't Summer's address. It was Robinwood Road.

An Everything In Its Place Tip for an Organized Trip

Don't forget these essentials
  • Tickets or e-confirmation numbers, maps, and guidebooks.
  • Picture ID.
  • Cash—make sure you have some small bills to tip shuttle drivers.
  • Cell phone charger.
  • Prescription medications in containers with pharmacy label.
  • Food for pets, leash, and shot records.
  • Camera.

Chapter
Seventeen

I quickly flipped through the stack of envelopes cradled in the middle of the folded flyer. A few were addressed to "Occupant," but several listed J. Dominguez or Jorge Dominguez as the recipient. Three credit card offers, postcards advertising teeth whitening and cheap tires, and an empty envelope with a jagged tear down the end, which was addressed to J. Dominguez. The printed return address was STAND in North Dawkins, Georgia. What was STAND? The postmark was from the same city. I turned the envelope over in my hands, chewed on my lower lip for a minute. I had no doubt that Summer had opened it. Did she find something inside that led her to call Tony and tell him she wouldn't be in the next day? Had she gone back to Jorge's apartment? But then why wouldn't she take her car? It didn't make sense.

After I found her phone book, I called the hotel and asked if there were any messages for me. *Maybe she didn't have my cell phone number?* The front desk clerk came back on the line after only a few seconds. "No, ma'am. No messages."

I sighed and hung up the phone. I paced around

the tiny space. What to do? What to do? Even though I felt something was definitely wrong, calling the police was out. At least for a few more hours. Summer hadn't been missing for a whole day. I didn't even know for sure she *was* missing. Maybe she'd just taken off. Mitch could catalogue the times when Summer hadn't done what was expected of her, but she was a grown-up. If she wanted to disappear for a while she could. No law against that.

I just couldn't shake my apprehensive feeling, so I wasn't going to go back to the hotel and worry. I picked up the stack of mail, found an extra key to her car in a drawer in her kitchen, and locked her apartment on my way out. There was a map of D.C. in her glove compartment. I looked up Robinwood Drive.

I'd lost track of the number of times I'd had to backtrack after I missed my turns. I'm a great navigator. Reading maps is a snap for me. It's just hard to read a map and drive at the same time. Add D.C. traffic to the equation and I had tons of U-turns and annoyed drivers in my wake. But I did finally find the apartment complex. It looked even scruffier in the thin sunlight that struggled to break through the gray clouds. I found a parking space on the far side of the street in front of another apartment complex. I jogged across the street and knocked on Mrs. Matthews's door. I couldn't think of anywhere else Summer could have gone, so I figured I'd go back to the last place I *knew* she'd been.

A young woman dressed in a short-sleeved denim shirt with the words *Gas 'n Go* embroidered on the left shoulder opened the door, already speaking. "Mama, how many times have I done told you, you don't have to ring the bell. Just use your key—" She ran out of words when she saw me and moved to close the door, but a toddler, his tummy showing between the hem of his shirt and his diaper, came motoring toward the open door. She quickly swept him up on her hip, pulled the shirt down, and wiped a peanut butter smear from the corner of his mouth, all reflexive mom moves. It made me miss Livvy, but I realized the woman was about to close the door, so I focused on her.

I dredged her name up from my memory. "You must be Danielle. I talked to your mother last night. My sister-in-law and I came by. We were asking about your next-door neighbor."

The boy grinned at me around his thumb, which he'd stuck in his mouth. Danielle's attitude wasn't as friendly as her son's. "Yeah. Mama mentioned you. I didn't know him," she said shortly. "Only saw him a couple times. He kept to hisself and didn't bother me none." She closed the door a couple more inches.

"Wait. I'm looking for my sister-in-law. I dug my billfold out of my purse and flipped through the plastic sleeve of photos. I had to flip through all of them. "Sorry. Most of these are of my daughter," I said as I kept turning until I got to the last one, a family shot of Mitch's parents and his two sisters. I pointed to Summer, her red hair tumbling over her shoulder.

"Cute little girl." Danielle had thawed a bit as she pointed to the facing picture of Livvy with angel wings. It was taken back when she still had rolls of baby fat. "Your little angel?"

"Yes, except she's rarely this angelic."

Danielle smiled. "They never are, except when they're sleeping." She shifted the boy higher on her hip. "No. No one's been by today."

"What about last night?"

"No. Not after I got home around eleven."

"Okay. Thanks." I stepped back and waved to the little boy as he said "bye-bye." We must have barely missed Danielle last night. If Summer had returned to this apartment, it would have been after Danielle got home. I walked up the sidewalk, sprinted across the street, feeling a little light-headed.

I realized I was absolutely starving as I slammed the door and put the key in the ignition. I'd been so focused on where Summer might be that I'd forgotten to eat, which shows how unnerved I was since I hardly ever miss meals. I wished I hadn't passed up Tony's offer of a sandwich earlier. It was past one o'clock and I hadn't had anything to eat since my bagel in the hotel lobby. I didn't even have any Hershey's Kisses, but that was probably a good thing. For once, I needed something a bit more substantial than chocolate. Well, I could always eat chocolate, but it would probably be better to eat an energy bar *first*, then chocolate so I didn't send my insulin levels out of whack. I pulled an energy bar out of my purse and devoured it.

I was crumbling the wrapper when a black car pulled into one of the parallel slots a few cars ahead of me. A man with a compact body emerged from the low-slung driver's seat. I squinted and leaned over the steering wheel for a better view.

Yes, it *was* Tony. He was wearing the same Washington Redskins T-shirt complete with pink paint smears, but more than that, I recognized the way he moved, quick and decisive, as he jogged across the street and up the same sidewalk to Jorge's apartment. He didn't knock. He flipped open the mailbox and paused. His movements up to that point had been automatic, but his smooth flow halted. He carefully looked around the porch area, checked the mailbox again, then checked Danielle's mailbox. He flipped through her envelopes, then replaced them. As he returned to his car, he made a call on his cell phone.

He probably wouldn't have noticed me since he was distracted, juggling his phone and his keys, but I couldn't help sliding down in the seat and ducking my head when he did a quick check up and down the block before gliding away from the curb in the black car.

I shoved the energy bar wrapper in my bag and pulled into traffic behind him. What was Tony doing at Jorge's apartment? And why was he so interested in Jorge's mail?

I still hadn't figured out answers to those questions thirty minutes later when Tony pulled into a parking slot near the long reflecting pool between the World War II Memorial and the Lincoln Memorial. I may not be that great at navigating in D.C. traffic alone, but I discovered that keeping up with someone else was a breeze. The masses of cars actually made it easier to follow him, and he didn't seem to notice or care that one particular RAV4 hung with him as he drove toward the center of D.C.

I needed to park. Fast. Tony was busy opening the trunk of his car as I drove past him. In my rearview mirror, I saw him slam the trunk and jog away, a football tucked in the crook of his arm. I was toast. He'd disappear into the swarm of tourists before I could find a place to park.

There was no way I could keep him in sight. Instead I focused on the cars, but I didn't see anyone leaving. Finally, I saw a sign for a parking garage. I parked and raced back outside. Even the overcast day seemed bright after the dark interior of the parking garage.

I walked back to his car and scanned the people dotting the grassy area around the reflecting pool. There were just too many people. He could be almost to the Washington Monument by now. No use running around looking for him. I wiped my hand across my forehead, which was damp from my almost jog from the parking garage and the mounting humidity of the day. I shook my head. I was hot, tired, and still hungry. I found a street vendor and bought a pretzel, an apple, and a Diet Coke. I walked back to the grass around the reflecting pool and sat down under a tree. Tony had to come back to his car sometime.

I ate my impromptu picnic and watched a group of young people playing soccer. I tossed the wrappers and apple core in the trash and returned to the tree. A few shriveled pink petals were caught in the crevices of the roots, the only evidence that the cherry trees had bloomed a short time ago. I leaned my head back against the tree and tried to sort out how Tony could know Jorge. Maybe Summer introduced them? Another thing to add to my already lengthy list of questions for Summer.

My phone trilled and I grabbed it.

"Hey, sorry I didn't call earlier. We didn't get out of class until just a few minutes ago."

I was so focused on Summer and expecting her to call me that it took me a minute to process what Mitch had said. "Oh. That's fine," I finally managed.

Mitch. Shoot. What was I going to tell him? I didn't want to tell him Summer had disappeared. He'd be quick to tell me I'd been wrong about her settling down. But she was his sister. I probably should tell him. I felt a little queasy and it had nothing to do with being pregnant. There was so much I needed to tell Mitch. Where to begin?

"How did the thing at the Archers' go this morning?" he asked.

Okay. I'd start with this morning. I filled him in on the room debacle and how the other wives came to my rescue. I wound up with the news about Summer's no-show.

"So, how long has she been gone?" he asked. I'd expected tension or even a bit of smugness, but his tone was casual.

"Since last night."

"So about fourteen, fifteen hours?"

I counted in my head. "Yeah, that's about right."

"Well, I wouldn't start to worry until it's been at least twenty-four. Maybe thirty-six."

"Really? Even with the police questioning her about Jorge's death?"

"Yeah. Really. Look, I hate to cut this short, but I've got to get back to the session. Try not to worry. She's just being . . . Summer. Oh, I almost forgot to tell you that Colonel Johns invited us to a dinner tonight."

"Us? Tonight?"

"The class." Colonel Johns was their FROT instructor.

"A dinner? Like a dinner party? That's kind of short notice, isn't it? How formal is it? Tonight?" I mentally ran through the clothes I'd brought in my suitcase, a futile exercise, really, since I knew there wasn't a cocktail dress back at the hotel.

"Whoa, there. Too many questions. Yes, I'm sure it's tonight. And they told us about it a few days ago, but I'd forgotten until now."

I figured as much. "Mitch—"

Mitch continued. "And don't worry. It's casual."

"Casual. Cocktail dress casual or business casual? All I have with me are shorts, sleeveless shirts, and a couple of pairs of capris. And some jeans. I don't think it will be *that* casual."

"Well, take Abby and go shopping for something."

"Mitch, do you know how hard it is to find a flattering cocktail dress? Much less a *maternity* cocktail dress?"

"Believe me, I'm thankful I don't know, but I think I'm going to hear more about it anyway." I could hear the smile in his voice and it made me smile, too.

"You think I'm making too big a deal of it, huh?"

"A bit."

"Okay. Well, I'll figure out something."

"You always do. Look, I've got to go. Don't worry about the dress or Summer. Everything will work out."

"Sure. Right. Hey, find out what Mrs. Johns is wearing to this party."

"How am I supposed to do that? She's not here. I've never met her."

"I don't know. You're a clever guy. Think of some ingenious way to get the info, like maybe the truth? Tell Colonel Johns that you forgot to tell your wife about the party until *this afternoon* and she's in a panic about what to wear."

"All right, I'll see what I can do."

I put my phone away, still a bit frustrated. That "don't worry, be happy" attitude summed up Mitch's take on life. Everything would work out. Yeah, it would, because I'd make it work out. I looked up through the latticework of the tree's green leaves and took a deep breath. Maybe I was overreacting about clothes. And maybe Summer was fine and would show up or call me and she'd be amazed that I'd worried so much.

I stood up, stretched, and shook the kinks out of my legs. I'd pulled out my map of downtown D.C. and was checking landmarks and street signs, planning a route to get back to Summer's house, when I saw Tony at the end of the reflecting pool with another man, who looked so much like him he could have been Tony's brother.

An Everything In Its Place Tip for an Organized Trip

Tips for business travel
- Make sure you have codes and passwords to remotely access your work phone system and computer while you're on the road.
- Find out what the dress code is at your destination. No need to pack a suit if business casual is the rule, but do include at least one jacket or blazer since air-conditioned meeting rooms can be quite cool no matter what the weather is outside.
- Don't trust essential business items to checked baggage. Carry with you any papers, notes, or other materials that you'll need. Or send these items ahead via a delivery service with tracking.
- Select your airline seat when you book your flight.
- If you can travel without your laptop, you'll save time at security screening points.
- A watch with two time-zone settings lets you keep track of time at your destination and back at the office.

Chapter
Eighteen

I shifted and looked around uneasily, but Tony was focused on his conversation and hadn't seen me. I took a couple of steps to get a better look at the other man. He had the same glossy dark hair and olive complexion. He was slightly taller than Tony and a bit heavier.

A cluster of tourists bunched around their guide a few feet away. It was either join the tourists or walk across the wide-open swath of grass alone. I suppose I could have stayed where I was, but I felt exposed.

Tony still had the football tucked under his arm, but he looked sweatier. The other man's shirt had dark spots at the armpits. They both looked like they'd finished a game of flag football.

I edged closer to the water and merged into the group of tourists. At the front of the group, a tour guide murmured about the construction of the Reflecting Pool.

I glanced at the two men again and heard Tony say, "Drop it." His sharp words carried clearly over the water. He realized it and lowered his volume, but I could still hear him as he continued. "Look, it's done.

We have to go on. And it's a good thing anyway. He was getting too involved with the woman after his assignment in Georgia."

The other man clenched his fists. His voice was angry as he said, "You can't go and make decisions like that. You can't take someone out."

"You think I killed him?"

The other man kept silent. I ducked my head over the map and inched a bit closer to the tour group.

"You really think that? You think I'd waste a minute of my time on Jorge? He was nothing."

"He thought you were getting soft. And I'm beginning to think he might have been right. Cushy job. Fast car. You like America, don't you? I don't know if you have the guts to do what needs to be done."

I sneaked a look up from my map and saw the anger in Tony's eyes as he said quietly, "I'm not soft. I didn't kill him, but it's a good thing he's gone. He got too wrapped up in women."

Suddenly, I realized the background noise of the tour guide's voice was gone. I looked up; they'd trooped away. I pivoted and cut diagonally across the grass to the street, studying the map as I went. I picked up my pace a bit more, and looked over my shoulder. The second man was walking away, but Tony charged along the edge of the reflecting pool, looking at me.

"Hey, watch where you're going," a woman said as I bumped into her. She scowled at me as she grabbed the earbud I'd knocked out of her ear.

I twisted around, said, "Sorry," and threaded through a crowd of people. I hurried along, not quite jogging, but close to it. I snuck another quick backward glance. Tony was dodging through a crowd and moving in my direction. I broke out of the crowd, crossed the street, and hurried down the opposite side. As soon as I was across, I realized it was a mistake. There were a lot more people on the Mall. I should have stayed over there, but I didn't want to cross back again, so I sprinted down the sidewalk. I looked back, but didn't see Tony. I passed his car and kept up my pace. Then a stitch in my side reminded me that running wasn't my thing. I really had to get out that pregnancy workout video.

I scanned the street for the parking garage, but didn't see it. *Oh God, what if I'd passed it?* I did *not* want to backtrack. I hurried on, sweat sticking my shirt to my back.

Still no parking garage. Maybe I wasn't remembering the name right. It had been First Class Parking, hadn't it? One more block, I decided quickly. I looked back, no sign of Tony. I slowed down to a brisk walk. Maybe I was crazy and he hadn't spotted me at the Reflecting Pool and followed me. I was trying to decide whether to make the block or look for a store or restaurant to slip into when I saw the yawning, dark entrance to the garage. I did another quick over-the-shoulder check as I slipped around the corner into the blackness.

Tony stood beside his car, breathing heavily with his hands on his hips, scanning the far side of the street.

Okay, he was definitely looking for someone and I had a feeling that someone was me. I found Summer's car, locked all the doors, and sat there with it running and the cool air blasting until my hands stopped shaking.

Where to go? I wanted to go back to the hotel, but I really should take Summer's car back to her house, in case she came back from wherever the blazes she'd gone. Tony probably didn't know which hotel I was in, unless Summer had mentioned it to him in passing. I'd cooled down enough that the air washing over my arms felt frigid. I savored the sensation for a few more seconds; then, I backed out and exited the garage.

Tony still stood beside his car, studying the street. Fortunately, his back was turned to me. I hit the gas, merged into traffic, and made the first turn I could. After several miles my heartbeat returned to normal. I didn't see a black car in my mirrors, so I picked up my phone at the next light. No new messages. Why was I not surprised? If Summer hadn't checked in earlier, why did I think she would now?

I dialed Abby's phone and she answered on the first ring. "Hey. What are you doing? Are you busy?" I asked.

"Not unless you consider reading *Cosmo* and *Fit Pregnancy* busy. I went to lunch with everyone and now I'm sitting around the hotel room, resting up for dinner tonight."

"You knew about that? Mitch didn't tell me until a couple of minutes ago. I have absolutely nothing to wear to a dinner."

"What about that cute outfit we bought you the other night? You know, the capri pants, blue tank, jacket, and sandals? That's dressy, but not too dressy. Or you can borrow my lilac sundress."

"I love having a personal stylist. You should charge for this kind of advice. Okay, now that my fashion emergency is resolved . . ." I cringed, remembering that she'd already helped me out once today. Was there a limit on how much you could ask of your friends? I'm sure Miss Manners would say that there was a limit on how much you *should* ask of your friends, but I really didn't want to be at Summer's alone. "I hate to ask you this, but can you get a taxi and meet me at Summer's apartment?"

"Sure. What's going on?"
"I wish I knew."

Somehow I managed to arrive at Summer's apartment first. A black Lexus, the only car in the driveway, was parked close to the house. All the excitement of the room redecoration and magazine interview must be over. I parked Summer's car on the street where it had been this morning and walked up the driveway to her apartment. I knocked on her door, but I didn't really expect anyone to answer. After a few moments, I unlocked the door and went inside, quickly sliding the dead bolt into place.

Nothing had changed. No purse tossed on the counter or shoes kicked off by the door. I fought down the uneasy feeling the lifeless atmosphere gave me and went to check her answering machine. A new message. I hit PLAY.

"Hi, Summer, this is Kimberly at the office. I thought you'd want to know that police officer, Detective Brown, came by this afternoon looking for you. I told him you always have Friday afternoons off and to check at your place. *Anyway*, just thought you might want to know."

Terrific. I checked my watch. The message had been recorded about ten minutes ago. Brown was probably on his way over here right now. As soon as the taxi got here, I was out the door. I didn't want to talk to Detective Brown in person. Lying, well, obfuscating, I could get away with for short periods over the phone, but not face-to-face.

I paced to the window. No taxi. I walked around the room a couple of times. I picked up the mug and set it in the sink, then forced myself to sit down on the couch. Paper crinkled as I plunked into the cushions. I pulled out the stack of junk mail that Summer had taken from Jorge's mailbox. Was this what Tony had been looking for? I glanced through the flyers and junk mail again. Nothing in there worth making a special trip to Jorge's apartment for, not that I could see.

I pulled the opened envelope out of my purse and looked at the address and postmark. I added it to the stack of junk mail and then shoved the whole bundle in my purse as I checked the end of the driveway again. Still no taxi. More clouds had rolled in and a few raindrops plopped onto the driveway.

The laptop was still open, so I powered it up and brought up the Internet. I began typing the word "STAND" into the search box, but after the first two letters, a drop-down box showed that "STAND North Dawkins, Georgia" had been typed into the search box before. I clicked on the words.

The search had retrieved sixty-two thousand results, but only one line on the first page was highlighted in a different color, indicating it had been selected recently. I clicked on that line and the screen filled with an aerial photo of a military base. Fighters and tankers filled the ramp. Huge hangars angled across the top of the photo alongside the runway. Above the photo, a banner bracketed with rippling American flags read *STAND: Secure Taylor And North Dawkins*. I scanned the text below the photo. STAND was an organization designed to make sure North Dawkins's military base, Taylor Air Force Base, didn't appear on base closure lists.

Suddenly, I had a feeling that Summer had done something impulsive. I walked over and picked up her phone and punched in the code to retrieve the last number dialed. A lively voice answered, "Around Town Shuttle."

"Hi, could you tell me a little about your services?" I asked.

"Of course. We provide shuttle and parking services for Dulles and Ronald Reagan National."

"And do you pick up travelers at their homes?"

"Yes and we also pick up at businesses, too. We have quite a few corporate clients. Would you like references?"

"No. I just need to know if you picked up a woman named Summer Avery last night at—"

"I'm sorry but we can't give that information out."

"Well, yes, I'm sure you wouldn't normally, but this is my sister-in-law and I haven't heard from her for several hours and if you could just confirm that she used your shuttle, I'd at least know she went to the airport."

"I'm really sorry, but I can't give out any information. Privacy policy, you know. Why don't you call the police?"

Good question. I couldn't say, "Because they want to talk to her, too." Just wouldn't sound good, so I thanked her and hung up.

My cell phone rang and I hurried over to answer it.

"Hi, Ellie. You're not going to believe what I found last night—"

"Summer, tell me you're not in Georgia."

An Everything In Its Place Tip for an Organized Trip

Since road trips can seem endless, here's a few games to help pass the time:

- State Blackout—Bring several copies of a map of the United States. Have kids color in a state when they see a license plate from that state. The winner is the person who either fills in the map or has the most states filled in at the end of the trip.

- Name Game—The driver says the name of a famous person. The person in the front passenger seat takes the first letter of the last name and thinks of a different famous person whose first name begins with that letter. For example, if the driver says, "Albert Einstein," the second player could say, "Eleanor Roosevelt." Rotate through the car until someone can't think of a new name. Variations on this game could include the cartoon character name game or, to make the game harder, limit the game to a category like only politicians or musicians.

- Alphabet Game—Begin with the letter *a* and look for a sign with that letter. The person who sees an *a* first gets a point. Continue through the alphabet, then total points. The person with the highest score wins.

- I Spy—Play this classic game with a time limit of a couple of seconds per turn since you'll be flying down the road and can zip past the item that was "spied" almost before anyone's had a chance to guess.

Chapter
Nineteen

A brief silence greeted me and then I could hear Summer take a deep breath, winding up for a long, wheedling apology. "You sound upset. Are you upset? I'm really sorry to leave you alone for the prep for Emma's room, but I'll be back before tomorrow and—"

"Summer, tell me you're not in Georgia," I repeated. "Because—leaving out all the worrying I've done about you—I really don't want to have to tell Detective Brown, who's looking for you, that you've left town. No, wait. Not that you've left town. You've left the state. In fact, you're not even in the same region, are you?"

"No." Her voice was subdued. "You're right. I'm in Georgia." The regret fell away and she hurried through the rest of her explanation. "But I'll be back before tomorrow. I'll be so quick that the police won't even know I was gone, and everything should be fine for Emma's room. Anyway, I had to come down here because I found this envelope in Jorge's mail and—"

"STAND, right? I found the envelope."

"Yes, how did you know about it?" Her voice was flat again.

I felt bad about deflating her excitement. "Summer, I'm sorry to be so . . . harsh with you, but I was worried about you and you shouldn't run off to another state when you're a suspect in a murder investigation. It doesn't look good. Haven't you listened to your messages?"

"No. I haven't had time. I think my phone is in the rental car. You called, huh?"

"Yes. One of my calls was to tell you that the photo shoot for *Mom Magazine* was moved up to early this afternoon." The silence stretched and I thought I'd lost the connection. "Summer, are you there?"

"Yes, I'm here. That's . . . I mean . . . they can't do that. It's not ready."

"Well, they can and they did. Fortunately, the other military spouses on my tour helped finish the room this morning. If they hadn't been here, there wouldn't have been a new room for Emma."

Summer groaned. "I should have known something would happen. It always does. What about Ms. Archer? Was she furious that I wasn't there?"

"No, Tony covered for you."

"Tony is such a sweetie."

"How well do you know him?"

"Not as well as I'd like," she said playfully. "He's always polite and professional. Very . . ." She paused and searched for a word. "Distant."

"Did he know Jorge?"

"Tony and Jorge?" Her voice was dismissive. "No, of course not."

"Well, Tony was at Jorge's apartment today, looking in Jorge's mailbox. I think he was looking for the mail you took."

"What?"

I summarized how I'd gotten in her apartment. "Since I didn't have any other ideas about where you might be, I went back there and he showed up. Then he met another man. I heard the other man accuse Tony of getting rid of Jorge."

"Whoa. That doesn't make sense."

"Jorge never went to the office? Did he do yard work there or something?"

"No. That is so bizarre because Tony, well, I'd trust him with anything. And Ms. Archer does. Are you absolutely sure it was Tony?"

"No doubt in my mind. It was Tony." I checked the window again. The taxi was still a no-show. "And you know, he mentioned Georgia. He said he shouldn't have sent Jorge to Georgia."

"That's why I'm here. I found the envelope from STAND. There was a check inside made out to Jorge and it was signed by Lena Stallings."

"Who's Lena Stallings?" I asked.

"She's the executive director of STAND and, more importantly, she's a redhead."

"A woman has red hair and you hop on a flight to Georgia?" I couldn't keep the exasperated tone out of my voice. "And how do you know she's got red hair?"

"Just listen, for a minute. I know she's got red hair because I looked up STAND online. There's a picture of their board."

I went back to the computer and clicked over to STAND's *About Us* page and waited for it to load.

Summer continued. "She signed the check to Jorge and in the memo line she wrote 'yard work.' There was also a sticky note stuck to the check that said 'Haven't been able to reach you. We need to talk.' And then there's a phone number. There's no

date on the note, but the check's date and the envelope's postmark were the week before Jorge died."

"So you think that she came to D.C., found Jorge
on the Metro platform, and pushed him?"

"Well, when you put it so bluntly, it does sound
tenuous, but, Ellie, she knew him in Georgia. She's
mailing him checks. She wanted to talk. I think they
were having an affair and she didn't want anyone else
to know about it. Down here, she's quite the southern lady ambassador for North Dawkins, Georgia.
Everyone I talk to here knows her and they all think
she's wonderful. I've heard how she grew up here,
became a nurse during Vietnam, and then came home
to set up tons of programs for returning vets. She's
very high-profile here."

"Summer, I'll be the first to confess that I make in-
tuitive leaps, but you've got to admit that what you've
got is pretty flimsy."

"Well, I know she was in D.C. last week. In fact
she's still there. That's why I'm coming back. And we
all know what that 'we need to talk' line means. They
were involved. I think Jorge came down here to do
yard work during the winter. There would be more
opportunities to work down here even in the winter
than there would be in Virginia or Maryland. He met
her and they had a thing going, but she got worried
when he left. A fling with the gardener just wouldn't
go over well for such a public figure here."

"I know you want to find some other legitimate
suspects, but—and I hate to say this—I think you're
reaching here. How do you know they were ever involved?"

"Ellie, the check is for fifty thousand dollars."

"Oh. Okay. That would be an awful lot of landscaping."

"Yeah. And I've seen her house. She didn't have

fifty thousand dollars' worth of yard work done. There's not even a water feature."

"Was the check a personal check or was it from STAND?" I asked.

"It was a personal check. I've been to their office, too. It was the first place I went when I got here. It's in an office park with landscaping contracted out to a local company."

"My, you have been busy," I said mildly. The Web page still hadn't loaded, so I hit the Refresh button and it came up right away with pictures of STAND's board across the top. "Hold on, that's MacInally's sister."

"What?" Summer asked.

"I'm looking at the Web page for STAND on your laptop. I've met Lena. She's MacInally's sister." When her mouth wasn't pinched with disapproval like it had been at the hospital, she was a very attractive woman. The photo showed off her high cheekbones and even her severe business suit didn't hide her curvy figure. "She was at the hospital. She was in D.C. on Wednesday. Except her hair was more brown than red when I met her." In the photo on the Web site, her hair was a deep cherry, which looked completely artificial and actually made her look older.

"So what? She dyed her hair. And there's one other thing." Summer's voice sounded smug and I knew she'd been holding back, saving the best for last. "She's in the photo you gave me. She was on the Metro platform."

"Are you sure?" I saw the flash of the taxi's headlights as it pulled into the driveway, so I shut down the laptop, turned off the lights, and grabbed my purse.

"Oh, I'm sure." Summer's voice swelled with confidence.

I locked the front door and walked to the taxi. It was just barely sprinkling so I wasn't really wet when I got in the taxi and mouthed "thank you" to Abby. I tucked the phone into the crook of my shoulder and slammed the taxi door. "Summer, I'm heading back to the hotel. I locked up your place. You've got another key?"

"Of course."

"Okay. I'm going back to look at the photo and think about all this. You're definitely coming back tonight?"

"Yes."

"Well, call me when you get in and be careful. Tony had your keys this morning. He could have had a copy made before he gave them to me."

"Tony wouldn't do something like that," Abby said dismissively. "I'm sorry I worried you so much."

I could tell from her tone that she wouldn't listen to what I said about Tony. Stubbornness was a trait that ran in the Avery family. Mitch and I were well matched in that characteristic, at least. "It's all right. I can see why you were so excited about tracking Lena down. I'm going to a dinner tonight, so I may not be able to answer my cell phone, but I'd really appreciate it if you leave me a message when you get in."

I said good-bye to Summer and Abby said, "So, busy afternoon?"

"Slightly." I leaned back into the seat and brought her up to date on everything that had happened.

"Are you sure you want to go to this thing tonight?" I pulled on my new sandals and checked my reflection in the mirrored closet doors.

Mitch wiped the last of the shaving cream from his face. "Don't have a choice."

I pulled on my jacket over the tank and capri pants and frowned into the mirror. We'd done our fair share of skipping out on squadron activities. Mitch had never been one to insist that we go to every event. "Really? We *have* to go?" He'd shaved for it. It must be important.

"No. *You* don't have to go, but I do. At least, I have to put in an appearance."

"Well, anything that you shave for and dress up for must be pretty important." I held up the shirt and skort I'd worn earlier in the day and inspected them for pink paint, but somehow I'd escaped any splatters. I folded them in half and squashed them into the bag that held our dirty clothes. As I pushed down, I felt a solid lump in the material. I pulled the skort back out and went through the pockets.

It was the memory drive I'd found this morning on Emma's floor. Had that only been a few hours ago? It felt like about three days. I tuned into what Mitch was saying.

"It's different, here at the class." He slid his arms into a long-sleeved white polo shirt. "It's a smaller group and if I don't show up, I'll definitely be missed. Are you tired? You don't have to go. You can stay up here and rest and I'll do the face time and keep it short."

"No. I'm not tired." More like keyed up. There were so many things swirling around in my thoughts. I needed to straighten them out. "Besides, I'm dressed and Abby says there's going to be a chocolate fountain. Can't miss that." I cleared my throat and went to lean on the wall behind Mitch, watching him in the mirror as he buttoned his shirt. He was so glad he didn't have to wear a uniform tonight. He'd rather wear a tie than one of his dress uniforms.

He finished buttoning the shirt and moved on to the cuffs as he said, "You look amazing, by the way. New outfit?"

"Yes." I twirled around. Mitch always noticed when I had new clothes or a new haircut. He didn't say anything else, but he smiled his slow smile, which was better than any compliment.

"New shoes, too. My feet will probably kill me by the end of the night, but unless I want to wear tennis shoes or my beat-up brown sandals, this is it." I ran my thumb over the smooth side of the memory drive as I held it in my hand.

He picked up his tie and said, "You okay?"

"Um . . . well, there's something I want to talk to you about—"

The phone on the nightstand rang. I snatched it up, relieved that I didn't have to try and explain the tangled mess of events that had happened earlier in the day. Mitch was good at sorting things out, but I knew he'd be less than happy that I'd followed someone around. And *I'd* lectured Summer on being careful and considerate.

"Ellie, this is Nadia. I just noticed the red message light on our phone. You want to see my photos from the Metro again?"

"Yes, I wanted to look at all your photos again in case we missed something earlier." *Like another woman with red hair.* "Do you mind if I borrow your computer?" Mitch flicked his tie over, watching me in the mirror.

"Not at all. Do you want me to bring it by tonight on our way down to the party?"

Mitch had his gaze fixed on me, and if I was really honest, I felt a tiny bit nervous. I took the coward's way out. "No, don't do that. I'll be right over to pick it up."

An Everything In Its Place Tip for an Organized Trip

Don't forget to do these things right before you head out the door:

- Set the thermostat to any desired temperature to save energy while you're gone.
- Take out the trash.
- Empty foods from the fridge that will spoil, like milk.
- Close curtains and set timers on lights as well as home security codes.
- Water plants.
- Start the dishwasher.

Chapter
Twenty

"Here you go. I brought up the file with the photos." Nadia pushed her laptop across the small table toward me. "Kyle and I are going on to the dinner, so take all the time you need."

"Thanks, Nadia. I gave those pictures we printed out to Summer. I just want to take another look."

"Sure," she said. Kyle, her bulky husband with a jocular attitude, stood in the hall, holding the door to their room open with his hand.

"Come on, hon. I'm sure she knows her way around a computer." He pointed a finger at me and said, "Just don't empty our checking account, okay?"

Nadia rolled her eyes on her way out the door and said, "Don't pay any attention to him. Bye-bye."

The door sighed shut behind them and I quickly clicked through the photos. I only had a few more minutes until Mitch met me here. I'd fled without explaining what I'd wanted to talk about and when he'd heard me asking to see the photos of the Metro platform again he hadn't been happy, but I'd left before he could say anything. And since he was having belt issues again—he'd been searching the suitcase pockets for his other belt, a plain brown leather one this time—he hadn't been as quick off the mark as he usually was.

I found the photo that showed Jorge. There was Irene in the corner. It was hard to believe she'd been so worried about talking to us about her fertility issues that she'd felt like she had to sneak around. She could have just told us she had an appointment and left it at that. Well, maybe not. This *was* Irene and she loved to share any gossip, or news, as she called it, with everyone, so she wasn't used to keeping anything quiet.

I frowned as I looked at the back of the redhead in the beret and denim jacket. Still no way to prove that the person wasn't Summer. The slip of material that was Wellesley's dress was there, too. Arranging marriages for illegal immigrants. Who would even think of a scheme like that? Of course, I knew the answer. Someone who's greedy.

The person I didn't see was Lena Stallings. I started over at the left side and carefully looked at each face. Finally, I found her. "Well, no wonder I didn't recognize her right away." In the photo, she was behind a man wearing a backpack who was turning away. The backpack blocked most of her body, but I could see her head. Her mouth was pinched together and she looked like she didn't like being in the crush of people. It was so dark in the Metro that her hair looked dark brown at first glance, but when I zoomed in on her, the hair brushing her eyebrows was a dark red color.

Okay, so maybe Summer had something here. Lena was on the platform and she was close to Jorge. One step and she'd be right behind him. The problem was that we didn't have any more photos.

I slid the memory drive into place and scanned

the documents listed on it. I'd just take a quick look and see if I could figure out who it belonged to. Ivan had said it wasn't his and I didn't think any of the wives from the tour group who had come to help out were carrying around a computer memory drive, but maybe it was Nadia's. If it was hers, I'd leave it with the computer. Or maybe it belonged to Tony or the woman who'd painted the mural, although she'd been working on the other side of the room.

When the list of documents came up, it read like a sightseeing itinerary: Washington Monument, Capitol Building, Senate Offices, White House, Library of Congress, Lincoln Memorial. The list went on. I opened the first item and scrolled down the page through several photos of the Washington Monument. I opened the next document and saw more pictures of the Capitol. It looked like a bunch of photos from someone's trip to D.C., but there was something missing. I went back through the first set of photos slowly.

No people posed in front of the monument. I switched to the set of photos featuring the Capitol. There were people in the photos, but they were walking or standing in groups, not paying attention to the photographer. No one was posing, smiling, or waving for the camera. I looked through the photos again and realized that the sequence of photos covered each angle of the building.

As I delved deeper into the documents, I swallowed. Someone was studying our national monuments and meticulously photographing them from every angle, at various times throughout the day and night. None of these were like Nadia's pictures. Hers had a warmth, a focus on people in their surroundings. These photos were cold and removed, almost analytical.

And the documents were really long. I paged down to the end of one and found a list of times the Capitol was open, broken down into lists of dates when Congress was actually in session, with estimates of how the number of people in the building fluctuated by the hour.

When I got to the section headed *Security,* all I could think was that these were very dangerous documents. I rubbed my forehead as I read the list: estimated number of security personnel, locations of security personnel, past security breaches. It went on and on.

I rubbed my forehead again and tried to decide what to do. Best-case scenario was that it was some sort of security review. Worst-case scenario was . . .

My thoughts skittered away from the awful possibilities. But I had to go there. What if it belonged to some nutcase who had something against the U.S. government? Or what if it belonged to a terrorist looking for weak spots?

I skimmed through the rest of the documents. Most of them looked the same as what I'd just read, except for one titled Press Release Draft. It was a single page and listed various talking points the Women's Advancement Center wanted to make about the safety initiative. The first line on the page read *From: Tony Zobart.*

I leaned back in the chair. I should call Detective Brown and give it to him. He could pass it on to the people who could determine if it was a threat. But I couldn't do that until I was sure Summer was back in town. It should only be a few hours until she was back. I'd have to keep it until then, but I certainly didn't want to take it back to the hotel room. I could picture it now. "Hi, Mitch. I'm ready to go. Just let me hide this memory chip under the hotel soap." No way that would go over well. And the questions it would lead to!

I pulled the chip out and put it in my pocket. It

was so tiny. What if I lost it? There was no way anyone would believe what I'd seen. I quickly put it back in the computer and copied the files into an e-mail that I sent to myself. I felt better with a backup copy, even if it was floating around in cyberspace. I pulled the chip out again and put it in my pocket.

I jumped and jarred the laptop when a knock on the door reverberated through the room. I closed down the laptop and went to look through the peephole. Mitch stood in the hall, one arm braced on the door frame.

I opened the door. "Hi. All done. Oh, good, you found your belt. Was it in the suitcase? We'd better hurry. We're riding over in the hotel shuttle with Abby and Jeff. We're supposed to meet them in the lobby." I realized I was talking too much, so I shut up and made a move toward the elevator.

He didn't move. "Oh no. We're not going down yet. Why did you have to look at Nadia's photos again?"

"Summer said she found another woman in the picture who has red hair and I wanted to see for myself." Stop there, I told myself.

Mitch sighed and dropped his arm from the door frame. "Ellie, what are you doing? You know the police are working on that."

"Yeah. I have a lot of faith in the police."

Mitch let that one go. We'd been through this before. We were both stubborn, but in so many other areas Mitch and I were opposites. His attitude was to let the police do their job and justice would be done. I wasn't so sure it would work out that way. "Mitch, they've zeroed in on Summer and aren't looking at anyone else."

"And how do you know that? Are you on the inside of the investigation? You know everyone they're talking to?"

"No, but I know that Detective Brown called Summer today, wanting to talk to her again." Oops. I didn't want to go there. "So they're obviously still fixated on her."

"And how did Summer take that?"

"She was nervous, understandably." I didn't mention that the police seemed to think she'd played a role in Jorge's death. There was so much to explain and it would take forever. After dinner, I'd tell him everything that had happened. "Come on. We've got to go," I said as I grabbed his hand. We walked down the hall. "So, did the woman have red hair?" Mitch asked as he punched the Down button.

"Yes, she did."

"And what did you want to talk about back in the room?"

The elevator doors slid open, we joined two other couples inside, and I said, "I'll tell you later."

"I don't see Jeff or Abby," Mitch said, so we took a seat on the leather ottomans in sight of the elevator.

Mitch pulled my hand into his and said, "After you left the room, I called the squadron. I figured I'd check in one more time. Our assignment came down."

He paused. He didn't look excited and he hadn't blurted it out the minute he saw me, so it wasn't good. *Oh no. More snow boots?* Or was it an assignment to one of the outposts of civilization, those tiny bases situated near a minuscule town without a freeway for miles and no restaurants or shopping?

"And?" I asked impatiently. Even if it was bad, I had to know. In fact, it didn't seem fair. Some unknown person in the Air Force Personnel Center already knew. And the whole orderly room back at the squadron, too. "Is it bad?"

"No. In fact, it's what we wanted. Hawaii."

"Hawaii! We actually got our first choice? That's great!" I squeezed his hand and he smiled briefly. "Aren't you happy? You don't look happy."

"I am. Hawaii will be terrific," Mitch said. "Jeff's assignment came down, too. It's not Hawaii. They're going to Georgia."

"Georgia. That *is* a long way." A wave of melancholy washed over me. Abby and I had hoped we'd be stationed at the same base and I'd refused to even think about it not happening. Getting through my week without Abby to laugh with and gripe with was just . . . unthinkable. She was the one who kept me sane. Well, Mitch kept me sane, too, but there were some things that you needed a girlfriend for, like shopping, which I was horrible at. And she helped me get through the long trips when Mitch was away. No one understood quite like another military spouse.

"We knew it was a long shot, the possibility of us getting the same base again." I wanted to put on a brave face, but I couldn't keep the sadness out of my voice as I said, "We'll be able to call and e-mail pictures."

Only a couple more months to hang out with my best friend. And her baby. I wouldn't get to do the whole surrogate doting aunt thing. I pushed those thoughts aside and tried to be cheerful. "There's Jeff and Abby."

Abby hurried up and said, "I heard you got Hawaii! How exciting. I'm devastated, of course. What am I going to do without you? You'll come visit me in Georgia, right? And we'll have to come see you in Hawaii."

I should have known Abby wouldn't hide her emotions. "You'll really fly all that way to see us?" I asked.

"It'll be a while before we can come for a visit, but do you think I'm going to pass up a beach vacation?"

"Congratulations, Jeff." I said the words with a genuine smile. I was glad for them. Georgia was a good assignment, closer to their families, and Abby was ready for a change from the snow and rain of Vernon, too.

"Here's our shuttle," Mitch said and we piled in.

"Why is our dinner at the Ronald Reagan building?" I asked as Mitch, Abby, Jeff, and I waited in line at the metal detector.

Mitch emptied his pocket change into a bowl and said, "It's a fund-raising dinner for Home Away From Home."

"I'm confused. Mrs. Johns invited us to a fund-raiser? Can we afford to go to a fund-raiser?"

The security guard said, "ID, sir."

"Oh. Sure." Mitch pulled out his wallet and showed his military ID card.

What was this place, the airport? Good thing I'd taken time to put my ID inside my tiny new leather envelope clutch. It was the one I'd bought while shopping with Abby. The turquoise flowers spilling across it matched my new outfit, and the chic little purse made the outfit just a bit dressier. I pulled out my ID card and handed it over.

"I finally got the full story today," Abby said. "Mrs. Johns usually has each FROT class over to her house for dinner, but this week she was working on this fund-raiser, so she got the class tickets to come here instead. It's a western-themed cookout."

I pulled the memory chip out of my pocket, slid it in my purse, and put my purse on the conveyor belt. I looked at the security guard. "Shoes on or off?"

He smiled. "You can leave them on. This isn't the airport."

I said, "Almost," and stepped through the metal detector. "What's the fund-raiser for again?"

"Home Away From Home," Abby said from behind me as she unfastened her heavy silver necklace, earrings, and bracelets. "It's an organization that keeps furnished apartments here in D.C. for families who come from out of town to visit injured soldiers in the hospital."

I moved over to one side to wait for Abby and Jeff since the security guard was rescanning her purse. She waved her hand. "Looks like it may take us a while. You go on. We'll catch up."

We entered a massive atrium where columns rose to a huge arched glass skylight overhead. As we joined the crowd I said, "I don't think I ever saw this many cowboy hats in one place when I lived in Texas."

"A little exaggerated?" Mitch asked with a smile.

"A bit. Check out the chuck wagon over there." Several banquet tables were set up around it and I could smell barbecue. "I hope there aren't any horses here."

"I doubt they'd get through security," Mitch said.

"I don't think you would've been missed if we'd skipped this," I said, taking in the sea of cowboy hats and red bandanas. "It's so crowded in here." As I looked around the room, I saw two senators chatting with Vicki Archer. Not too far away, a political consultant I'd seen several times on news shows laughed with another group. "Pretty high-profile crowd, too."

"Mitch!" A hand slapped down on his shoulder. "Glad you could come."

I recognized an underlying Texas twang in the man's voice. Mitch turned and shook hands with the man, who looked right at home in his Stetson and western-cut shirt.

"This is Lieutenant Colonel Johns. My wife, Ellie."

"Nice to meet you," I said, ignoring the grin on Mitch's face. Okay, Mitch was right. He would have been missed. "What part of Texas are you from?"

"Still haven't lost the accent, then, have I? Lubbock. Grew up on a cotton farm."

"Windy over there. I'm from Kitland originally."

He said, "Oh, so you know what that kind of wind is like. I spent a couple of years there in the flat country."

We chatted on that topic for a bit, and then I said, "This is quite a setting."

He gestured up at the skylight. "I'm told there's an acre of glass up there. It's the largest building in D.C." Something behind me caught his attention. "It appears I'm needed elsewhere. I see my wife signaling me. Glad you could make it."

He moved away through the crowd and I smiled at Mitch and admitted, "Okay, so maybe you would have been noticed if you'd skipped, even if it is pretty crowded. Did you see Vicki Archer over there?" I asked, tilting my head in her direction. The senators had moved on and a short, shriveled man with gaunt cheeks handed Vicki a drink. He'd skipped the cowboy gear for the more traditional suit and tie, and by the way it hung loosely on him I wondered if he'd been sick or had been on a crash diet lately.

I saw another familiar face and leaned over to Mitch. "Oh, look. There's Jay MacInally and he's heading this way. He's the bulky guy with the thick black hair with a bit of gray. His face looks so much better."

"The man who knew Debbie's dad?"

I nodded as MacInally shouldered his way through a knot of people and joined us. "Ellie, how are you?"

"Great. Good to see you." I introduced Mitch, then said, "Looks like you've recovered." The bandages were gone and the bruise around his eye had faded.

"Yep. Like I said before, I'm a tough old bird. Say, did you get my message?"

"Message? Oh. Yes, I did and I forgot to call you back. I'm sorry," I said.

"It's probably nothing, but I did think of one more thing you can tell Debbie. Just something about when we were on leave, some of the crazy stuff we did." He studied his scotch, then cleared his throat and looked back up at me. "Now's not a good time to talk about it." He shifted his feet and glanced around the room.

"I haven't talked to her yet," I said. Maybe this would be a story I could pass on to Debbie without wondering if it was going to cause her emotional trauma.

"It's no big deal, really. It was just something I'd forgotten about until last week. I've been doing that more lately, remembering little things that happened a long time ago." He scanned the crowd as he said, "I think it was being in the hospital. Stirred up the memories, you know?"

"I can see how that would happen. Why don't we meet tomorrow?" I looked over at Mitch. "What's the schedule?"

"There's no formal classes until Monday when we have the last session. Saturday there's a special tour of the Air and Space Museum and you wanted to go, right?"

"I might as well see all the museums while I'm here." I turned back to MacInally and said, "Why don't we meet tomorrow afternoon?"

MacInally nodded in a distracted way, his gaze fixed on someone in the crowd. "Air and Space. Tomorrow."

"Mr. MacInally?" It looked like he was staring at Vicki Archer and the group of people around her.

He focused his attention on me. "Sorry. Thought

I recognized someone. Tomorrow is fine. I can meet you at the museum."

"You don't have to do that," I said.

"No. It's fine. I'll be around that area anyway. Three o'clock?"

"All right."

"I'll meet you under the *Spirit of St. Louis*," he said.

"Sounds good. I'll call you if something changes."

He and Mitch shook hands and he moved off into the crowd.

"Whew. We finally found you," Abby said. "They hand-searched my purse."

Jeff said, "Probably because you have so much stuff in there they couldn't tell what was in there on the X-ray."

"Ignore him," Abby instructed. "Just for that, you're dispatched to the bar. Go find me a drink," she commanded. "It'll have to be club soda, but it'll still be a drink." Mitch decided to go with him. I put in my order for another club soda and told him we'd meet them at the tables on the far side of the room.

Abby said, "Can you believe we're at a swanky D.C. fund-raiser?"

"No. You just never know what's going to happen to you when you're a military spouse," I said.

"Isn't that the truth? Of course, I think our chances of ending up in, say, North Dakota are much higher than ever getting to do this again."

"You're probably right, but let's enjoy the swanki-ness while we're here. Earlier, we saw two senators talking to Vicki Archer."

Abby leaned to look around me and said, "No, she's talking to her husband now. Well, not really talking, more like standing with him."

I swiveled around. "No. That can't be her hus-band." I could see more of the man's face, but he still looked like he'd just had a rather nasty flu. Dark circles accompanied the bags under his brown eyes. Vicki was a good foot taller than him. She tossed her head to get her golden fringe of bangs out of her eyes and ignored the man at her side.

"Yes, it is. I read a magazine article about her while I was on the treadmill yesterday. There was a picture of them. That's her husband, Alan Archer. He's in civil service."

I tilted my head to the side to get a better view. "You know, I did see him back at the beginning of the week. When I went to get Summer, he was in Vicki Archer's office . . ." I'd been about to say when the police questioned her for the first time, but I didn't want to bring that subject up so I just stopped talking. I was really going to have to think of better conversational strategies than silence.

I looked back at Vicki and her husband. That was when I noticed Jay MacInally watching the group, too.

Chapter
Twenty-one

Jay MacInally stood a few feet away from the Archers, taking an occasional sip of his drink, but he was zeroed in on them.

Then Vicki and Alan moved to join another couple and I realized MacInally hadn't been staring at them, but at a man who'd been standing slightly behind Alan Archer. MacInally still had his attention fixed on the man, who was quite a contrast to Archer. For one thing, he was young and healthy, buff in fact. He'd also gone with the dark suit, which strained across his chest, and the sleeves looked like they were about to split down the seams. He looked like the Incredible Hulk in a suit.

There was something about the stiff way he held himself and the way his alert gaze scanned the crowd, then returned to the Archers that made me wonder if he was some sort of bodyguard. I couldn't see one of those earpiece things, but then, maybe that only happened in the movies. He shadowed the Archers as they circulated through the room and the whole time MacInally shadowed him.

I was about to turn away when a woman in a cowboy hat, a long denim skirt, and boots joined MacInally. He hugged her with one arm and she kissed his cheek in greeting. He left his arm draped over her shoulders. The brim of her hat hid part of her face, but from what I could see she looked like Lena Stallings. She tilted her head and laughed at something MacInally said. It was Lena. Her hair curled under the edge of her hat. It was much darker than in the photograph I'd seen on the Web site, but it still had an auburn sheen to it.

"Why are you frowning?" Abby asked.

I nodded toward MacInally and Lena. "I met her at the hospital. That's MacInally's sister, but look at them." MacInally still had his arm wrapped across her shoulders and he was stroking her upper arm with his hand.

"No way she's his sister," Abby said emphatically. "See how they're looking at each other?"

"Weird." Why would she say she was his sister? The buff guy MacInally had been watching moved a couple of steps and MacInally broke the intense eye contact with Lena. He whispered in her ear, then moved slightly so he could keep the oversized man in his line of sight.

Abby and I were about halfway around the room when our path intersected with MacInally's. Lena had her arm tucked through his as she snuggled into his shoulder.

"Hi again," I said to MacInally and introduced Abby. I turned to Lena. "And it's so good to see your sister again. Remember, we met at the hospital?" Lena straightened up, distancing herself from MacInally, but he laughed and put his hand over hers when she tried to unlink herself from him. "This is Lena Stallings. A good friend," MacInally said as he caressed the back of her hand.

She smiled at me automatically, then grimaced. "Hospitals can be so strict about visitors. They weren't going to let me in."

MacInally said, "Lena's work brings her to D.C. quite a bit. I was lucky she had meetings this week and could be here for me."

"So your work for STAND is why you're here?" I asked.

She raised her eyebrows. "I didn't realize I was so well known."

"I saw the Web site for STAND," I explained. "You must live in North Dawkins."

"Yes," she said. She obviously wasn't going to get into any details about what brought her to D.C., so I said, "Do you like it there? Abby and her husband just got an assignment to Taylor Air Force Base."

"It's a lovely little town with a real sense of community." She looked over my shoulder and said to MacInally, "Oh, darling, there's the Archers. We have to go and say hello. Excuse us." Her crimson nails dug into the material on MacInally's arm as she dragged him away.

Abby watched them walk away. "Man, she doesn't like you."

"I don't know why. That felt like high school, didn't it? It's not like I'm her competition or anything. And she sure didn't want to talk about STAND."

Abby said, "Yeah. Looks like she thinks every woman is her competition. I'd stay out of her way."

We moved through the crowd to the other side of the room where Abby pointed out a tall slab of concrete covered with graffiti and said, "Modern art is so strange. It doesn't even go with the rest of the building. Everything is so light and open here, not grungy."

"Yes, it does. Go with the building, I mean. It's from

the Berlin Wall." We read the sign and I stood there thinking about the desire for freedom and the news footage I'd seen on a documentary of Germans literally hacking away, crumbling the wall into tiny pieces.

"I wonder if Nadia's seen this," I said.

Abby said, "I don't know. I haven't seen them yet. I'm going to get us a table. I don't see place cards, so we can sit anywhere we want. They must be keeping it casual to go with the western cookout theme."

"Okay. I'm going to look for Nadia. She'd love this."

I made another circuit of the room, but didn't find Nadia. I turned to head over to the tables and saw Vicki Archer talking to Tony. I quickly reversed course and put several knots of people between me and them. I did not want to see Tony now. I slinked along the edge of the room until I was behind an artfully arranged display of hay bales and wagon wheels. I pulled out my phone and checked for messages. Summer's plane should have landed by now, but my voice mailbox was empty. I punched some buttons to check my missed calls, but there weren't any of those either.

I was so busy with my phone that at first I didn't notice the two people arguing on the other side of the hay bales, but the forceful, angry tone caught my attention.

Even with the cowboy hat, I recognized Lena. Her voice was soft and she was trying not to draw attention to herself, but her angry tone and the tense set of her shoulders pulled a few glances her way besides mine. "No problems. Those were your exact words. You said there wouldn't be any problems and there better not be any. Because if there are—"

Alan Archer glanced quickly around, noticed the

staring faces, and interrupted her. "There won't be any. You've got to calm down. I told you Taylor is safe."

He reached out for her elbow. "Now, let's go have some dinner. You don't have anything to worry about." He pulled on her arm, but she jerked it away and said, "There better not be," before pushing past him.

A cowbell clanged. "Ladies and gentlemen," a voice rang out over the crowd and I turned to the stage set up near the chuck wagon. A woman in a crisp white cotton shirt with a red bandana tied around her neck stood in front of a facade of a barn. "Thank you so much for coming out to support Home Away From Home. Help yourself to some grub and then we'll tell you more about this wonderful organization."

I saw Mitch and joined him in a lumpy line that formed by the food. We dipped out plates of brisket, corn on the cob, beans, and rolls, then joined our group at the round tables. I grabbed a seat beside Nadia.

"Hi, everyone. Where's Irene and Grant?" I asked.

"She'll be here later. She wanted to see the news story about Wellesley," Nadia said.

"That sounds like her. She's probably been missing the news and her police scanner while we've been on vacation. Have you seen the piece of the Berlin Wall?" I asked Nadia as I buttered my roll.

"Yes. Isn't it awesome? I just wish the light was better." She touched the camera near her plate. "I took some pictures, but I'll spare you having to look at them. Or be in them," she said to Gina across the table.

"Thank God," Gina said. "As long as I don't have to be *in* the pictures I don't care how many you take."

Ever since Gina had seen Nadia's pictures they'd seemed to have declared a truce.

Nadia continued. "I can't believe how much history is in the city. And in the most unexpected places. I'd love to bring a field trip here sometime."

"You know, I've been surprised at how at home I feel here," I said. "I'm not usually a fan of big cities, but here in D.C., I have a sense of belonging. I think it's because when I look at the monuments I feel like they're my monuments. They're for me, for Americans."

"Leading a field trip sounds like hell to me," Gina said in a matter-of-fact voice.

"Would that be from your school in Georgia? Do you teach on-base?" I asked Nadia.

"At Taylor? No. I'm at an elementary school not too far from there in a town called North Dawkins." She sighed. "First graders would be too young for a trip like this, but I'd still love to do it someday. Maybe when my girls are teenagers."

Gina shuddered. "All that angst and emotion. And history's a big yawn for them at that age."

I decided to intervene before the truce crumbled, but Abby beat me to it. "Well, I want to hear all about Taylor and Georgia because it's our next assignment," she said. "We got the news this afternoon."

Nadia squealed, sounding like one of Livvy's toys. I don't know many people who actually squeal, but she did. "This will be so fantastic. Are you going to teach after the baby? I'll put in a good word for you at our school. I shouldn't say this"—her voice dropped to a whisper—"but it really is the best school in the area. I'm so excited. When will you get there?"

"Sometime in the fall. We're going to try and time it so we move after the baby. November, probably."

Nadia put down her napkin and turned on her

camera. "It's southern. Lots of 'good old boys,' but there's tons of suburbanites moving in since we're close enough to commute to Atlanta. It's humid. Very green. I'm terrible with words. Here's some pictures." She passed the camera to Abby.

"What's the base like?" I asked, thinking of Lena and Alan Archer's conversation.

"The base is nice. Not that old. There's a new commissary, but base housing is tiny."

"When is it not?" Gina asked.

"Oh, she's right," Nadia said. "We live off-base. It's a pretty small community around the base. Very tight-knit, probably because the city depends on the base so much. If the base closed . . ." Nadia shook her head. "I don't know what North Dawkins would do. Everyone we meet down there works at the base. Tons of civilian employees. Anyway, the whole town is on pins and needles, waiting for the base closure list. It actually looks like they might close it because of the runway issue."

"Something wrong with the runway?" Jeff asked.

"No," Nadia's husband, Kyle, said. "It's the en-croachment issue. There's been a lot of growth around the base and one of the things the commission looks at is how much of a buffer there is around the base. Airspace congestion is getting to be a problem, too. Atlanta seems to get busier every day."

This was the most serious I'd ever seen him. The few, brief times I'd been around him before, he'd been smiling and cracking jokes, like he had earlier today when I'd borrowed Nadia's laptop. "It doesn't look good for Taylor," he concluded.

Abby turned to Jeff. "If it does get on the closure list, what will happen to our assignment?"

He shrugged. "Nothing, probably. It takes years to close down a base. We'd probably finish the assignment and move somewhere else before it actually shut down."

"Probably," Abby said darkly. "My least favorite word when it's associated with our future."

Nadia said, "Because 'probably' usually means 'probably not.' "

The conversation moved on as everyone listed the bases they thought would be on the closure list. I realized I hadn't eaten much of my food and now it was cold. I'd only been pushing it around on my plate as I listened to the conversation and thought about the contrast between what Nadia and Kyle had to say about Taylor AFB and what I'd overheard Archer say about it.

Mitch leaned over. "You okay? Tired?"

"No. I'm fine, just thinking." I put my napkin beside my plate and pulled my cell phone out of my purse, which only had room for my ID, lipstick, and the memory chip.

No messages. Had Summer really been on her way home? Or had she just said that? She should have been back by now. The phone rang in my hand just as a group of people approached the microphones on the stage.

An Everything In Its Place Tip for an Organized Trip

Packing
- Most of us have a tendency to bring too many clothes. One way to limit how much you bring is to stick with two or three basic colors, which will allow you to mix and match. Layers are always a good strategy if there will be large temperature variations.

- Pack for the climate. It's usually cheaper to purchase umbrellas or sunscreen at home than in the hotel gift shop.
- Seal liquids like lotions, shampoo, and makeup in zip-top plastic bags. If pressure changes cause leaks, your clothes will be protected.
- To prevent wrinkles, roll or stack clothes and fold gently in thirds. Place folded or rolled clothing on one side of your suitcase and use the other side for shoes, cosmetics, and toiletries. Or, pack clothes in the protective plastic covers that dry cleaners use. Another wrinkle-reducing tactic is to wrap clothes in tissue paper. Unpack as soon as you arrive at your destination.
- Downsize your cosmetics and toiletries with travel-size items so you'll have less bulk to pack and less weight to carry—every ounce counts!
- Pack a tote bag inside your luggage so that if your purchases overflow your suitcase, you'll be able to carry on your new items on the return trip. Or, ship purchases home if it's not too pricey.

Chapter
Twenty-two

"It's Livvy," I said to Mitch. "Do you want to talk?"

"No. I talked to her this morning during one of my breaks. You go ahead."

Photos flashed on large screens on either side of the barn as the first notes of Aaron Copeland's "Hoe down" filled the room and almost drowned out Livvy's voice. "Hold on, sweetie. I have to go outside," I said as I squeezed behind Mitch's chair. I made my way to an exit and then into an empty hallway out of the range of the music.

"Okay, now I can hear you. What did you say?" I asked.

Livvy's high-pitched voice said, "I've got dirty feet."

"You've got dirty feet?"

"Yep," she confirmed confidently.

"How did they get dirty?"

"Outside. We planted—"

The phone cut out and I said, "What? Are you still there?"

"Yep."

"What did you plant? I couldn't hear you."

Her exasperated sigh came over the line. "I told

you. Tuna. We planted tunas. And I watered. Grammy let me water everything. I got to hold the hose." Her voice was filled with pride and a bit of recrimination. She never got to hold the hose at our house. "Grammy says I'm a good gardener."

"I bet you watered everything." I could just picture my parents' garden. It probably looked like a swamp. "So are you going to take a bath to get your feet clean?"

"Nope. Not until my ice cream. I get ice cream *with* chocolate *every night*."

I had a feeling that the transition home was going to be a tough one. Ice cream with or without chocolate wasn't on the menu every night at our house. But the grandparents had to spoil the grandkids. It was a rule, so I wouldn't say anything.

"So what else did you do today?" I asked as a few people walked by me.

"Well . . ." She drew out the syllable, took a deep breath, and launched into a minute-by-minute account of her day. "First, I woke up, then Grammy made pancakes with bananas, and then . . ."

When she got to about eleven o'clock (trip to the hardware store for plants) my mom finally took the phone away from her.

I could hear her say, "Here's your spoon. You can tell your mom the rest tomorrow."

When my mom came back on the line I said, "If she combines what happened today with her day tomorrow, it'll take her three hours to tell me everything."

My mom laughed. "She has done an about-face with the phone conversations, hasn't she?"

"You really got her to eat banana pancakes? Did she know they had bananas in them?" Livvy liked everything plain. She was a no additives or preservatives kind of kid and she'd always refused to eat bananas, saying they were too mushy.

"Yes, of course. It's all in the way you present it, darling."

I had a feeling Livvy was eating banana pancakes because the presenter was Grammy, not Mommy. "So you planted tuna, huh?"

"Petunias. And Livvy was an excellent helper. She followed directions really well."

"That's great. I'm glad she's behaving."

"Although the bathtub may take a while to get clean."

"Just hose her down outside," I joked.

"Excellent idea. No, Livvy don't lean on the walls. I've got to go."

"Wait. I was kidding about the hose—" I stopped talking when I heard the click. Livvy would probably want to be hosed down now instead of taking a bath at home.

"Ellie!"

I turned and saw Summer charging down the hall, her mass of red hair bouncing with each step. "Summer, I'm so glad to see you, but you could have just called."

"Oh, I had to bring this up here for Mr. Archer anyway." She held up a file folder. "A fax came in for him at their house after they left. Ms. Archer called and asked me to bring it with me." She made a face. "A couple of days ago I'd told her I'd be here, so I figured I'd better show up. Emma's room looks divine, by the way. Thanks."

"So you've already been by your apartment and everything was okay?"

"Yes. Mitch told me you were a worrier and I can see what he means. Everything is fine. Tony wouldn't do . . . anything like you're thinking."

I opened my purse so she could see the memory chip. "Is this his?"

"It looks like the kind we have at the office, but ours are all labeled, so this one can't be Tony's."

"I doubt a terrorist would label his research."

"What?" She reached to take it, but I pulled it out of her reach. "No, leave it there. There's some dangerous stuff on this. Detailed info about D.C. landmarks." I outlined what I'd seen.

"You think this belongs to Tony?"

"Well, who else could it have been? One of the wives who helped out? The muralist? She worked on the other side of the room the whole time and Ivan spent all his time on a ladder around the edge of the room. He didn't lower himself to doing something so menial as making up the bed. Tony and I did that. It was on the floor under the dust ruffle where he'd tossed his jacket. And it couldn't have been there before the makeover, because it was on top of the new carpet. Besides, there's a memo with his name on it."

"There's got to be some mistake," Summer insisted. A cell phone rang and we both checked ours.

"Mine," Summer said as she answered. "Yes. I'm here. I'll bring it right in to you." She slipped her phone back into her purse and repositioned the papers that were sliding out of the file, but not before I'd seen the bold title on the cover of the fax sheet, BRAC. "Let me drop this off and we'll figure out what's going on with the memory chip," she said.

"Wait. Mr. Archer. What does he do?"

Summer took a few steps toward the doors into the atrium. "He works at the Pentagon. Most of the time it's very hush-hush, but for the last couple of months he's been working for the BRAC Commission. Wait for me here. I'll be right back," Summer said as she headed for the doors.

"Okay, but I have to find a restroom first. I'll meet you back here." After this trip, I could write a travel book, *The Pregnant Woman's Restroom Guide to D.C.*

I went down the hall and around the corner, following the sign for the restroom. BRAC stood for Base Realignment And Closure, a commission that would recommend base closures. Earlier, Archer had promised Lena that Taylor wouldn't be on that list. One person couldn't make that kind of promise.

I had reached out to push open the door when I saw a movement out of the corner of my eye. A hand closed firmly around my outstretched arm and another hand pressed into my back.

"What the—"

"This way." I processed that the quiet voice was deep and masculine behind my ear as I was propelled to the next door down the hall. The man kicked it with his foot. I struggled, but couldn't break his grip on my arm. I braced my feet, but the slick granite floor didn't give me any resistance. The pneumatic door sighed open and I was shoved into a tiny room.

Chapter
Twenty-three

A tier of metal shelves rocked as I slammed into them. Bottles, cans, and paper towels rained off the shelves as they swayed. The sharp odor of bleach stung my nose. I gripped one of the shelves and turned. The man was pushing the door closed, narrowing the swath of light from the hall.

My brain struggled to take everything in. The door closed and the blackness was complete. I swallowed. My throat felt dry and my heartbeat hummed in my ears.

I heard the click of the lock and felt a frisson of panic run through me. *This cannot be happening.* My phone was in my purse. Where was it? Had I dropped it in the hall when he'd grabbed me? Or was it on the floor in here?

I spread my foot around cautiously, but only felt the hard metal cans that had fallen off the shelves. It didn't matter. I didn't think the man would wait politely while I made a 911 call. I could hear him moving around on the other side of the tiny room. I squished into the corner where the two sets of shelves met. There was a thud. "Damn it." More thumps sounded as the ping of metal cans hit the hard floor.

I ran my hands over the shelf behind me. Stacks of paper towels. Next shelf. Paper towels. Lower shelf. More paper towels. Good grief. This wouldn't do me any good. I reached down, grabbed one of the metal cans off the floor just as the overhead fluorescent light flickered, then came on.

I didn't wait. As soon as I saw where he was, I aimed the nozzle and sprayed. I had no idea what I was spraying him with, but it seemed to work pretty well as a defensive weapon.

He ducked, threw up one arm to block the spray, and covered his eyes with his other hand. "Ellie. It's me. Tony."

If he moved a bit to the side, I could get out. "I know who you are." In fact, his identity had just registered. The sleeve of his suit jacket bubbled with white foam. I stopped spraying and shook the can. The sloshing sound and lightness of the can told me that there wasn't much left.

I glanced down at the floor. Plenty more cans down there, if I could get one before he grabbed me. I didn't really know if I'd be fast enough. I wasn't all that quick off the mark to begin with, and pregnancy has a way of slowing everyone down a few notches.

He saw my glance. "Ellie, don't." He wiped one hand down his damp face and shook off the droplets onto the floor. Tiny beads of liquid dotted his thick eyebrows and one eye was bloodshot. Only a partial hit, then. I must have aimed too high. He kept one hand extended toward me. "I just want to talk to you."

I shook the can. "Then open the door and let's go out in the hall."

"Look, I'm sorry. I obviously startled you, but—"

"Startled me? You *startled* me? More like scared me half out of my mind. I'm pregnant, you know." I suddenly felt terrified, not of Tony and not for me, but for the baby. My heartbeat was going crazy. That couldn't be good. I took a deep breath and willed myself to calm down a bit, but I still felt adrenaline coursing through me like an electric current.

"You're right," Tony said. "I apologize. But I had to stop you before you talked to anyone else."

I shook the can and sprayed again.

He stepped sideways out of the spray and I darted for the door, still coating his arm with the cleaning solution.

My fingers slid over the handle, slipped. It was wet from the cleaning chemicals.

His arm flashed out, and before I realized what had happened, the can was out of my hand and rolling on the floor.

"Ellie. I'm FBI."

"What?" I turned toward him. We'd changed places in the closet. Now I was beside the door and he was on the side with the shelves. Behind my back, I gripped the door handle with one hand, but waited. Didn't FBI agents carry guns? I decided not to make any sudden movements.

"I promise I'm not going to hurt you. I'm with the FBI," he repeated.

I didn't let go of the door handle. Still no sign of a gun. Just to clarify, I said, "You're an FBI agent?"

"Yes. You're going to have to trust me. I'm under-cover." He wiped his chin, which was a drippy white goatee, then ran his fingers through his thick hair to push it off his forehead. I'd really doused him good the second time. "I need the memory chip and you can't tell anyone else about it." He stood there, both arms extended out, palms toward me like I was holding a gun on him.

I spotted my purse behind him on the floor under one of the shelves. My breath was coming out in puffs and I felt like I'd just stepped off the treadmill. "What memory chip?"

He dropped his hands. "Ellie, please. I heard you tell Summer about it."

I licked my lips. "Okay. It's in my purse." I nodded at his foot. I still had the copy of it that I'd e-mailed to myself. It was more important to get out of here than to keep the memory chip. "Down there. Under the shelf." I readied myself to swing the door open and get out of there as soon as he reached for my purse. Sure, it was a cute clutch, but no way was I going to wait around to get it back from him. Purses could be replaced.

The only problem was, he didn't move. We stayed frozen for a few more seconds; then he relaxed, leaned one shoulder back on the shelves, and crossed his arms, looking for all the world completely comfortable. He seemed oblivious of the damp clothes, wet hair, and chemical smell. "I can't tell you everything, but I need to tell you a small part of it, so you'll understand what a volatile situation you're in the middle of."

My hand was sticky now as the cleaning spray dried. I flexed my hand, then gripped the door handle again. My breathing and heartbeat were returning to normal, but I was still tensed and ready to move if he did.

"What about the man you met on the Mall? Is he FBI, too?"

Tony held my gaze. "No. He's a terrorist."

I blinked. He was completely serious. "And you're not?"

"No. Only pretending to be. I infiltrated their cell."

"That man on the Mall and Jorge were part of a terrorist cell?"

"Yes. Let me tell you a bit about Jorge Dominguez. His real name was Kazi Agha. He was born in Pakistan, trained in Afghanistan and Africa. He was determined to finish the job in Washington, D.C., that was left undone on September 11. Getting a marriage certificate was part of a strategy to keep his identity secret and let him apply for citizenship, erasing his real origins. Once he was a citizen he'd be able to get a federal job, which would give him access to more sensitive areas, like federal buildings and airports."

That slowed me down. Jorge was an illegal alien from . . . Mexico. Wasn't he? I thought back over what I knew of Jorge. I didn't really know anything about him. I'd assumed he was from Mexico simply because of his appearance and because he worked as a day laborer, but what better place to disappear in America than in a community of people who kept to themselves? They wouldn't turn him in even if they suspected he wasn't a Latino. They'd have too much to lose.

Tony waited to see what else I asked. For someone in law enforcement, he was remarkably willing to answer my questions. Of course, he could be lying. Maybe he wasn't with the FBI and maybe he really was a terrorist.

"Okay," I said slowly. "If Jorge was part of a terrorist cell, why would a cell like that trust you?"

"An American boy? Normally, they wouldn't. But they might eventually trust an American who had an American mother and an Iraqi father. They'd trust someone like that who sought out his roots at the local mosque and became a follower of Islam. I was recruited there. Of course, they wouldn't trust me so much if they knew about my time at Quantico."

"So let's say that you're FBI and Jorge and the other man were terrorists, why would you be so stupid and lose a memory chip with all that information on it?"

"I slipped up. I was distracted." A faint blush appeared on his cheeks. At first, I thought it was a reaction to the cleaner that must still be on his skin, but then he said, "I shouldn't have changed my focus, but I was worried—" He broke off as the flush increased. He uncrossed his arms and stood straight, one hand on a shelf, the other on his hip, which drew back his jacket. I still didn't see any evidence of a gun.

As I thought about what Tony said, a few pieces clicked into place. "It was Summer, wasn't it? You were worried about her. That's what distracted you."

He shrugged. "Any friend would be."

Right. Just a friend. Well, if that was the way he wanted to play it, I could go along. "Tony, is that your real name?"

The atmosphere shifted and he shut down a little. "That's not important here." I thought Summer would disagree with that statement, but let it go. He continued. "What is important is that you give me the memory chip and that you convince Summer to forget about it."

"That shouldn't be hard. She thinks you can't do anything wrong." I thought a shadow of a smile crossed his face, but he hurried on.

"Good. She's got to continue her normal routine. No more disappearances. Mr. and Ms. Archer have to believe that nothing has changed. Summer and I are still loyal employees worthy of their trust."

"And Jorge?"

"Jorge was a yardman who died in a tragic accident."

"That's not what the police think. They think Summer pushed him. And they're doing their best to prove it." He grimaced at that, but seemed to steel himself. "That's the best way."

That last part made me mad. I'd calmed down quite a bit. I wasn't breathing in little gasps and my heartbeat wasn't thundering in my ears, but I felt my blood pressure rise. "You think that's best? That Summer is a suspect?"

He held up one hand. "Yes. It is best. I know it's hard. Believe me, I know. But if Summer is a suspect because she knew Jorge in his role as a yardman, then it keeps the focus off his other activities. We're close to shutting this thing down and I need you not to say anything to anyone else about what you've found out."

"The memory chip is in my purse." I gestured at the floor near his foot. "Take it."

He gave me a long look, then squatted and picked up my purse. Tony opened it and pulled out the chip, then handed my purse to me.

Even though he said he was FBI, he might be making all this up. Despite being splattered with cleaning spray, Tony still looked composed. I took in the cut of his suit, the heavy watch, and thought about his car, a very expensive, new car. The man on the Mall had insinuated that Tony liked America too much and was getting too comfortable. A power struggle inside their little group could be another explanation.

My head was beginning to throb from the fumes in the small space. I wanted out of the room. Agreement seemed the way to go. "Okay, I'll talk to Summer and convince her not to say anything to anyone about the memory chip, but you'd better keep her safe."

"You don't need to worry about that."

I believed him. And that was strange, because I didn't know if I could trust anything he'd said earlier, but I believed him now.

I unlocked the door, swung it open, and stepped out into the hall quickly, just in case Tony lunged for me. He didn't. He followed me into the hall, straightened his cuffs, and disappeared into the men's restroom.

It was so anticlimactic that I laughed. I slapped my hand over my mouth because if anyone turned the corner and saw me standing in the middle of a deserted hallway laughing, they'd think I was crazy. And when they got a whiff of the chemical smells on me, they'd think I'd been sniffing cleaning products to get high. I felt a bit nauseated and unsteady. Must be all the fumes. I hurried across the hall to the women's restroom.

I felt calmer after I used the restroom and then washed my hands and my arms, but as I looked in the mirror, I realized that the wet paper towel I was holding was trembling as I blotted my forehead and checks.

I tossed the towel in the trash and collapsed into one of the wicker chairs beside a table with a flower arrangement and a box of tissues. I closed my eyes, leaned forward, and rested my head on the heel of one hand. All that adrenaline was working its way out of my bloodstream. I took a couple of deep breaths.

A few women came in and out and I just sat there, resting. It was all too crazy. I'd gotten myself mixed up in a terrorist cell? Could that even be true?

I noticed a pair of cowboy boots positioned a few inches in front of me. I pulled my head up and let my gaze run up the denim skirt and western-cut shirt to Lena Stalling's face. She looked aggravated.

An Everything In Its Place Tip for an Organized Trip

Carry-on luggage

If you're flying, check with your airline for travel restrictions, including what items you're allowed to carry on. Here's a few essentials you'll want to make sure you bring in your carry-on bag:

- Prescription medications.
- Glasses and/or contacts.
- Decongestant and/or motion sickness medicine.
- Reading material—a good book or book on tape can make those frequent flight delays less irritating.
- Water—purchase after clearing security.
- Gum.
- Essential travel documents like tickets, hotel confirmation numbers, and passport.
- Valuable items you don't want to pack in your checked luggage like business paperwork or expensive camera equipment.

Chapter
Twenty-four

With her hands braced on her hips and her head tilted to one side, she said abruptly, "You okay?"

"Sure. I'll be fine in just a minute."

She ignored me. "You don't look okay." She contemplated me for a few seconds with a frown, then shook her head and sighed. "No use. I can't walk away." She sat down in the other wicker chair. "Are you sick? Do you have low blood sugar?"

"No, I'm not sick. I'll be fine. I just had a bit of a shock."

She reached in her purse and handed me a package of peanut butter crackers. "Eat some of these. I'll be right back."

I opened the package and pulled out a cracker. It flaked as I bit into it.

A few minutes later, Lena swept back in and popped the top on a can of Coke. "Drink this."

"Oh, I couldn't take your drink. I'll be fine in a minute. I usually drink diet anyway."

"Drink it. You need the sugar. You're pregnant?" I nodded and took the can from her and washed down the dry, salty cracker. "You can't go without eating. I can't believe women today. You have to gain weight to have a baby." She sat down in the chair on the other side of the table.

"No, it's not that. Believe me, I'm not into dieting while I'm pregnant. I'm not into dieting ever, actually. Anyway, it's just tonight I was so distracted with, well . . . it's hard to explain."

I devoured more crackers and downed them with swigs of the Coke. "Thanks. I feel better."

"Good." She pulled her lipstick and a tiny mirror out of her purse. "Sorry to be so bossy." Her words were indistinct since she wasn't moving her mouth as she talked while she reapplied a coat of red lipstick. I had the feeling she wasn't sorry at all and was used to ordering people around, for their own good, of course. She rubbed her lips together and checked her tiny mirror. "I used to be a nurse. Old habits die hard, you know." She capped her lipstick and slid it and her mirror into her purse. "You rest in here a little longer and finish off that drink."

"I will, but before you go, can I ask you about Jorge?"

She studied me warily for long moment; then she said, "Jorge?"

"Yes, a man who did yard work, construction work. Manual labor. I know that you knew him, that you knew him in Georgia."

"Doesn't sound familiar," she said as she quickly zipped up her purse and got ready to stand up.

"Yes, it does. It took you a few seconds to figure out how you were going to act when I mentioned his name. That hesitation gave you away. And I also know that you sent him a check, a rather large one, and wanted to meet with him." She didn't look so commanding now as she studied me and chewed on her lower lip, eating away some of the fresh lipstick.

She went on the attack. "How do you know that? And why do you care?"

"I've got—let's call them connections," I said. She didn't need to know that my connection was a stack of stolen mail. Besides, I'd just had an enlightening conversation with an FBI agent. That was a connection, if there ever was one. "And I have a relative who's suspected of pushing Jorge off the platform in the Metro and killing him. She didn't do it."

Lena relaxed and leaned back in the chair. "You think I pushed him?" she asked as she ran the purse strap through her fingers.

"You were on the platform."

She raised her eyebrows at me questioningly.

"There's a photo."

"I see." She kept running her fingers over the stitching on the strap. "Well. I didn't push him, so I have nothing to worry about, do I?"

"If you didn't push him, then no, you don't have anything to worry about. Did you see who did?"

Lena shook her head. "I was checking my watch when it happened, so I was looking down and didn't see anything."

"Did you see a woman with long red hair on the platform near you?" I asked.

"No," she said impatiently. "I didn't look around and catalogue the people beside me. I was thinking about my meeting I had in twenty minutes. The meeting I didn't make because of what happened."

She was annoyed and I could tell she was about to cut off my irritating questions, so I said, "You're really here in D.C. on business? I thought you might be here to make sure Jorge didn't cash your check. Or maybe it was to convince Jorge to keep your relationship with him quiet? Or was it only Jay MacInally you don't want to know about it?"

Her eyes narrowed. "So that's it. You want me to tell you about Jorge and you won't tell Jay about him?"

Since I'd obviously hit a sore spot, I nodded and she said, "Fine. Okay. Jorge was on a crew that dry-walled. I was having the inside of my garage finished. Anyway, he let me know he was available to do other work, landscaping, handyman projects."

I'll bet he made himself available, I thought, but kept that to myself. "And he was a contract employee to you?"

"No. We had a romantic relationship." I hadn't expected her to admit it so readily and I didn't know whether to believe her or not. Would Jorge romance Lena, then turn around and pursue Summer a few weeks later? She must have read the skepticism on my face.

"You think I'm too old? That he wouldn't be interested in me?"

"No, I think you're a very attractive woman." A very deceptive woman, too. "But you wanted your relationship to stay a secret? Is that why you sent the money?"

"No, of course not." She was offended. "It was a loan. Jorge wanted to start his own landscaping business."

I suddenly felt sorry for this beautiful, aging woman. She got scammed and she didn't want to admit it. "Why here? Why start his business in Washington, D.C.? Why not Georgia, near you?"

"Georgia was seasonal work to make ends meet. This was where he had family."

I didn't say anything, but I didn't think anyone had claimed Jorge's body and Detective Brown had asked if he had family. Mrs. Matthews gave the impression that Jorge only had a few visitors, not hordes of family coming and going. And that thought reminded me of Mrs. Matthews's comments about the one visitor Jorge did have.

"You visited him at his apartment here, didn't you? Not this last week, but before."

She looked a bit uncomfortable. "Once. I went there once."

Rebecca Matthews had said the woman was crying, so her visit hadn't gone well. It seemed Lena wasn't going to say anything else about that, so I asked, "Was he involved with anyone dangerous?"

"No." She said it quickly, but her gaze dropped to her hands.

"Are you sure? It looks like Jorge was mixed up with some shady stuff."

She kept her attention fixed on her hands. "No, definitely not."

She wasn't going to talk about any unsavory connections that Jorge had, so I went back to his relationship with her. "He'd taken your money and wasn't calling you back. You decided to give him a little push and take care of the whole thing. Your money stayed in your account and you didn't look foolish either."

She sputtered, "That isn't true. There's no way—"

"What I don't understand is why you're with Mac-Inally," I continued.

She said, "Jay's a dear. I watch out for him. He's too trusting. I've always felt . . . protective of him. I don't want anyone taking advantage of him."

"That's not the impression I have of him. He seems to be someone who can take care of himself."

She sighed. "He comes across as tough, but I knew him after he was wounded. He was fragile. And he still is." She stood up, settled the strap of her purse on her shoulder. Her hips swayed as she moved to the door. "Don't let his facade fool you."

The door sighed shut and I took a deep breath. I actually felt better, steadier, and the blood no longer seemed to be pounding through my head. I brushed cracker crumbs off me, threw the can and wrapper in the trash, and examined my face in the mirror. Amazingly, I didn't look too bad, considering I'd been at the center of two confrontations in the last, what, half an hour? And one of them had involved spray cans of foaming bathroom cleaner. Except for a dark patch of fabric on my shoulder, which I figured was from the cleaner, and scraggly hair, I looked about the same.

I finger-combed my hair, touched up my lipstick, and did the best I could to blot away the dark spot on my shoulder. It wasn't totally gone, but I heard voices moving down the hallway outside and I hurried to join the group of people on their way back to the atrium. I didn't want to meet up with Tony, or anyone else in the hallway. I was going to plant myself beside Mitch and not move for the rest of the night while I tried to sort through the confusing jumble that was my brain.

I wasn't quite quick enough to reach the atrium without being waylaid. I was a few steps behind the group of people when I saw Lena marching down the hall toward me with her face set in a determined way. I quickened my pace, but she slipped around the group, grabbed my arm, and pulled me over to one side of the hall.

What was it with people grabbing my arm tonight? I'd had it with being manhandled. I wasn't about to get dragged away again, so I ripped my arm away roughly and said, "What?"

She took a step back and said, "Sorry."

Maybe I overreacted just a tad.

"Sorry," she repeated. "I didn't mean to frighten you." Despite her apologetic words, her expression was set and resolute. "I couldn't walk away without telling you." She gestured to my stomach. "You're pregnant. I don't want to be responsible for . . . anything. You have to be careful." She lowered her voice. "You asked if Jorge was involved in anything dangerous. He was. He had a group of, I don't want to call them, friends, I guess. I don't know what other word to use. I don't know anything about them, except that you don't want to be on their bad side."

"Who were they?"

"I don't know. All I know is that one of them worked for Ms. Archer. There was a struggle going on between Jorge and this other man."

"On the platform? You saw them fighting?"

"No," she said impatiently. "It was a power struggle. Jorge wanted to be in control and the other man was threatened. The other man got rid of Jorge. I know he did."

She paused and I didn't think she was going to say anything else, but then she rushed on, the words tumbling out. "I know what you were insinuating back there. You think Jorge swindled me." She swallowed and blinked rapidly. "I didn't want to admit it to myself, but I could see it in your face. The way he came to me, made sure I knew him, suggested jobs he could do. It's obvious now, looking back. He sought me out. And he's the one who wanted the blackmail thing. I didn't want to do it, but he talked me into it. And the thing is, we didn't have to do it. He'd have done it for me."

"What blackmail thing?" I asked and she clamped her red lips together, shock in her eyes. She hadn't meant to say that, but I put her words together with the interaction I'd seen earlier in the evening. Tony said he'd sent Jorge to Georgia. Lena knew Mr. Archer.

"Mr. Archer. Jorge talked you into blackmailing Mr. Archer. To keep Taylor off the closure list. And then after that, he had something to blackmail you with, too."

She backed up a step. "No. No, it wasn't like that. It was a loan." Lena gripped my forearm again and fixed her gaze on me. Her eyeliner had smudged, leaving black streaks under her eyes. "It wasn't like that at all."

"What did you know that you could blackmail Mr. Archer with?"

"That doesn't matter. You have to be careful." She squeezed my arm painfully, then released it and hurried back into the atrium.

I took a deep breath and leaned against the wall, trying to assimilate everything that had just happened. I didn't know if I believed Lena about the blackmail being Jorge's idea. She could easily have come up with it, and now that Jorge was dead she could say it was all his idea. He wasn't around to contradict her, but I did believe her when she said those people were dangerous. She was genuinely scared. For me. I swallowed hard, rubbed my arm.

I made a decision right then to stop looking, poking around. It was too dangerous. I didn't know who I could trust and I didn't have the resources to sort it out. And all this emotion, the fear, the worry couldn't be good for the baby. I had to consider that. I had to step away and trust the police. At least Summer was back and I knew she was okay. That was one less worry. As soon as I got back to the hotel I was going to call Detective Brown and tell him everything. Of course, that would mean telling Mitch everything, too, probably on the way to the hotel, but I needed to do it. I wasn't looking forward to either encounter. In fact, I wasn't sure which one I was dreading more.

"Ellie, where have you been?" It was Summer coming from the opposite end of the hall, her high heels clicking toward me. "I came back here, but you were gone."

"You're upset that you can't find me after five minutes? This coming from someone who disappeared for a day?"

"Okay, you've got me there. I'm glad I finally found you, though."

"You just missed Lena," I said.

"Lena Stallings? She's here?" Summer turned to look toward the doors into the atrium.

"Yes, she's here and I just had a long conversation with her. Two conversations, in fact. She says she didn't see anything on the platform—not who pushed Jorge or a woman with red hair. I'm going to call Detective Brown tonight and tell him everything that's happened. Everything she said. She said to be careful, that there are dangerous people involved in Jorge's death." I yawned and it was one of those jaw-cracking yawns that I couldn't hide.

"You don't look too worried," Summer said.

"I know. I'm drained. My tired phase is about to hit me. I can feel it." I decided I'd better save my energy for talking with Mitch and Detective Brown.

"So, did you ask her about the check?" Summer asked and I nodded.

"What did she say?" Summer asked eagerly.

"She said it was a loan so he could start a business."

"That's ridiculous. I'm going to look for her."

I summoned up enough energy to say firmly, "Summer, I asked her everything I could think of

and I don't think she's going to talk about it anymore to us. It will probably be a different story when
Detective Brown asks the questions." I fought off another yawn. "Look, I'm not up to explaining everything right now, but I promise I'll fill you in on
everything tomorrow. I think we can deflect some of
Detective Brown's attention away from you onto
Lena. You still have the check?"

"Of course."

"Okay. That in itself should interest him. I'll tell
you the whole story tomorrow. And we still have to
talk about Tony."

"You're mistaken about Tony," Summer said flatly
and then sighed. "But I can see that you're beat. Anyway, I just got off the phone with one of my good
friends. I'm on my way over to her place right after I
pick up Chunky Monkey ice cream, a king-size Snick-
ers, and some movies. Her boyfriend dumped her."

"That's terrible." It was a great solution to my worries about Summer being alone. She'd be out of her
apartment and her friend would keep her occupied.
The Tony discussion would have to wait until tomorrow. Maybe by then I'd have figured out if he was
really on our side or not. *Stop*, I reminded myself. I
was leaving everything alone. No more involvement.

"She's devastated. They'd been dating two years.
So I'm out of here. I'll probably stay overnight at her
place."

"Great. Call me tomorrow. And don't talk to Tony.
Or go near him."

"Whatever you say," Summer said in a humoring
tone that I'd used with Livvy when she was getting
cranky.

"Have you called Detective Brown?" I asked.

"Yes," she said in the same patient tone. "He hasn't
called me back. Here's Melanie's number." She handed

me a slip of paper with a name and phone number. "I'll have my cell phone, too, just in case. Now I've got to go check out with Ms. Archer, then I'm out of here."

I walked with her back into the atrium and I had the strange feeling you get when you leave a movie theater. The fantasy is over and it's back to reality. It seemed as if the intensity of the encounters with Tony and Lena had been a figment of my imagination. I also noticed that my shoes were pinching my toes, my calves ached, and my purse felt like it weighed twenty pounds. Now, if it had been the diaper bag, that would have been possible, but my tiny little clutch wouldn't top out at more than five pounds. I braced my hand against the back of a nearby chair. I didn't think I could walk around to the other side of the room again. It seemed as enormous as a football field and I didn't want to make the trek.

I hid another yawn behind my hand. This was pathetic. It wasn't even ten o'clock and I was yawning like a toddler. The buzz in the crowded room subsided as people moved around on the stage. Another presentation was about to begin.

I paused and watched Summer approach the Archers; then I scanned the room, looking for Mitch. He was still at the table where we'd had dinner. He saw me, said a few words to Jeff, and began working his way through the tables and people toward me.

Since he was on his way over here, I pulled out the chair and dropped into it, wiggled my feet out of my shoes, and let my gaze bob between Mitch's progress and Summer's interaction with the Archers.

I still couldn't get over them as a couple. They didn't go together at all. Vicki's height, youth, and commanding presence contrasted with Alan's squat, skinny form and shriveled face. I shook my head. He was barely taller than Summer and when he stood

beside Vicki she looked like an Amazon. I just didn't
understand how some couples became couples. Summer finally got Vicki's attention. Vicki's stiff blond
hair bobbed up and down as she nodded a few times
and turned away, a dismissal. Summer said a few words
to Mr. Archer and left.

Mitch finally reached me. "You look beat. Ready
to go?"

"Yes." I winced as I pushed my toes back into my
shoes. Mitch noticed my expression and gave me a
questioning look.

"I hate to admit it, but I'm going to have blisters
tomorrow."

He said, "We'll get a taxi."

That's one reason I love him. He didn't ask where
I'd been or rub it in that I shouldn't have worn new
shoes. He took my hand, got us out of there, and
into a taxi. I fell asleep on his shoulder on the ride
back to the hotel.

Saturday

The next morning, I woke, taking in the sun pour-
ing in the gap in the curtains, Mitch's prone form
beside me, and the time: nine-twenty. There was
something I was supposed to do.

"Mitch." I grabbed his bare shoulder. "You're going
to be late."

There was an incoherent response from him as he
rolled over.

"It's after nine. What time did your class start
today?"

"It's Saturday. No class today," he said, his arm circling my waist, pulling me close.

"Oh." I fell back onto the pillow.

We stayed that way for a while and I thought Mitch had gone back to sleep, but then he said. "Room service for breakfast?"

"Sounds great." I reran the events of last night in my mind and realized I hadn't talked to anyone yet. My stomach clenched. Suddenly breakfast didn't sound so good.

Mitch released me, found the phone, and ordered pancakes, fruit, and a "good morning basket," whatever that was.

"Muffins," he explained as he pulled me close again. I didn't stop him from turning in an order for me. After last night, I knew I needed to eat and I was going to make myself do it, just like I was going to tell Mitch everything and make that call to Detective Brown. Right after breakfast.

"We should get up since you ordered breakfast," I said without moving.

"Yep," he agreed, but didn't move.

I watched the dust motes float in the shaft of sunlight filtering through the edge of the curtains, felt his breath on my shoulder blade. "I'm getting as bad as Livvy about sleeping in the car. I can't seem to stay awake after about nine-thirty, if you put me in a moving vehicle. It's something about the sound of the tires and the engine. Mesmerizing."

"I'll have to remember that. Could come in handy someday." Mitch shifted around, propped his head up on his hand, "So, are you going to tell me what's going on anytime soon?"

Chapter
Twenty-five

"I'm busted, huh?"

"Totally busted," he said. I tried to gauge his tone. He wasn't angry, which was the reaction I'd expected and dreaded. He sounded curious. Of course, once he knew everything he might be mad, but I decided it would be better to tell him now when he was interested and neither one of us was about to fly off to class or a tour. "How do you know something's up?"

"Because, my dear, you've had that same look on your face for the last couple of days that you get when you're organizing a closet or a room and things aren't working out like you've envisioned them. You're puzzled that everything doesn't fit and you're determined to make it work."

Did this man know me or what? Here I was thinking he was completely oblivious of everything that was going on and the whole time he'd been aware of my preoccupation. In the future, I had to remember he was much more perceptive than I gave him credit for.

I squirmed away a few inches. His undivided gaze

was pretty intense. "Okay. Here's the deal. I hate not telling you everything, but we've both been so busy. And I couldn't just throw it out there when you were shaving and on your way to class. This hasn't really been a vacation for either one of us, you know?"

"I know. I had no idea I'd be in class every day, all day, and then have a project on top of that. It used to be a pretty relaxed course. At least, that's what Tommy told me. He did it a few years ago."

"Well, things change. It's still been great getting away just the two of us, but I've found out some things," I paused, trying to decide where to start.

Mitch groaned and rolled away from me, onto his back, but he wasn't upset. His tone was still teasing as he said, "You've found out some things! How do you do this?"

I shifted onto my elbow. "I don't mean to. It just . . . happens. I see things, hear things, and put them together."

I went back to Nadia's photo and described how oddly Irene had acted. I glossed over why she'd been acting strange by saying it was "female stuff," and he held up a hand. "Don't want to know."

"Good, because I wasn't going to tell you. It's private." I went on to describe Wellesley's side business. His good humor melted a bit there and he said, "Ellie, why are you so focused on this? Why not let the police do their job?"

"Because back at the beginning of the week, they were focused on Summer. They still are, actually. They think she's guilty." He opened his mouth to say something else, but I cut him off. "Detective Brown thinks I helped her get rid of Jorge."

He studied my face, then said, "Go on."

After I told him about Summer's inquiries into a

restraining order, he ran his hand over his forehead, then rubbed his eyes. "She didn't want to tell me about it?"

"No, she didn't. And earlier, I promised her I wouldn't, but, well, I told her I was going to tell you. I think you should know. Things have gotten too complicated, too dangerous."

"What else?"

"She found out Jorge's address and we went by his house and talked to his neighbor." I left out how we'd gotten the address. "Then she pulled her disappearing act."

By now Mitch was sitting up, his back braced against the headboard, and I'd shifted around so that my head was at the foot of the bed and my feet were on my pillow. Mitch tossed me a pillow and I tucked it under my head. "The neighbor?" He pulled my foot over and began to rub it.

"No. Summer. That feels good. I promise I'm not ever breaking in new shoes at a fund-raising dinner again." His hands stopped moving and I explained the mail Summer had taken and how she'd traced it to Lena Stallings. "So she took a shuttle to the airport and flew down to Georgia."

Mitch closed his eyes, but he was rubbing my foot again, which I took to be a good sign. "Figures. That is just like her."

I hurried on. "I didn't want to call the police because it would make her look guilty, leaving town like that. So even though I knew she was okay and on her way back—she didn't find Lena—I still had to wait until she was back before I called Detective Brown."

"So you're going to call Detective Brown?"

"Yes. As soon as we eat and I finish telling you what happened last night."

"There's more?"

I shrugged. "A little." I described my encounters with Tony and Lena. He didn't really pay close attention to the part about Lena. He kind of got stuck on the part about Tony. He dropped my foot and got off the bed.

"His name is Tony? Tony what?" He was tossing clothes around the room.

"Tony Zobart, but, Mitch, I'm okay and I'm going to tell Detective Brown everything."

He ignored me as he slid open the closet door. It banged against the frame and I got out of bed, too. I wasn't sure what Mitch was going to do. He pulled his cell phone out of his jacket pocket, then dropped back onto the bed as he dialed.

"Operator thirty-one, good morning."

I sat back down on the bed. He was talking to a military base operator. I didn't know which base, but I figured it was good that he was on the phone instead of running out the door to attack Tony. He asked to be patched through to a number I didn't recognize.

There was a knock on the door and Mitch looked at me. "It's room service."

I'd forgotten about our breakfast. I threw on my robe and got the door. I rushed the man in. "Anywhere. Here, let me sign that," I said and practically shoved him out the door.

I hurried and sat back down on the bed. Mitch had settled back against the headboard again. He tilted the phone away from his mouth and said to me, "I'm on hold."

"For who?" I asked, but he snapped the phone back to his ear.

"Great . . . okay. Thanks." Some of the tension eased

out of his shoulders. He glanced at me as he spoke into the phone. "Yeah. I'll try. You know how that goes." He closed the phone. "Thistlewait says hello."

"You called Thistlewait? On a Saturday?"

"He was working. Tony's legit. Let's have breakfast."

"Wait. Tony's really FBI? Thistlewait can check him out? That fast?" I had too many questions and Mitch was acting way too relaxed for me. Shouldn't he still be upset?

He threw on a T-shirt and tossed his phone on the dresser. "Let's eat. Yes, Thistlewait was able to verify that Tony's with the FBI."

"And you're not upset about . . . everything?"

Mitch removed the covers from the plates, pushed on my shoulder so that I sat in one of the chairs, and waved a basket under my nose. "Muffin?"

I shook my head and opted for orange juice. Maybe I needed sugar. Maybe I was hallucinating. Mitch plucked a blueberry muffin from the basket. He picked up his knife, slit the muffin, and buttered it. "Ellie, you got in the middle of an undercover investigation. What Tony did—well, I can't blame him. He had to do something fast before you gave away any more information."

I sat up straight. "He didn't have to drag me into a closet."

"Where else could he have gotten you alone, convinced you that he wasn't a terrorist, and gotten the memory chip back without anyone else seeing?"

I cut into my pancakes and reluctantly said, "Okay. You've got a point."

Mitch said, "I think the best thing for us to do today is check in with Summer. I'll make sure she's still with her friend and then we lay low."

"What about MacInally? We're supposed to meet him at the museum." I had to call Debbie this afternoon, too, and tell her something. I'd put off calling her until I talked to MacInally one last time. At least, that was the excuse I was using to justify not calling her. I dreaded that conversation because I knew she wanted the truth and, deep down, I knew I was going to tell her the truth. As painful as it would be, that's what she'd want.

Mitch chewed thoughtfully. "Do you think he's involved?"

I thought about it as I swirled more butter onto my pancakes. "I don't see how he could be. He wasn't on the platform when Jorge was pushed. He was in the hospital. He does know Lena and she's mixed up in this somehow. Although they just don't seem to go together, as a couple, you know? And, speaking of that, did you see Alan and Vicki Archer? There's a mismatch, if I ever saw one."

"Why do you say that?"

"Because she's young and attractive and he's old and shrunken," I said.

"He must have that Henry Kissinger thing going for him. Power."

"He's barely taller than Summer." I shook my head. "There's no accounting for taste, is there?"

"Nope. Tell me about Lena. What did she say?"

"She said the check she sent to Jorge was a loan to start a business. She let it slip that Jorge talked her into blackmailing someone. I think it was Alan Archer. He *is* powerful. He's on the base closure commission and Lena wants to guarantee that Taylor Air Force Base isn't closed. She also said that one of Jorge's friends worked for Vicki Archer."

"That would be Tony. Okay, so Jorge goes down

there with the intention of connecting with Lena so that he can get something on Alan Archer?"

"Yes, Tony said he sent Jorge to Georgia, but Jorge got too close to 'her.' He had to be talking about Lena. At first, I thought that Tony killed Jorge. Apparently, there was a bit of a power struggle going on between Jorge and Tony. Lena thinks that's what happened."

Mitch positioned a bowl of chopped fruit between our plates so we could share. He speared a chunk of watermelon. "But we know that Tony's a good guy. He wouldn't kill Jorge."

I poked at some cantaloupe. "Unless he had to?" Mitch and I looked at each other for a few moments.

"It's possible," Mitch finally said.

I bit into the juicy fruit and chewed thoughtfully. After I swallowed, I said, "I can't really see him letting Summer take the heat of an investigation, though. There's something there between them. I think he really likes her. And I *know* she likes him."

Mitch laughed. "That's all we need. Federal law enforcement in the family. We've already got enough contact with the police."

I ignored that comment. "Back to Lena. We still don't know what Lena used to blackmail Archer."

"What if it wasn't Archer who was blackmailed?" Mitch said.

"Okay, who else? Ms. Archer? Vicki Archer doesn't have anything that Lena wants," I said.

"That we know about," Mitch countered, "but all right. Say it was Alan Archer. What have they got in common?"

I shrugged. "I don't know. I guess it really doesn't matter why she blackmailed him or what she used. It only matters that she did." I ate the last strawberry. It was almost time to call Detective Brown. I swallowed hard. "I feel kind of bad for MacInally. I think he really likes Lena."

Mitch said, "You know I talked to him some more last night while you were having your closet conversation with Tony. You said you didn't think Lena and MacInally went together?"

"No. There were tons of mismatches on display last night. He's open and honest. She's cunning. I get the feeling that she's looking out for herself first."

"Well, he's known her a long time, since Korea. He's got to know what she's like."

I paused with my glass of orange juice poised in midair. "Since Korea?"

"He told me she was his nurse in Korea."

"*In* Korea?" I asked.

"Yes."

I put my glass down and leaned back in the chair. "I had the impression she met him after he came back to the States. I know Summer said something about Lena being a nurse in Vietnam. Could she have been in both Korea and Vietnam?"

"It's possible, I guess. I don't know much about how they assigned nurses back then." Mitch put the covers back on our empty plates and moved them to the tray. "When are you going to call Detective Brown?"

I was still stuck on the discrepancy between what Lena had told me and what MacInally had told Mitch. I trusted MacInally more than Lena, so I had a feeling that his version was what had actually happened.

I pulled myself back to the present when I realized what Mitch had asked. "What? Oh, that's right. Detective Brown." I stood up. "I'll call him after I shower." I grabbed a green cotton shirt and denim capri pants.

An Everything In Its Place Tip for an Organized Trip

Travel with kids
- A great way to generate excitement about the trip for your kids is to let them get involved in trip planning. Help them contact the visitors center or chamber of commerce at your vacation destination a few weeks before departure to request brochures and maps.
- If you're flying, don't forget to carry on an over-the-counter decongestant. Check your pharmacy section for medicine strips that dissolve in the mouth. They're lightweight and not as messy as a liquid medicine.
- For entertainment for kids, go beyond electronic handheld games and include dot-to-dot books, a notepad and colored pencils, and books geared to their age.
- A map and highlighter will let your kids track your progress across the country.
- Don't forget that special blanket or stuffed animal.
- A night-light always comes in handy and can help kids feel more comfortable in unfamiliar surroundings.

Chapter
Twenty-six

When I emerged from the shower, I was still thinking about Lena and MacInally. I'd decided I wouldn't get any deeper involved in trying to sort out the mess around Jorge's death, but I could *think* about it. I couldn't talk to Mitch while I was drying my hair, but as soon as I switched off the blow-dryer and started on my makeup, I asked Mitch, "So, what else did you and MacInally talk about?"

The TV volume went down and I heard the closet door slide down its track. "Oh, you know, how long he's lived in D.C. Where he grew up. Stuff like that."

I gave my lashes a few swipes with the mascara wand. "Where's he from?"

"Arizona." Mitch appeared in the mirror behind me and braced his arm on the wall, settling in. "I know that look. You want details, don't you?"

"Of course." I smiled as I ran some lip gloss over my lips.

"Okay." Mitch sighed. Details were like torture to him. I wondered if interrogators had ever tried that technique to get men to talk. Drown them in details. They'd break after a couple of hours.

"Let's see. We talked a bit about Arizona. Not much, since I've never been there. He's lived in D.C. for about ten years. Before that, he was in San Francisco. That was about it."

"Okay." Nothing earth-shattering there. Mitch went in the bathroom and started the shower water. I sat down on a chair, slid my feet into my comfortable tan sandals, and dialed Detective Brown's number while I fastened the straps.

I was hoping for his voice mail, but he answered the phone.

"Detective Brown, this is Ellie Avery, Summer's sister-in-law." I paused.

"Yes?" His tone was impatient. I tried not to picture his jowly face and cold gray eyes, but I could imagine his expression of annoyance without too much trouble since his tone conveyed it so well.

"Summer got in touch with you?"

"Yes. Do you need something else, Mrs. Avery? I'm on my way to talk to Summer now."

"Oh." Was that good or bad? "You just want to talk to her, right? You don't have any new evidence, do you? Because even if you did, Summer's not guilty," I finished hurriedly.

"I have to confirm a few things. That's all. Now, if that was all you needed."

"No. I've found out a few things you probably should know about."

There was total silence on the line and I wished I'd thought about what I was going to say before I'd called him. "I met a woman last night, Lena Stallings. She was on the platform the day Jorge was pushed. She had a relationship with him. I think she might have wanted him dead."

"And you know this how?" His tone was less impatient, but still had a heavy dollop of reluctance mixed with doubt.

"She told me."

"Why would she tell you something like that?"

I paused, trying to think fast, but thinking fast on my feet had never been one of my strong points. Basically, I froze. Wasn't stealing mail a federal offense? I couldn't tell him about Summer taking Jorge's mail. And that would be tampering with evidence, too, wouldn't it? I was suddenly glad I was sitting down, because I felt dizzy. I wanted to help Summer, not get her in more trouble.

"Mrs. Avery, are you still there?"

"Yes. Sorry." Okay, skip the mail part. Stick to last night. "I met Lena Stallings at a fund-raiser event last night. She's from Georgia and works for STAND, an organization that wants to keep Taylor Air Force Base open. That's in Georgia, the base, I mean."

"Yes, I know." His voice was less curious.

"Anyway, I know she was on the platform right before Jorge was pushed because my friend took some pictures that day and Lena's in one of them. She told me Jorge had dangerous friends and that he was blackmailing someone." There. That was vague enough, wasn't it? No mention of Summer, but I had given him the link between Lena and Jorge.

"Mrs. Avery," he began, but silence cut into his words. He was getting another call. Thank goodness. I breathed a sigh of relief as he put me on hold. I plucked at my shirt and went to turn up the air-conditioning in the room. He came back on the line. "I'd like to talk to you more about this. Will you be at your hotel this afternoon?"

"We're on our way to the Air and Space Museum,

but we'll be back later. We'll probably stop by here before we go to dinner."

"Fine. I'll call you."

He hung up and I collapsed onto the bed and let the cool air fan across me. *That was nerve-racking.*

"Hey, can you hand me a new bar of soap?" Mitch called.

"Sure." I unwrapped one and handed it to him.

He stuck his head around the shower curtain. "I remembered one other thing MacInally mentioned. Alan Archer. It's freezing out there. Have you got the air blasting again?"

"Alan Archer?" I said and went to turn the air off.

Mitch was back behind the shower curtain when I got back to the bathroom door. "Yeah. Apparently, he and Archer go way back. They've known each other since the war."

I leaned on the door frame. Archer was a Vietnam vet. How could MacInally have known him since the war? Steam billowed out of the top of the shower and engulfed me, but I hardly noticed the mugginess of the room.

"Mitch, I'm going down to the business center to look up some bios online."

I hurried down to the little room located in the lobby, but stopped short in the doorway when I saw a man in a white dress shirt at the computer. I turned to leave, but he said, "I'm done," and clicked on the box at the top of the screen to close the window. There was something about the way he moved quickly and the way his gaze darted back to me and then to the computer that gave me the feeling that he didn't want me to see the screen.

He stood up and grabbed several pages as they slid out of the printer. He hurried out of the room, pulling on a brown vest that the hotel employees wore. I frowned, watching him. I'd seen him before. He worked at the front desk, but seeing him out of his brown vest had jogged a memory. I walked over to the computer and swirled the mouse around, still thinking about the man. He was young, tall, with inky dark hair.

The screen was still active, but blank. I clicked on the bar at the bottom and a screen from a free online e-mail service came up. He'd been in such a hurry he must have hit the button to minimize the screen, not close it. I pointed the arrow at the button to close it, but paused as the subject lines of the e-mails caught my eye. "Stop Zionist Aggression Now," "Your donation equals dead American soldiers," "End U.S. aggressors." I couldn't help but skim down the list, which went on in the same vein with more calls for donations and action.

The e-mails were from groups with names like Humanity Against Zionist Aggression, Save Palestine Now, and End U.S. Imperialism. There weren't any personal e-mails on the list. All of them were from causes either requesting money or thanking "Faiza88" for the donation. I saw a movement at the doorway and I jumped, my grip tightening on the mouse. I twisted sideways, but it was just a businesswoman hurrying through the lobby, pulling her rolling suitcase. I took a deep breath and turned back to the computer, but it was blank.

"What?" I circled the mouse, but the screen was gone. I'd closed it when I jumped. A few clicks brought up a new connection to the Internet, but I wouldn't be able to get back to the e-mail account of Faiza without a password. Not that I wanted back in. Thinking of what those organizations raised money for made me shudder. It was hard to grasp the fact that people gave money to these organizations with the hope that it would actually contribute to someone's death, preferably that of a U.S. soldier. I could see the hotel check-in desk and the young man was there, smiling at the woman who'd dashed by the door a moment ago. I watched him. He was the one who'd come over to us when Abby and I had talked to Joe Tickner. Abby had signaled him and he'd hovered in the background until we were sure Joe wasn't going to do anything more threatening than clear out the breakfast buffet. But there was something else.

The woman left and a family moved up to the desk. The mother turned to scold the boy who'd tossed a foam football in the air. I watched it bounce wildly across the shiny floor and then I had it. The desk clerk had been the man Tony talked to at the Reflecting Pool on the Mall. His clothes were different, but the face and build were the same.

I shifted my chair to the left so that the family blocked the desk clerk's view into the business center doorway. It looked like Tony had been telling the truth about his connection with radicals. I felt I should do something about the e-mails I'd just seen. I couldn't see something that threatened soldiers and Americans without feeling that I should report it. But what was there to report? The fresh connection to the Internet glowed on the screen and the printer hummed softly in the small room. I couldn't get back to the screen. Would anyone believe me if I told them what I saw? I had no proof that the e-mail account existed and I didn't even know the guy's name, except that he called himself Faiza online.

It would take forever to explain what I'd seen to the police. Even Detective Brown had thought I was being rather tedious when I'd called him earlier. I doubted he'd be exactly eager to hear from me again so soon. And there was the little fact that I dreaded calling him again because I knew he'd probably ask more questions about the whole Lena/Jorge connection. I wasn't that good at dancing around the truth without tripping all over myself. No, Detective Brown was pretty low on my list of people to call.

Tony seemed to be a better choice. At least he would know the guy's name. Maybe Tony already knew about Faiza's contact with those radical groups? And Tony would have the resources to call in someone who might be able to find the e-mail account either on the computer hard drive or out in cyberspace.

I rolled the chair closer to the keyboard and ran a quick search on the names I'd been curious about when I first came down, MacInally and Alan Archer. I threw in Lena's name, too. I had a hard time focusing because I kept checking the front desk, but it was a busy time and there was always a line of people. I paged through the results rapidly and printed a few articles that popped up associated with the names; then, I snatched the papers out of the printer tray. After a quick check of the front desk, which still had a line three people deep in front of it, I zipped across the lobby to the elevator bank. Well, I probably lumbered. I was pregnant and didn't want to slip on the mirrorlike floor tiles, but I went as fast as I dared.

I squeezed into the elevator beside the kid with the football and his family. As we went up, I scanned the articles. There were more pages about Lena than the other two, with lots of info rehashing her background, which had been on the STAND Web site. Alan Archer only had a few mentions. Vietnam vet and war hero were the most popular descriptions attached to his name. MacInally only had one article about his consulting service, a fluffy piece that ran in the business section of his local newspaper when he started the business.

The elevator doors opened as I flipped to the last page. I paused on the elevator's threshold. The page didn't belong to me. It was from Humanity Against Zionist Aggression, one of the groups I'd seen on the e-mail account, and the addressee was Faiza88. The subject line read *Increase in funds urgently needed*.

"Are you going up?" I realized the dad in the family group in the elevator had his finger on the button that held the doors open.

"No, I'm sorry." I stepped into the hallway and almost ran into Tony.

Chapter
Twenty-seven

We both paused for a second, assessing each other. Thistlewait said Tony was legit. That thought was the only thing that stopped me from darting past him to our room down the hall.

Tony smiled disarmingly and said, "Just the person I was looking for. Don't worry. There's no storage closets around here. Could I speak to you for a moment?"

"Okay," I said slowly and paced down the hall to our door. I inserted the key card and pushed it open. "Give me just a minute." Inside with Mitch seemed like a better choice than outside in the hall alone.

The room was empty. The bathroom door was still closed. I tapped on it and said, "Tony Zobart's stopped by." I suddenly felt a little silly. Clearly, Tony wasn't here on a social call, but my words sounded like I was about to offer him some juice and a muffin.

"Really?" Mitch's tone sounded more interested than alarmed. "I'm getting dressed. Be out in a second."

I went back to the door and let Tony in. He spoke

before I did. "Sorry to show up unexpectedly, but this will only take a minute—"

"Here," I interrupted him. I shoved the printout of the e-mail at him.

Mitch emerged from the bathroom dressed in a dark brown shirt and khaki shorts. I felt better with him in the room. I still didn't quite trust Tony, despite the fact that Thistlewait had vouched for him. I explained where I'd gotten the printout. Mitch shook his head. "Again, I have to ask, how do you do this? You were gone ten minutes."

I shrugged. "I don't know. Either I'm lucky or I'm cursed. I can't figure out which one."

Tony's gaze flicked down the paper and back up to my face. "Do you believe me now?"

I shrugged. "I'm still not sure who to believe. So, is that his name, Faiza?"

"No," Tony said and didn't elaborate.

"And that was him at the Reflecting Pool on the Mall?"

"Oh yes. That was him." Tony folded the paper and slipped it into the inside pocket of his dark suit jacket. Apparently, his talkative mood had dried up and he wasn't going to answer my questions like he had on the night of the fund-raiser. But I figured I could keep asking him questions of my own.

"So, you know about his . . ." I waved my hand at his suit where the paper had disappeared. I had done the right thing, hadn't I? Tony was the one to give it to, wasn't he?

Tony finished my sentence for me. "About his association with groups that raise money for radical causes? Yes."

"So, he does . . . what? Sends them money?" Mitch asked.

Tony nodded. "Yes. We know what he's doing."

"You're letting him send them money? And you know he works in this hotel?" My voice became sharper with each question. "He could be dangerous. How can you let him work here? What if he does more than send money? He could endanger people here."

In contrast to my rather piercing tone, Tony's voice was low and smooth. "We know what he's doing. We're watching him. We're *letting* him do it." He said the last line with special emphasis.

Mitch said, "You're using him to lead you to the groups that are questionable. The ones that are funneling money to radicals?"

Tony didn't agree with him aloud, but dipped his head in Mitch's direction. I took that as an acknowledgment that Mitch had hit on the truth. Tony glanced back at me. "We're watching him and he's not going to do anything without us knowing about it."

"But why would he use the business center here at the hotel?" I wondered aloud. "Isn't that a little risky?"

Tony said, "I can't say anything about the person you saw today, but I can say, in general, people who don't want to leave a trail of information that connects them to certain transactions often use public computers."

It did make sense. Unlike using a personal computer, the computer at the hotel business center was open to any hotel guest. It would be difficult to trace activity on it back to anyone. And Faiza—even if it wasn't his real name, that was how I'd begun to think of him—could slip in there and log on to his free e-mail account during slow times or right before or after his shift. I didn't know all the ins and outs of the Internet, but it seemed like his free e-mail account would also give him some degree of anonymity.

"I can assure you that the hotel staff and all public parts of the hotel are under careful scrutiny," Tony said, then shifted the conversation away from the desk clerk. "Now, the reason I'm so rudely interrupting your vacation," he said briskly.

"It hasn't felt like a vacation for several days," I muttered. "And it's getting more surreal by the moment."

Tony continued in his businesslike tone. "I talked to Summer today and she said she took some mail from Jorge's apartment."

I said, "Summer talked to you? Obviously, she didn't listen to me."

"That's nothing new. Summer never listens to anyone," Mitch said.

"She definitely knows her mind." There was a moment when I could swear the two men sized up each other. I glanced back and forth between the two of them, not sure what was going to happen.

Mitch said, "That's a pretty accurate assessment of my sister." The tension eased.

Tony seemed to relax a little as he turned back to me. "She said you might still have the mail that was in Jorge's mailbox?"

"I've got the envelope that held the check from Lena. Summer has the check." I walked over to the dresser.

"I know. Summer gave it to me." I must have looked surprised because he added, "It's evidence. Bagged and tagged. I'm not keeping it. I need the rest of the mail."

"You want Jorge's junk mail?"

"I wouldn't exactly call it junk. You've still got it?"

"Yes," I pulled it out from under a stack of magazines and newspapers on the dresser and handed it to him, but I wished I could look through it again. Why did he want it?

"Thank you very much." Tony headed for the door. "Sorry to disturb you."

"Wait. What's in there? I saw you check his mailbox the other day. You were looking for junk mail?"

"You saw that, did you?" He looked from me to Mitch, seeming to evaluate us for a moment. Then he pulled out the glossy flyer for teeth whitening. "There is no Potomac Dental Center."

The flyer looked like the countless ones I received and trashed every day. I wouldn't have glanced at it twice. Tony continued. "It's a message to Jorge, setting up a time and meeting place, a meeting that I don't want to miss. You have to have the grille, a piece of paper with holes in it, to read the message. You put the grille over this and then you can read the message."

"And you've got the grille?" Mitch asked.

Tony nodded. "I do. I just needed the message. Thanks." He shook hands with Mitch and then with me. "Hopefully, I'll be less rushed next time I see you. Don't worry about Summer. My . . . inquiries . . . are about to wind up. Once that is finished, we'll inform Detective Brown about Jorge's real identity and that will help take the pressure off Summer." The door closed behind him and Mitch looked at me.

I dropped onto the bed. "That was weird."

Mitch sat down in a chair and pulled on his shoes. "Who would have thought someone would use junk mail to send a message?"

"I know, but it does make sense in a twisted sort of way," I said. "Junk mail is so annoying that I don't pay any attention to it. I just toss it, but what if someone called the phone number on the flyer?"

Mitch looked up as he tied his shoes. "It probably isn't a real number, but I guess someone could set up a phone number and take messages. Or maybe they had one of those phone mail message centers with the automated voice and forty options. I know after a few minutes of that I'd just give up and call somewhere else." Mitch stood up. "So, are you ready for one more museum?"

"We're going to a museum? More sightseeing after everything? That doesn't seem right."

Mitch picked up his phone and clipped it on his belt. "It'll be better than sitting around this room all day. Tony's going to take care of what he needs to with that information, and when he wraps up his end of things, the focus of Detective Brown's investigation will change." Mitch held out my purse for me.

I stood in the middle of the room for a few seconds, then reluctantly took my purse. He was right. We'd done what we could. Tony would do his job and bring in the members of the cell—at least, that's what I thought he meant when he said his inquiry was near an end—and then that would help reveal that there were more people who had a motive to want Jorge dead besides Summer. I sighed. I didn't really want to look at aircraft and spaceships, but it would be better than looking at the hotel room walls for the rest of the day.

A few hours later, I stood on the wide walkway that bisected the second floor of the museum. I leaned against the railing and gazed at the *Spirit of St. Louis.* Suspended at eye-level with me, it hung above the open-entry atrium where tourists flowed in, swirled around the moon rock and *Mercury 7.* John Glenn had orbited the earth's atmosphere in *Mercury 7.* Since Nadia was touring Mount Vernon today, she wasn't here to act as impromptu tour guide. I'd had to read the information card. I flipped to my map of the Mall to see how far we were from the National Gallery of Art. Maybe we'd have time to go by there before the day was over.

Air and space definitely weren't my things. The museum was interesting, but the place didn't enthrall me, like some of the other museums had. I gazed at the *Spirit of St. Louis,* thinking how light and fragile it looked compared to some of the sleek modern displays, like the lunar capsule and the missile below it. The small plane I could relate to. It made me think of the Jimmy Stewart movie and the first solo transatlantic flight. The plane looked a little out of place against the lines of the glass and steel atrium.

"Imagine flying all the way across the Atlantic in that little thing," I said to Mitch.

"Umm." His head was down as he focused on the map of the building. He glanced up, saw where I was looking, and said, "Yeah. I have to hand it to Lindbergh. *That* was flying."

"I'm not as interested in the rest of it. The missiles, the moon stuff."

"That's okay. Want to catch a show at the IMAX?" Mitch asked.

"No. I have to meet MacInally, but you go ahead."

"Oh no. Today we stick together."

"Sounds good." I checked my watch. "It's almost three. I figured it would be easier to see him from up here. Do you want to look at anything else later?" I asked.

"No. I'm good. I've seen everything. I thought you wanted to see this museum."

I smiled. "I came because I thought *you* wanted to see it. I figured, planes, you know. That's your thing. My plan was to hang out with you today and see what you wanted to see."

"I see planes every day."

"Yeah. That's right." It was a classic case of knowing someone so well that I missed the most basic thing. "Well, what do you want to see? After we talk to Mac-Inally we can go anywhere you want to."

"The Natural History Museum sounded interesting. That was the one with the dinosaurs, right?"

"Among other things," I said. I could happily prowl around there some more. "I don't see MacInally. Let's go down a little farther."

We turned and I let my hand trail along the shiny banister as we walked. "I guess I'm not very good company today. I'm having a hard time focusing. I keep thinking about the whole incident with the desk clerk. Actually, my mind keeps skipping from that to what I read about Lena. It doesn't match with what MacInally said."

"And that bothers you."

"Yes. It does."

When we reached the end of the banister, we both leaned on our elbows and watched the crowd.

"So, what did it say about her online again?" Mitch asked.

"Her bio with STAND says she grew up in Georgia and graduated from the University of Georgia, where she got a degree in nursing. She was an Army nurse in the late sixties to the early seventies, which was during the Vietnam War, but the Web site doesn't say where she was sent. Those dates fall during the time that MacInally was wounded in Korea, so she could have been there. She could have met him in Korea."

"So ask him about it today," Mitch said.

"I'm going to."

"There was something else. I didn't have time to tell you. I looked up Alan Archer, too."

"And?"

"It was harder to find information about him, but there are several prominent mentions of his time in Vietnam. Lots of medals." Mitch would have known the significance of many of the names that didn't mean much to me, but I couldn't remember all of them.

"Was he career?" Mitch asked, meaning had Archer made the military a career?

"Yes. He retired a full bird colonel. He's had civil service jobs at the Pentagon since then. Now he's on the BRAC. That was it."

We'd been watching the crowd and I said, "Look at that man. That's got to be the world's worst toupee. Do you see him?"

"How could I not?" Mitch said. The man had to be at least in his sixties, but his hair was a solid black and the hair above each ear rose straight up in a huge curl. The two rolls of hair met in the center of his forehead and dipped toward his nose. It was like a really bad cartoon sketch of John Travolta's character in *Grease*.

I scanned the room again. "Oh, wait. There's MacInally." He had on a tan windbreaker over a golf shirt. He was the one person who wasn't moving around on the floor below us.

I waved and caught his eye, motioning that we'd come down the escalator. A few minutes later we'd moved to the food court area and were seated at a table under a very noisy air conditioner. MacInally set a cup of coffee down on a napkin. Mitch handed me a chocolate shake before settling into his chair.

"I probably shouldn't drink this," I said and took a long slug on the straw.

"Calcium." Mitch winked. "You need it. And you're on vacation."

"Right. I'll just tell my doctor the extra fifteen pounds I gained this week is all calcium," I joked.

MacInally had been removing the lid from his coffee and didn't seem to have heard our exchange. "I forgot what a racket there is in here," he said as the vent droned above us.

The only up side was that we wouldn't have to worry about anyone overhearing our conversation. "It's all the glass," MacInally said. The room was a boxy modern-day conservatory with glass ceiling and walls. Add throngs of tourists, several fast food restaurants cranking out steaming fries and burgers as if they were on conveyor belts, and the place bordered on sweltering.

"So, you've enjoyed your visit here?" MacInally asked.

"I have," I said. "I'm not so sure about Mitch. It's been work for him. He hasn't really seen anything except the Ronald Reagan building. And restaurants, lots of restaurants."

Mitch shrugged. "It's been fine. I'll see a few things this weekend."

MacInally took a sip of his coffee and pleated the edge of his napkin. "How much longer are you here?"

"Just until Monday. We fly out in the afternoon."

MacInally nodded, his gaze on his coffee cup. I glanced over at Mitch as I took another big slurp of my shake. Something was wrong. MacInally seemed distracted, like he didn't really want to be here. He folded the corner of his napkin a few more times. Maybe he didn't know how to begin?

I leaned over the table and said, "Mr. MacInally—" That got his attention and he opened his mouth to correct me, but I said, "Sorry. Jay. If you don't want to talk about Noel, that's okay."

"No." He sat up straighter. "I do want to talk about Noel." But then his phone rang. "Excuse me. I have to take this."

His side of the conversation didn't amount to much. He only said yes a couple of times. Mitch slid his arm around my shoulders and leaned in to whisper in my ear, "I think he's nervous. Maybe if I leave the table he'll feel more comfortable."

MacInally said, "Fine. I'll meet you there in an hour." He punched a button on his phone and placed it on the table near a pile of napkins.

Mitch stood up. "I think I'll get one of those shakes for myself. You two go ahead. Don't wait on me. The line's long."

MacInally nodded. Did he look paler? His dark eyebrows and eyes contrasted with his skin, which looked as white as the napkin he was fidgeting with again. He took a swig of his coffee and set the cup down with a thump on the table. "Ellie, there's no new story about when Noel and I were on leave. I just told you that so I could meet with you again."

Chapter
Twenty-eight

"**O**kay," I said slowly. His gaze was concentrated and I leaned back in my chair. He scared me a little. I looked over his shoulder and saw Mitch waiting in the longest line, watching me. I swallowed and refocused on MacInally. We were in a crowded restaurant. I had no reason to be afraid. As I looked closer at MacInally, I saw a couple of drops of sweat at his hairline. He grabbed a few napkins and wiped his face.

"Are you feeling all right? Are you sick?" I asked, my alarm had switched from fear to worry for him. Was he about to have a heart attack or something? He'd been through a lot in the last week. Maybe he wasn't as tough as he thought.

"No." He took a deep breath and leaned forward, his elbows braced on the table. "What I told you before about Noel, how he shot at the patrol that night, that was how I remembered it." His tone was regretful, almost apologetic. "It was in the official report."

"Right. That's what you told me." Did he think I doubted him?

"I've been thinking about that day." He drained

the last of his coffee. Tremors from his hand made the cup tremble for a second before he put it down. "More of it is coming back to me." He looked up from his cup and held my gaze. "And what's coming back to me, my memories, don't match the official report."

The air conditioner droned as he waited for my reaction. "I don't understand," I said.

"I didn't either. It means I was lied to." He waited for that to sink in and then he said, "And it means that Noel's family believed a lie."

"What lie?" I realized my hands were icy. I put the shake down.

"The lie that Noel killed Shipley and wounded me."

"What? That's not true? But you believed it was."

MacInally held my gaze and said, "At the beginning of this week, I believed it. Now I don't." He pushed his empty cup of coffee and napkin away, making room for his forearms on the table. His color looked better, but I think mine probably looked worse. Why had he put me through that worry?

"God, it's a relief to say it," he said, almost to himself. He tilted his head and asked, "You okay? You don't look so good."

"I'm trying to understand," I said, crossing my arms.

MacInally snorted. "Me, too. Look, last week I believed Noel shot Shipley and me. That's what everyone said. I had what the docs call dissociative amnesia, but my memory loss was selective. I could remember bits and pieces, but most of that day, after the claymores went off, was gone. I remember the mosquitoes and the rocks tossed to probe our position. And until I went into the hospital a few days ago, I didn't remember anything else. But this week, I think it was being in the hospital again . . ." He paused and ran his hands over his hair. "I can't explain it, but stuff started to come back. Anyway, what I know now is that Noel didn't fire that gun."

"Then who did?" A sudden horrible thought hit me. "Did you?"

He actually laughed. "No. Now, that would have been a terrible thing to remember. Here I thought remembering what really happened was awful, but you're right, if that was what I remembered, that would be worse." He smiled ruefully. "Sorry. This is a little stressful. It was the other man on patrol with us, Alan, who shot me and Shipley."

"Hold on, I'm confused. Alan? Alan who?" I asked.

"Alan Archer."

"Alan *Archer* was on that patrol? I thought you said the other guy's name was Stretch."

MacInally snorted. "We called him Stretch because he was so short. He had to stretch for everything."

"I thought Archer served in Vietnam," I said, trying to work it out.

"He was in Korea and Vietnam. Lots of guys were in both theaters."

"So what do you remember?" I asked.

"I remember the ambush, waiting, the mosquitoes. And I remember that right before we left on the patrol a few days before that, Archer found out Shipley was getting promoted. Archer wasn't. Archer thought he deserved it. He was furious, but he got it under control before we left on patrol. The whole time, though, he was tense and you could see the anger almost shimmering off him."

MacInally looked pasty again. He swallowed and pushed the napkin away. It was folded into a neat rectangle. His voice was soft as he said, "When the ambush broke and the firing started, I saw Archer fire at Shipley. Noel charged at Archer. Then Archer shot Noel and aimed at me. Noel died and I went into a coma."

It was a few seconds before I managed to say, "But that's the opposite of what you were told." MacInally nodded and I said, "He blamed Noel for everything. He couldn't blame you. You might contradict him."

"Not with amnesia, I couldn't. That's why he's always kept in touch. Always wanted to know if I was a threat to him. He probably figured this long and I'd never remember, but he was consistent, always calling on my birthday, checking in whenever he was in town." He smiled. "My first wife didn't like him. Thought he was a creep. She was right. She always said it was odd when he came around and didn't feel right. I should have listened to her."

"Does he know you've remembered?"

"No. I think he suspects. Week before last I was at dinner with him and his wife and I mentioned Debbie's e-mail, how she'd contacted me out of the blue. 'Brings back a lot of memories,' I said. He must have thought that meant something more than I intended, because I was almost dead a few days later."

"And before you were able to talk to me."

"Ironic, isn't it? At that point, I hadn't remembered anything to tell you and I nearly died because of one comment."

"You think going into the hospital was what brought back the memories?" I asked.

"They don't really know why my memory is coming back now. It might have happened without going into the hospital. Or not. If Alan hadn't sent that thug to beat me up, he might still have his secret."

"You remember what the thug looked like?"

"I saw him last night at the fund-raiser, following Archer around. It was like a light switch flipped on in my brain. What had been fuzzy and indistinct before was clear now."

"The guy who shadowed Archer last night? The one who looked like he should be in the WWF? He was the one who beat you up?"

"Yes. It was him."

"Who is he?" I asked.

"I have no idea. A hired thug, I don't know. That's for Detective Mansfield to figure out."

"Have you told anyone about this?" I asked.

"Only you."

Despite the overheated room I felt a shiver crawl up my back. "You'd better tell someone else soon."

"That's what I'm on my way to do next," he said. "I'm meeting with Detective Mansfield in . . ." He paused to check his watch. "Thirty minutes. I should go soon. Debbie deserved to know the truth first. She was the only one who believed in her dad, who kept on believing."

He swallowed, rubbed his hands over his eyes, and said, "I knew Noel. I shouldn't have believed he was capable of something like that."

I reached out, touched his arm. "You can't blame yourself. You were wounded. Of course you'd believe what they told you."

He shook his head. "No. I shouldn't have. Why is it that we're so quick to believe bad things about our own people?"

I didn't have an answer.

"Well." He slapped his hands down on the table. "I've got to go."

Before he left, I said, "What about Lena? Do you think she knows?"

He paused. "I don't think she knew in the beginning, but I think she's figured it out."

MacInally ran his hand over his hair again. "She

asked me about it last night. She wanted to know whether I remembered anything from the firefight. t was the way she asked, like she was checking up on me, making sure I still didn't remember anything hat tipped me off. That's when I knew she was playing me."

He looked so beaten down that I said, "I think she does care about you." She had seemed genuinely fond of him when she talked about him. Not like she was in love, but I did think she liked him.

MacInally smiled sadly. "But not as much as she cares about herself."

"How did she know?" I wondered. "She wasn't on he patrol."

He shook his head. "I'm not sure. I was pretty fuzzy those first few weeks after I was hit, but I do remember Lena talking with the other nurses about Archer. She fancied him. Apparently, he'd been in to see me when I wasn't awake. He must have gotten leave somehow." He smiled his bleak smile again. "I was disappointed to overhear her going on and on about Archer. They were serious. I thought they were going to get married. I was sweet on her myself."

He went silent, lost in the past. Then he came out of his reverie. "When we ran into each other a few years ago, we became friends. At least, I thought we were friends, but now I wonder if she was just keeping an eye on me for Archer. She'd asked about my memories of Korea every so often. Maybe we became more than friends so she could get even closer to me."

Or maybe she was hurting and on the rebound from Jorge? I didn't say that aloud. "She and Archer never married?"

"Nah. Don't know what happened there. She told me one time about ten years ago that Archer wasn't

the marrying type. Then a couple of years ago h
married Vicki, a political alliance. It's certainly n
love match, I can tell you that."

I wasn't exactly feeling sorry for Lena, but I knew
it couldn't have been easy for her to see Archer mar
ried to Vicki. Maybe that incident was a factor in he
little fling with Jorge.

There was no way I'd ever get the answers to thos
questions, but my mind raced to the implications of
MacInally's story. It had to be what she'd used to
blackmail Archer.

I refocused on MacInally. His gaze was bleak. Th
closeness he'd shared with Lena last night was over
He wasn't going to excuse her role in the cover-up
He was going to turn her in, too.

"I think you need to be very careful until you tal
to Mansfield," I said, suddenly worried for him. "Di
you tell Lena you remembered what really hap
pened?"

"No. I can't trust her," he said simply. "But don'
worry about me. I can take care of myself." He stood
"Where's your husband?"

I glanced around the room as I stood up, too.
spotted Mitch talking to a couple I didn't recognize
"Over there by the door. He must have run into some
one he knows. No matter where we go he bumps into
someone he knows."

"Military life does that for you—gives you lots of
friends." He kissed my check and said, "Give my lov
to Debbie. I'd like to meet her someday, if she's stil
interested."

He left and I dropped back into the chair, m
thoughts spinning. MacInally thought Lena had lie
to him. Did that mean she was the one who pushe
Jorge? To keep her relationship with him, not t

mention their blackmail, a secret? She was on the platform, but how did she get Summer's Metro card?

A phone rang and I reflexively reached for my purse, which was draped over the back of my chair. I'd switched back to my large Coach backpack, which had room for maps, guidebooks, and a new supply of Hershey's Kisses. My phone was quiet when I pulled it out. I glanced around again because the ringing continued and it was close. I saw a flash of silver under the napkins in the center of the table. The phone changed over to voice mail as I brushed the napkins away and picked up MacInally's phone.

I might be able to catch him before he left the museum. I waved to Mitch, showed him the phone, and shouted that I'd be right back. I hurried out the doors and into a corridor that led to the museum. A stubby woman in a security guard uniform with the longest fake eyelashes I'd ever seen guarded the double glass doors. "No food," she barked and pointed to a trash can.

Fake eyelashes or not, she looked like she'd take me down if I tried to sneak a french fry into the museum. I opened my hand. "It's just a phone." She reluctantly nodded her head and I pushed through the doors. She was obviously practicing for when Homeland Security called with an opening in airport screening.

I hurried down the walkway, looking for MacInally. I spotted his tan windbreaker as he stepped on the escalator. Why was he going to the second level?

I wedged myself onto the crowded escalator. I realized the man with the terrible toupee was one step above me, blocking my view. I had to lean around him to keep MacInally in sight.

What was it about our society that we went for so

much fake stuff—fake eyelashes, fake hair, fake whit
teeth? And why did so many people wear things lik
wigs and eyelashes that were *obviously* fake? Wouldn'
it make more sense to go for the natural look?

The escalator slid to the top. I stepped off an
turned right. A few more steps and I placed my arr
on MacInally's shoulder. "You left your—" I droppe
my hand and stepped back. "I'm sorry."

It wasn't MacInally. The man had the same jacke
the same dark hair tinged with gray, and the sam
tall, hefty build, but it wasn't him.

Something about those words . . . I closed my eye
and concentrated. Then I had it.

We'd been so focused on the people we could se
on the platform that we'd completely ignored th
person we couldn't see. Who was the person wit
long red hair and a denim jacket? I turned slowl
went to the edge of the walkway, and looked dow
into the crowd on the first floor. Suddenly, every
thing came together for me. I knew who'd pushe
Jorge. It was the only thing that made sense.

I reached back to pull my phone out of my purs
but realized I'd left my purse and phone in the foo
court area. I gripped the oversized handrail, leane
over, and peered into the crowd below. I had to ge
back and call Detective Brown, but I had to look fo
MacInally, too. He could be in danger and since
had his phone there was no way to warn him. He'
probably stayed on the first floor and was alread
gone. I scanned the ebb and flow of the crowd an
saw another tan jacket topped with dark hair.

"MacInally!"

He turned and I shouted his name again. His gaz
climbed to the walkway over his head and I rose o
tiptoe, waving his phone to get his attention. At th
moment he saw me, a solid blow between my shou

der blades tipped me over and sent the phone arcing away as I scrambled for a hold on the slick handrail.

An Everything In Its Place Tip for an Organized Trip

Cruise vacations

- Even if you're on an all-inclusive cruise, bring some cash.
- Find out if gratuities are included in the cost of your cruise.
- A cabin on the middle deck will help minimize the ship's motion.
- You can save money on excursions if you book them independently, but the trade-off is that the ship won't wait for you if you're delayed.
- Also, check on the length and type of transfers required to get to your excursion, so you don't spend your shore time stuck in traffic on a bus.
- If you're planning a family cruise, check for age restrictions on children. Some cruises don't allow infants.
- Find out how formal or casual the dining will be. If you'd rather not dress up, there's often a buffet option.
- Make reservations for shipboard activities as soon as you arrive on board because slots fill quickly.

Chapter
Twenty-nine

The hairs on the back of my neck prickled and my stomach seemed to jump into my throat as the room tilted. My torso went over the handrail at an angle. Another shove jolted against my back and shoulder and sent me completely over the railing. Glass and metal kaleidoscoped. My left arm jerked and stretched taut as I gripped the handrail.

Pain seared through my arm and into my shoulder. It all happened so quickly that it was only when I focused on the *Spirit of St. Louis* a few feet from me that it registered that I was dangling in midair by one arm. I glanced down. Big mistake. My legs swayed slightly and I felt light-headed as I looked past my feet to the foreshortened people on the ground floor. They looked so far away.

I swallowed hard and realized people were pointing at me, their necks cranked back at an awkward angle. I felt sick and hot. My arm and shoulder throbbed and my fingers burned. A memory of Abby and me craning our necks backward to see the ceiling of the Rotunda flickered into my mind and I thought, *That's how we must have looked.*

I snapped my head up and became aware of the shouts below me and a scuffle on the other side of the glass banister. My palm slipped a little on the smooth metal and I tried to force my fingers to keep their grip, but they were numb and I didn't know if I was holding on to anything or not. My palm slid over the metal and I twisted, trying to rotate my legs around so that I could swing my foot up and get a toehold on the sliver of the walkway on my side of the banister.

A hand gripped my wrist. "I've got her."

I looked up. Long red curls nearly obscured Alan Archer's shriveled face. I tried to scream, but I made a strangled gasping sound instead. I couldn't seem to get enough air in my lungs to get a deep breath.

Another arm extended out to me and I swung my right hand up to grip it, but missed and had to try again. I saw the crowd behind Archer; they were waiting, holding back to see if he could pull me in. My right hand connected with the other arm reaching out to me. I grabbed the arm and looked up. It was the bad-toupee man. I swore that I'd never again think disparaging comments about anyone, no matter how awful their toupee looked. As he pulled, the strain on my other arm slackened. "I can't hold her," Archer said and let go. He fell away from the banister and the crowd closed around him. Mitch's face appeared above me, his arm extended. "Ellie, give my your hand."

His voice was so normal, calm, and matter-of-fact, like he rescued women hanging from balconies every day. I heaved my arm up. It burned down to my shoulder, but I caught his hand and he and the other man hauled me up and over the railing. I collapsed in a heap with my back against the glass.

"Are you okay?" Mitch asked.

"Yes. At least, I think so." I looked at the other man. "Thank you. Thank you so much."

He looked flustered as he pulled down his sleeve and patted his hairpiece. "Glad I could help. Do you need me to call someone? Are you hurt? An ambulance?"

"No. I think I'm fine. What happened to Archer?" I pulled myself up and looked down the walkway. I saw a petite figure moving quickly through the crowd, red curls swaying.

"Stop him . . . I mean her." No one moved and the wig bobbed farther away. He was almost to the top of the escalator. I remembered the panic in the Metro station and shouted, "Stop her. She's got a bomb."

It was like a bolt of lightning had struck in the middle of the crowd. Most people scattered, screaming, but several men tackled Archer. He struggled to crawl away and his wig rolled off. The men who'd tackled him were being kind of restrained, but when they saw they were dealing with a man, one landed squarely on Archers' shoulders, pinning him to the floor. A security guard sprinted down the hall. He took charge and began pulling men off Archer. MacInally stepped off the escalator and approached the officer.

I sank back down to the floor and Mitch put his arm around me. "What happened?"

"It was Archer. MacInally told me it was Archer who shot his commanding officer in Korea, not Noel. MacInally had blocked it out, the trauma of the day, but he'd been remembering over the last week. When he told me it was Archer who fired the shot and blamed it on Noel, I knew that incident was what Lena and Jorge had used to blackmail Archer."

Mitch pushed my bangs off my forehead and I realized I was shivering. He pulled me closer and I nestled into the crook of his shoulder. "When he first told me, I thought it meant Lena killed Jorge so no one would know about their relationship and the blackmail, but then MacInally forgot his phone. When I ran out here to find him, there was a man who looked just like him from the back—the same clothes, the same hair, the same build—but when I caught up with him, it wasn't MacInally—just someone who looked like him. That's when it hit me about fake eyelashes and toupees and wigs and I knew it had to be Archer."

"Okay," Mitch said with conviction, but I knew I wasn't explaining it very well.

I looked around, but the man with the toupee was gone. "The man with the toupee? Remember him?" Mitch nodded and I said, "It just clicked. I remembered the red wig I'd seen at the Archers' house. It was with a mermaid costume and I assumed it was his daughter's, but he could have used it to disguise himself. He's the same height and build as Summer. I saw them standing beside each other last night, and with the right clothes, a wig, and her beret, he could pass himself off as Summer. No one looks very closely at anyone on the Metro."

I felt Mitch nod and rub his chin over my hair, so I continued. "But it was the Metro card that cinched it. As the owner of Summer's apartment he had to have a key to it. He could get in, steal her Metro card, even take her jacket and beret."

"What happened up here? Did you recognize him?"

"No." The fabric of Mitch's shirt rubbed against my cheek as I shook my head. "I didn't even know he was here. He must have seen MacInally talking to me and thought he'd told me what really happened on that patrol. I saw MacInally down on the first floor. I yelled to get his attention and held up his cell phone. The next thing I knew, someone shoved me over the railing." I shivered again. "Mitch, I'm so sorry, I had no idea."

"Not your fault."

MacInally came over and leaned down on one knee. "Ellie, you scared the hell out of me." He pulled off his tan windbreaker and Mitch wrapped it around my shoulders. "I'm calling an ambulance for you. I know the police will want to talk to you, but let's make sure you're okay." He took out his phone. As he dialed, he smiled and said, "It survived the fall. Landed on a kid's backpack. Thanks for getting it back to me."

An Everything In Its Place Tip for an Organized Trip

Camera Tips
- Before you leave home, check your camera to make sure the batteries are charged and everything is in working order.
- Stock up on batteries, memory cards, and film, if needed.
- To make sure you don't lose pictures, download them while on the road. You can use hotel business centers or Internet cafés. If you're in an area with one-hour photo businesses or drugstores with self-serve photo kiosks, you can transfer your photos to a CD.
- If you use rechargeable batteries, it's a good idea to bring regular batteries, too, as a backup. Some rechargeable batteries lose power quickly.
- If your camera has an LCD screen, you can switch it off to conserve battery power.
- Keep your camera in a camera bag and avoid exposing it to extreme temperature variations.
- Keep your camera safe. Don't carry it with the strap over your shoulder or leave it unattended

even for a few moments on tables in restaurants.
- Bring a disposable camera for kids. Let them record the trip their way. They'll have the most interesting pictures!

Chapter Thirty

Monday

"Ellie, move a little to your left," Nadia instructed and I inched closer to MacInally. The wind whipped my hair into my eyes and I pushed it behind my ear as Nadia snapped the picture. "Stay there," Nadia said. "Let's get a couple more."

It was the kind of Monday that made you glad you weren't at work. A few puffy white clouds dotted the vibrant blue sky overhead. The air was so crisp and pure it threw everything from the blades of grass at our feet to the solid statues of the Korean War Memorial into sharp relief.

"Okay. I think we've got enough," Nadia called out as she walked toward us. "Mr. MacInally, it was a pleasure to meet you," she said as she shook his hand. She pulled me into a crushing hug. "I'll send you the pictures as soon as I download them." She moved down the line and gave Mitch a more reserved hug. "If you ever end up in Georgia, call us," she said and headed down the path.

I waved to Nadia, then turned to MacInally. "Thanks

for coming out. I know the pictures will mean a lot to Debbie." MacInally, Mitch, and I stood on a path beside the memorial. A black chain scalloped gently from pole to pole, separating us from nineteen stainless steel statues capturing a patrol's cautious movement. Despite the solidness of the statues, their rain ponchos billowed around them, giving the impression that they'd just moved when you looked at them. Even though the sun was blazing down, they were so lifelike that it was kind of eerie.

It was a very different memorial from the Vietnam Memorial. The Wall was all about the names. To me, it seemed that this memorial was about capturing the men themselves as they fanned out across the shallow terraces.

"I was glad to do it."

I started and realized MacInally was replying to my statement that Debbie would appreciate the pictures.

He was withdrawn and solemn today, and although I was bursting with questions, I hesitated to interrupt him. Mitch stood beside us, taking in the memorial. This was the first time Mitch had seen this part of the Mall. I sneaked a look at my watch and relaxed. Plenty of time. We had about an hour before we had to be back at the hotel to check out. Mitch had received his all-important certificate of completion for the FROT class, so he was officially finished with the course.

MacInally walked a few feet away from us, put his hands in his pockets, and surveyed the memorial. My phone rang. "That's probably Livvy again," I said to Mitch. I stepped back a few paces as I pulled it out.

Mitch said, "Go ahead, talk to her. MacInally won't mind. I'm going to check on him." Mitch ambled toward MacInally.

When I finally got my phone out, I realized it was a text message, not a phone call. I switched to the message and read

Junk mail delivered. Thx. Tony.

I guess he'd gotten whatever he needed from the mail. I hoped someday I'd get to hear the full story, but for now I punched in, "UW," text lingo for "you're welcome." As I reached back to put my phone away, my shoulder muscles bunched and tightened. I slowly straightened my arm and cautiously rotated my stiff shoulder.

MacInally and Mitch had made their way back to me and MacInally noticed the movement. "How's the arm?" he asked.

"Not too bad, considering the alternative. It was the five hours in the emergency room that nearly did me in." Although the visit had been worth it because they'd thoroughly checked the baby and everything was fine.

He grinned and said, "I don't want to see the inside of a hospital again any time soon either. And the baby?"

"Fine. The doctor told us that babies, even unborn ones, are very resilient. He did emphasize that I shouldn't get pushed over any more railings, though."

We turned and walked slowly down the path, away from the memorial. Mitch caught my hand as we strolled. The mood wasn't as somber, so I asked MacInally, "Did Detective Mansfield say what's going to happen with Alan Archer?" The story had been on the front page of the newspaper this morning.

"He's in custody. The heavyweight who attacked me says Archer hired him to kill me. Fortunately for me, he liked to use his fists instead of guns and he didn't quite finish the job. They're searching Archer's house and office, going through his files. I think they're looking for your sister-in-law's Metro card. I doubt he kept it, but Detective Mansfield indicated that they've found evidence that he doctored reports going to the BRAC. I don't know if they'll get him on the murder in the Metro, but with what they've found so far he won't work for any more commissions."

"Have you talked to a Detective Brown?" I asked.

"Yes, I've had several conversations with him, too. I think I'll be talking to policemen for quite a while."

We paced along for a few steps, and then I said, "I think I've been able to figure out Jorge's movements, but not what they mean. He was here last fall, working landscaping jobs and hiding out in the Latino immigrant community. Then in the winter he went to Georgia where he romanced Lena and got the information on Alan Archer. After that, he came back here and *tried* to romance Summer."

MacInally nodded. "He was quite a Don Juan, wasn't he?"

"Yes, but why did he want something on Alan Archer?" I wondered.

"From what I've been able to gather from the police, he wanted inside information on the Pentagon. Alan Archer was in a position to provide sensitive information that he could feed back to his terrorist cell."

Mitch nodded. "Certain terrorists are known for returning to targets that were missed or not completely destroyed. Remember, the World Trade Center was hit the first time in 1993." We were all silent for a few moments, thinking about the horrific second attack in 2001. I closed my eyes briefly. I didn't want to think about the possibility of another attack on the Pentagon or the Capitol, but I knew every building that held significance for me, each place I'd visited on our sightseeing tour, was a possible target.

MacInally rubbed the back of his head and said, "Apparently, once Jorge made the demand and Archer realized what he wanted, Alan couldn't do it. He could kill a man during a firefight, but he couldn't give away information that would endanger thousands of people's lives. He must have decided he had to take Jorge out. He'd been tracking Jorge's movements and knew his routine."

"So it was just death on a large scale he couldn't condone? Noel's death and framing Summer didn't bother him?" I asked incredulously.

MacInally shrugged. "There's no accounting for how someone's mind works, especially someone as warped as Alan."

"But at least Summer is cleared now," Mitch said, then added, "But it looks like Vicki Archer may have a hard time finding work."

"And that means Summer will have to start over in her job search, but I think that, in the long run, she'll be glad she's not working for Vicki Archer." I tilted my head to look over at MacInally. "What about Noel's death?"

"The military is reopening it. I wasn't in any state to know how the investigation of the incident was handled back then. Since Archer was the only witness they took his statement and wrapped it up. I couldn't contribute anything and with Shipley and Noel dead, they didn't have any indication that Archer wasn't telling the truth. We'll have to wait and see what comes from them reopening the case."

I wasn't sure if I should ask the next question, but I said, "And Lena?"

"She's in custody, too." My sympathy must have shown on my face because he said, "Now, don't look at me like that. Sure, I was fond of that gal, but it was a bit too good to be true. I always asked myself what she was doing with an old codger like me." He laughed sharply. "Now I know. She was keeping an eye on me."

He didn't seem to mind talking about Lena, so I asked. "Did you hear why Lena sent Jorge that check?"

"It seems that Jorge had her convinced he was starting his own business. She must have thought he was in this country legally. The detectives think the money was going to fund his terrorist activities. With all the new laws and restrictions on transfers, it's really put the squeeze financially on terrorist organizations. Their funding isn't what it used to be." We'd reached the sidewalk. "Well, this is it, I suppose," he said.

We said good-bye and Mitch got a taxi for us. The trip back to the hotel would take under five minutes and we could have easily walked to the Metro and ridden it back to the hotel, but Mitch said I needed to take it easy. Instead of bristling at the kid-glove treatment, I decided to enjoy the pampering.

I settled back into the taxi and said to Mitch, "How do you think Jorge found out about Lena and her connection to Alan? How did he, or actually Tony, know to send Jorge to Georgia and find her?"

Mitch said, "I don't know, but I bet that since Alan Archer was their target, they probably researched him and his background, looking for anything they could exploit."

"You're probably right. I doubt it was a coincidence that Jorge was their landscaper. He probably sought out that job, just like he sought out the job drywalling Lena's garage."

We hit a bump and I grabbed the armrest and looked out the windshield at the brake lights of the car in front of us. There was a bumper sticker on it for the Air and Space Museum. I swallowed and tried to push down the thoughts that filled my mind. I realized Mitch was talking to me. "What?"

"I asked if you were okay. You went quiet all of a sudden."

I glanced at the bumper sticker again, then looked back at Mitch. "I was just thinking about Saturday." I closed my eyes. "At the museum. I keep remembering the way the floor looked . . . so far away." I opened my eyes. "What if I hadn't been able to hold on? What if you hadn't been right there?" I blinked because my vision had gone blurry.

Mitch took my hand and unclenched my fingers from the edge of the seat. I hadn't realized I had my hand clamped around the upholstery. "You were able to hold on and I was there." He laced his fingers through mine. "You can't focus on the what-ifs. You have to let that go."

I wiped the corner of my eyes with my other hand and said with a bit of a smile, "That is so you—just let it go. But when I think about what could have happened . . . to the baby . . . to me . . ." I swallowed hard, then managed to say, "I was so foolish."

"Ellie," Mitch said as he gripped my hand. "I'm not saying it wasn't a big deal. I nearly died when I saw what was happening, but did you know Alan was there, following you?"

"No."

"Did you have any idea you were in danger?"

"No."

"Then you weren't foolish. You didn't intentionally put yourself in danger. You can't dwell on that or you'll drive yourself crazy. And I know you. You already worry about every tiny thing. Don't add this to the list, okay?"

"Okay." I blinked again and Mitch squeezed my

hand. I gave him another smile and said I was okay, but I knew it would be a long time before I stopped thinking about all the horrible things that could have happened that day.

I felt something strange, a twitch that felt both new and somehow familiar. I yanked my hand out of Mitch's.

"What? What's wrong?"

"Nothing. I think . . ." I put both of my hands on my stomach. "I felt something. Maybe it was nothing, but I thought the baby moved. It was a flutter. I don't know . . . it's been a long time since I felt that sensation."

Then it came again, a definite movement. I grabbed Mitch's hand and placed it under mine. "Do you feel it?"

We waited. I felt the small pressure inside me, pushing out.

"Nope. Nothing," he said, but he didn't look disappointed.

"There. There it goes again," I said.

He shook his head, but his smile was wide. "It must be so small that only you can feel it right now."

"I'm sure that will change."

"Folks, I hate to interrupt your moment of joy here," the taxi driver said sarcastically and nodded his head at the hotel. We'd arrived and hadn't even noticed it.

We climbed out of the taxi and crossed paths with Gina and Irene. They were about to step into the airport shuttle for their flights home.

Irene patted me on the shoulder. "You've got my e-mail address. Keep me up to date on your pregnancy. And I'll let you know if we have any . . . additions of our own."

"Yeah, that kitchen remodel is taking forever," Grant said as he handed off their luggage at the back of the van.

"Not that," Irene said.

They exchanged a quick, secretive smile and he said, "Right. Not *that* addition."

I guess he was okay with the idea of foster care or adoption.

Gina handed me a business card. "It's been—well, I was going to say fun, but that's not quite the word. Unusual is more like it. See you," she said and hopped in the van.

A melancholy mood swept over me, surprising me. I was going to miss these women. We walked through the lobby and I stabbed at the elevator button. "All these good-byes. It makes me a little sad."

"Don't worry, it's just the hormones. You'll feel better later."

I swung toward him. "Don't talk to me about hormones. Anyone would be sad to see friends leave—" I broke off when I saw he was grinning. I could always count on Mitch to know what to say to make me smile and lighten the mood.

My phone rang and the name on the screen was Summer Avery.

"Hi, Ellie," she said when I answered. "I'm so sorry I couldn't make it over to say good-bye this morning. I'm, well . . ." her voice turned softer. "I'm with Tony right now and he's filled me in on everything. I'd love to come over but we still—" Her voice broke off and she covered the phone. I heard some giggling; then she said, "Sorry about that. Tony and I have a lot to talk about." She sounded distracted again as she quickly added, "I sent you a fax. Have a good trip home."

"That was Summer. She's with Tony. She's sorry

she can't come say good-bye in person, but I don't think her attention would be on us, if she came."

Mitch nodded and said, "Thistlewait called this morning. He'd checked in with Tony for me. Tony said the situation they were working on was resolved last night and he'll be heading out of town. Summer doesn't have anything to worry about as far as shady characters bothering her again are concerned. That's probably what he's telling her."

"I think there's a little more to it than that," I said dryly, then asked, "So, the terrorist cell is wrapped up? There wasn't anything in the paper this morning or on the news."

"If it was done right there wouldn't be," Mitch said.

"Mrs. Avery?" I turned toward the voice. A woman wearing the hotel's uniform of a brown vest and skirt with a long-sleeved white shirt hurried from behind the front desk to us. "This came for you today," she said and handed several papers to me.

"Thanks," I said.

"Could I ask you a question?" I said quickly before she turned away. "You had a clerk working at the front desk. A young man, dark black hair. Is he here today?"

A blank expression wiped across her face, erasing her open and helpful expression. "I'm sorry, but he's no longer employed here."

"Really?" I glanced at Mitch.

"Yes, he was let go. He won't be back."

"What happened?" Mitch asked.

She said, "I can't discuss anything about dismissals." She turned away and I thought I heard her say under her breath something like, "Especially when federal law enforcement is involved."

I raised my eyebrows at Mitch and said, "Let's stroll by the business center."

When we came to the door, the room was dark and empty. The computer, printer, and phone were all gone.

"Looks like Tony has been busy," Mitch said.

As we walked back to the elevators, I scanned the large swooping handwriting on the cover page of the fax.

I read Summer's note aloud. " '*Mom Magazine* is still going to run the article. They've dropped Vicky and Alan Archer from the story and they're going with a new angle, "Big Storage Solutions for Small Spaces." See page two.' "

I flipped to the second page. Summer had circled a paragraph, starred it, and put three exclamation points in the margin. I skimmed it and looked up at Mitch. "They quote me as an organizational expert. They mention Everything In Its Place and list my Web site!"

Mitch punched my upper arm, playfully. "Way to go. You'd better get ready for a barrage of e-mail."

We stepped on the elevator and as the doors closed I said, "You know, I am going to miss everyone, but I'm ready to get back home. I'm ready to see Livvy. I miss her arms squeezing my neck when she hugs me at bedtime. Of course, Vernon won't be home for much longer." I was thinking of the move to Hawaii. I should be excited about Hawaii. I focused on the good stuff: hulas, orchids, sea breezes.

It didn't work because those thoughts led to beaches and swimsuits and the last thing a pregnant woman wants to think about is swimsuits. I kept my thoughts to myself. I wouldn't ruin our last few hours by being sad and grumpy. At least, I'd try not to ruin them. I'd spend as much time with Abby as I could and we could travel to see each other once our babies were born. I stopped myself from thinking about how long the flight would be between Hawaii and Georgia.

The elevator door opened and we went to our room. "I'll call Abby and Jeff to see if they want to ride to the airport with us," I said, heading to the phone. The message light was blinking so I retrieved the message.

"It's the orderly room. They want you to call them." I handed the phone over to Mitch.

I checked the drawers, closets, and the hook on the bathroom door to make sure we hadn't forgotten anything while Mitch put his call through. I found Mitch's belt in the back corner of the closet and shoved it in the suitcase. I ran the zipper around the suitcase as he hung up. He sat on the bed for a moment without moving.

"Mitch? Is everything okay?"

"Well, it depends. How sold are you on sunshine and Hawaii?"

"What do you mean?"

"Well, I hate to disappoint you, but my assignment's been changed. I'm sorry."

I had a sudden sense of foreboding. Were we going to be shoveling even more snow than we did now? "How bad is it? Are we going to Alaska?" I tried not to grimace.

"No. It's not that bad."

"North Dakota?"

"No. It's Georgia. Taylor Air Force Base, same as Jeff."

"No!"

"Yes, I'm sorry, I know you liked the idea of Hawaii—"

I interrupted him. "Georgia is perfect. Absolutely perfect. I'll get to see Abby and Jeff's baby. I didn't realize until a few days ago how much I was going to miss them. You know, when you have to start over every few years." I felt my eyes getting misty. *Oh, good grief, maybe there is something to the pregnancy hormone thing.* I blinked, sniffed, and managed to recover a bit. "It's hard to make friends. It'll be so much nicer to go somewhere where we already know at least one couple."

"Two couples," he amended. "Nadia and Kyle are stationed there, too."

"Oh, that's right. Well, that'll be an interesting . . . dynamic."

"You were just saying how you were going to miss everyone." Mitch looked perplexed.

"I know, but Nadia. Nadia's great in small doses. Oh, who cares, we'll work it out. I'm going to tell Abby."

I hurried out the door, across the hall, and banged on Abby's door.

She opened it, shouldering her carry-on bag. "We're ready."

"We're going to Georgia, too!"

"What?"

"Mitch's assignment's been changed. We're going to Taylor."

Abby shrieked, "We'll be together!"

"We're going to Georgia together!" We linked hands and were practically jumping up and down. We probably looked like Livvy and her friends on the playground.

I dropped her hands and said, "Wait. Georgia. We'll be together, but we'll be in Georgia. *Georgia.* Why couldn't you get reassigned to Hawaii? Why did *we* have to get reassigned to *Georgia?*"

Abby laughed. "Hey, it's the U.S. military. It's not supposed to make sense!"

An Everything In Its Place Tip for an Organized Trip

Sightseeing tips

- If you'll be in a major metropolitan area, take advantage of the public transportation. It's usually the most efficient and economical way to get around.
- Bring comfortable shoes. Even with public transportation, you'll still be doing a lot of walking and it's often the best way to see the sights.
- Plan your sightseeing in a logical order to make the most of your time. To keep from backtracking, break your itinerary into areas or regions and visit all the sights within a region in one day.
- To keep everyone happy, let each person in your group pick his or her number-one sightseeing destination, then make sure you see everyone's number-one pick.
- Purchase a good map of your destination or pick one up from your travel club. Laminated city maps are great resources for finding your way through new territory and many fold into a handy size that fits in a pocket.
- Check with the visitors center for passes that allow you to visit several attractions at a discount.

Acknowledgments

Seeing a book in print is an amazing journey, and I'm delighted I could share it with these people.

A special thank-you to my wonderful editor, Michaela Hamilton, for her insight, guidance, and endless support. Thanks to Faith Hamlin for seeing potential and sticking with me.

I've loved getting to know readers, booksellers, librarians, and reviewers. Thanks for helping get the word out about the Ellie Avery series.

Thanks go to my blog buddies, the Good Girls, for keeping me sane.

A sentence doesn't quite do justice to my extended family who've encouraged me and helped me celebrate being an author. A special thanks to my most energetic publicity team, my mom and dad. And thanks, Mark, for the cruising tips.

I'm so glad I can share this experience with Jonathan and Lauren, who still think it's cool that Mom writes books. And, as always, to Glenn, for talking plot points and other things—you know what they are.

Turn the page for a sneak preview
of Sara Rosett's new Ellie Avery mystery,
MAGNOLIAS, MOONLIGHT, AND MURDER,
available in hardcover from Kensington
in April 2009!

Chapter One

O *ne hour. Just give it one hour,* I told myself. That's the advice I give my organizing clients when clutter overwhelms them. Break up the large jobs into smaller tasks. It's what I told Livvy when her attempts to write her name nearly drove her to tears. One letter at a time. One chunk of clutter at a time.

Of course it's easier to give advice than to follow it yourself, I decided, as I folded the flaps back on a box that contained our tax returns from the last five years. It was the same box I'd opened almost an hour ago, but life, in the form of dirty diapers, lost socks, and a spider in the bathroom sink, had whittled away at my time.

Mitch stuck his head around the doorframe of the spare bedroom and said, "Wow, doesn't look like you've gotten much done."

His tone was matter-of-fact, but I was aggravated. "That's because I haven't." I surveyed the room and decided we were in denial. The bed frame and mattresses were propped against the wall so we could fit stacks of boxes into the rest of the space. "This isn't a spare bedroom. This is a storage room."

"There's nothing wrong with having a storage room," Mitch said in the same reasonable tone.

"There is if you're a professional organizer. I should have had these boxes unpacked months ago. We've lived here for *ten* months. I always unpack all our boxes right away."

"It's a well-known fact that professional organizers who have a three-year-old and a toddler get an exemption from perfection. Let's tackle it this weekend. I'll help."

"No. That's okay," I said quickly. "I'll try to get in another hour tomorrow." It was sweet of him to offer, but if I let Mitch unpack these boxes I'd probably never find the tax records again. He'd put them anywhere there was an open space. They could end up under a bed or in the laundry room. I clambered over two boxes to get to the door. "Sorry I'm so crabby, but knowing we have all this stuff crammed in here is like an annoying gnat that keeps buzzing around my head."

"You'll get it done," Mitch said and rubbed the back of my neck as we walked down the hall. "How about a relaxing game of Galaga after we get the kids in bed?"

I'd found a game system with Mitch's favorite classic arcade games for his birthday. "Yeah, that'll help," I said dryly. I had to be the worst player ever. "Let me get in a walk first before it gets dark."

"Great idea. I'll get the stroller." Mitch had already gone for his run, but he was always up for any type of workout.

"No, I meant a walk by myself." The words popped out before I had time to check them.

"Oh." I could tell from his subdued tone that I'd hurt is feelings.

"Mitch, I'm sorry, but I need some time alone."

He leaned back on his side of the hall and crossed his arm. "Why don't you want to spend time together, just us? Every night, it's like you can't wait to sprint out the door for your walk. You're already by yourself all day."

I gaped at him. "How can you say that?" I usually get tongue-tied when I'm in an argument, but not this time. "No, I'm not. I have two kids and a dog with me *all the time*. That's not being alone." I braced myself on the other side of the hall. "While you're talking to adults, gong to lunch with the guys, and working out, I'm making peanut butter and jelly sandwiches and changing dirty diapers. I load and unload that dishwasher so much I feel like I run a restaurant and I know every word to *'There's a Hole in My Bucket,'* which has to be the most annoying song in the world."

I blew out a breath, trying to calm down. I hated it when we fought. "Look, I want some couple time for us, too, but I feel like I'm being pulled in a million directions. The kids are so . . . labor-intensive right now. A twenty minutes walk is my sanity break."

"My job isn't all fun and games, either," he said quietly. Mitch never raised his voice. He just got quieter and more still.

"I know that. I know being in the squadron is stressful, too." How could I explain?" Imagine if you never left the squadron. You were *always* at work. That's how it is for me."

Arms extended straight in front of her, Livvy "flew" between us, the pillowcase I'd pinned to her shoulders flapping out behind her. "I'm Super Livvy," she shouted. Nathan "cruised" behind her, stumbling along on his pudgy legs as he transferred his grip from one piece of furniture to another to help him keep his balance. He gripped my knees for a second as he passed, then inched his way down the hall with one hand on the wall.

We stared at each other for a few seconds. Then Mitch cracked a small smile. "Reminds me of my office. *'There's a Hole in my Bucket,'* huh?"

My shoulders relaxed and I smiled, too. "As sung by Goofy, but don't say it too loud or Livvy will break into song."

Mitch stepped away from the wall. "You go on. I'll get Super Livvy and her sidekick in their pajamas."

I slid my arm around his waist and kissed him. "Thanks."

A few minutes later, I punched in the remote code to close the garage door and then let out the leash as Rex ran down our long driveway. He'd been waiting for me at the door, ears perked and an air of barley suppressed expectation nearly vibrating off him. With two weeks of almost constant rain, his walks had been severely curtailed. I rotated my shoulders and tried to put our spat out of my mind and enjoy being outdoors.

It was still slightly muggy, but the humidity was so much lower than it had been during the summer. After our move to Georgia in January, we'd enjoyed two months of ideal weather and I now understood snow birds. A winter without snow tires was such a welcome break after our last assignment in Washington state, where it would already be cold by now and there might possibly be snow. Here in the middle of Georgia, the only signs of fall were pumpkins dotting the wide porches. Even though we were barely halfway down the block, a fine layer of sweat beaded my hairline, and my shirt plastered itself to my shoulder blades.

I wondered what my old neighbors, Mabel and Ed

Parsons, would think of our new neighborhood. We'd
gone from an Arts and Crafts bungalow that could
verifiably be called an antique to a house built three
years ago. Only one occupant before us. We had all
the bells and whistles now: remote garage door opener,
garbage disposal, security system, and those clever windows that fold down inside so you can clean the outside of them without leaving the house. However, I
didn't see much window cleaning in my immediate
future. In fact, my days seem to consist only of keeping the basic necessities of our life clean: the clothes,
the dishes, and (sometimes) the house.

Our new subdivision, Magnolia Estates, certainly
lived up to its name, with magnolia trees dotting almost every yard. Tonight, the scent of jasmine hung in
the still air. Set back from the road, new brick houses
in a traditional style kept up the Southern theme:
roof lines soared above Palladian windows and wrap-
around porches. A few homes had white rocking
chairs on their porches.

I paced own the street as it curved around the
edge of a large drainage pond to the end of the road.
A silver Cadillac coasted to a stop at the curb behind
me, and Coleman May leveraged himself out of the
car. As always, he wore a golf shirt—today's was yellow—and khaki pants. A visor shaded his eyes but
left his mostly bald head bare to the sun. Surely his
few stands of comb-over hair didn't protect his head
from sunburn during all the hours he spent on the
course?

He popped the trunk and pulled out a black
garbage bag. "Evenin'," he said as he tore a garage
sale sign from the corner light post and crumpled it,
then picked up some litter.

"Mr. May," I said and reeled the leash in, then bent

to help him with the bright flyers and posters tha
clogged near the drain. The rains had softened the
paper and made the ink a runny mess.

"Can you see this light post from your house?" he
asked.

"I suppose so."

"If you can see anyone putting up signs, flyers, o
posters, give me a call. I'll come down and take care
of it. The only one who's authorized to put anything
up is Gerald Lockworth," Coleman said as I picked
up a flimsy, water-soaked paper. "He's filled out the
permit with the homeowners' association." Even
though it was smeared, I recognized the flyer.

It looked like hundreds of other flyers taped in
business windows all over North Dawkins. FIND JOD
read the bold letters above the picture of a smiling
young woman in her twenties. Straight blonde hair
framed a pretty face. Her smile was wide and showed
her even white teeth. It was hard to reconcile the
open face with the words below the picture: MISSING.

I wasn't about to start tattling on my neighbors, so
I said, "You know, I don't really notice things like
that. Too busy with my kids."

"You should notice. It's everyone's responsibility
to maintain the standards of Magnolia Estates."

It sounded like a line form the monthly Home
owners' Association Newsletter that Coleman wrote
and delivered each month in his role as HOA presi
dent. It probably *was* a line from the newsletter, but
couldn't really say for sure, since I never read the
thing. For all I knew, Mitch and I were in violation o
several obscure HOA regulations.

Coleman said, "I've made a special exception fo
Gerald because Jodi lived here."

I looked at the blurry photograph again before
put it in the trash bag. "Really?"

"You didn't know that?" He yanked the ties on the trash bag closed, then held it against his potbelly. His gaze flickered to my house again, and I had the feeling he was about to say more, but stopped himself.

"How long has she been missing?" I asked.

He put the trash bag in his trunk and walked around to the driver's door. "Let's see, it was right about the first of the year, so that would be around ten months. Keep an eye out for those illegal flyers," he called before he shut his door and drove away.

Rex pulled on the leash. I turned and followed the street's blacktop, which extended a few feet. Then the road switched to a gravel track that had been an entrance for the construction crew during the building of the first phase of Magnolia Estates. It would eventually be paved and lined with homes, but now, between building phases, the road was quiet and mostly used as a jogging and walking path.

I let Rex off the leash, and he hurtled down the path. The missing woman, Jodi, had lived in Magnolia Estates. How weird was that"? I'd seen her picture around town, but knowing that she lived here, drove the same streets, might have even walked this same path, gave me a strange, eerie feeling. I picked up my pace.

A few scraggly rays of sun angled through the dense growth of trees, bushes, and vines. The patch was the only swath of openness. The dense foliage made me feel like I was miles from civilization, but I reminded myself it curved around past the far side of the pond, then ran parallel to our street, creating a perfect walking loop.

I looked up. Directly overhead, a strip of sky was still light blue with one tiny paisley-shaped cloud tinged pink. I took a deep breath and drank in the beauty of the blush-colored cloud.

I noticed Rex hadn't trotted back to me in a while. I called him, but the gloomy path was empty. I jogged to the bend in the path and called again. I saw a flicker of dark movement up on the left. I hurried over. "Rex, come down." He was nosing around the small cemetery plot that was set back off the path at a slightly higher elevation.

"Rex," I said in my firmest voice, and his head swung toward me. "Come."

Reluctantly, he trotted toward me, and I clipped the leash back on him. I glanced back up at the cemetery, thinking that it was slightly odd that the place didn't creep me out. I'd walked past it for weeks without seeing it, since it was higher than the path and the black wrought iron that had once enclosed the rectangle of land now tilted at a crazy angle and trailed a skirt of kudzu that camouflaged it.

I noticed it one day when I spotted a pale yellow stone marker, an obelisk, poking through the curtain of leaves and bushes. I'd taken a few steps up the embankment and stopped there to study the worn markers. No poison ivy for me, thank you. It hadn't made me feel the least bit scared, only a little sad to see the graves so abandoned.

Rex pulled on the leash, ready to move on, but I paused, frowning. "Now that's not right," I said. In the fading light, I saw a white Halloween mask, a skull. It sat under a bush outside the kudzu-draped fence, contrasting sharply against the dirt and dark leaves.

"Kids," I muttered as I climbed two steps up the embankment and angled my foot to kick the mask clear of the greenery. It looked like the Halloween pranks were starting early this year.

I hesitated and leaned down. It looked so realistic. Correction, Not realistic. Real.